James Macdonald Oxley

My Strange Rescue

And Other Stories of Sport and Adventure in Canada

James Macdonald Oxley

My Strange Rescue
And Other Stories of Sport and Adventure in Canada

ISBN/EAN: 9783337178475

Printed in Europe, USA, Canada, Australia, Japan

Cover: Foto ©Andreas Hilbeck / pixelio.de

More available books at **www.hansebooks.com**

MY STRANGE RESCUE

AND OTHER STORIES

Of Sport and Adventure in Canada

BY

J. MACDONALD OXLEY

Author of "In the Wilds of the West Coast," "Diamond Rock,"
"Up Among the Ice-Floes"
&c.   &c.

THOMAS NELSON AND SONS

London, Edinburgh, and New York

1895

PREFATORY NOTE.

THE Author begs to express his acknowledgments to the publishers of *Our Youth*, *Youth's Companion*, *Harper's Young People*, *Golden Days*, and other periodicals, in whose pages many of these stories and sketches were first published.

J. M. O.

CONTENTS.

MY VERY STRANGE RESCUE.

A SHOUT of laughter rang through the kitchen and went echoing up the great chimney when, much more in fun than in earnest, I hinted that if they could not manage to kill the bear themselves I would have to do it for them.

Now it was no new thing for me to be laughed at. My big brothers were only too fond of that amusement, and I had got pretty well used to it; but this time I detected a particularly derisive tone in their hilarity, which touched me to the quick, and springing to my feet, with eyes flashing and cheeks burning, I burst out hotly,—

"I don't care how much you laugh. As sure as I'm standing here, I'll put a bullet in that bear before this time to-morrow night!"

At this they only laughed the louder, and filled the room with sarcastic shouts of,—

"Hurrah for the Bantam!"—"I'll bet on the bear"— "What will you take for his skin, Bantam?" until father silenced them with one of his reproving looks, and drew me to him, saying soothingly,—

"Don't mind the boys, Walter; and don't let your temper betray you into making rash vows that you cannot keep."

I sat down in the sulks, and soon after skipped off to bed; but it was a long time before I got to sleep, for my brain was in a whirl, and my blood coursing through my veins like fire.

I was the youngest in a family of six sturdy boys, and consequently came in for much more than a fair share, as I thought, of good-natured ridicule from my big brothers.

They were all fond enough of me, and generally very kind to me too; but they had a notion, and perhaps not altogether a mistaken one, that I was inclined to think too much of myself, and they took great pleasure in putting me down, as they were pleased to call it.

Of course I did my best not to be put down, and they had nicknamed me "the Bantam," as a sort of left-handed compliment to my fiery opposition against being put down.

I was rather small for my age, and they could easily beat me in nearly all the trials of skill and strength country boys delighted in—not quite all, however, for, much to my pride and satisfaction, I could hit the bull's-eye chalked out on the big barn-door twice as often as the best of them; and no small comfort did my skill in shooting give me.

But this far from contented me, and in my foolish

feverish haste to get on a level with those big fellows, I was constantly attempting all sort of reckless, daring feats, that called forth my father's grave reproof and my mother's loving entreaties.

Time and again would father say to me,—

"Walter, your rashness will be the death of you some day. Don't be in such a hurry to be a man before you've quit being a boy!"

But reproof and entreaty alike went unheeded; and that night, as I tossed restlessly about in bed, I made solemn vows to the stars peeping in through the window that next morning I would take Tiger and go off alone after the huge black bear which had been prowling around the sheepfold lately, and which father and the boys had twice hunted in vain.

Soothed by the prospect of the glory success would bring me, I fell asleep, and dreamed that, armed only with my jack-knife, I was chasing hard after the bear, which seemed half as big as the barn, yet ran away in the most flattering fashion.

Next morning all my temper had vanished, and so much of my valour had vanished with it that my bear-hunting would never have probably got beyond dreamland had not Jack, the moment I appeared, called out mockingly,—

"Behold the mighty hunter! Make way for Bantam, the renowned bear-slayer."

The chorus of laughter that greeted this sally set me in a blaze again; but this time I held my tongue, and the teasing soon stopped.

The mischief was done, however; I felt as though I would rather die than go back on my word now. Never before in my life had I been stirred so deeply.

Determined to keep my purpose secret, I waited about the house until all the others had gone off. Then, quietly taking down my gun, I put half-a-dozen biscuits in my pocket, and, with well-filled powder-flask and bullet-pouch, slipped off unobserved towards the forest, Tiger following close at my heels.

Tiger was my own dog—a present from a city uncle after whom I had been named. He was half fox-hound, half bull-terrier, and seemed to combine the best qualities of both breeds, so that for sense, strength, and courage, his superior could not be found of his size. My affection for him was surpassed only by his devotion to me. He acknowledged no other master, and fairly lived in the light of my countenance.

This morning he evidently caught from my face some inkling of the serious nature of our business, for instead of bounding and barking about me in his wonted way he trotted gravely along at my side, every now and then looking up into my face, as though about to say, " Here I am, ready for anything!" And where could I have found a trustier ally ?

It was a glorious day in December. A week of intense cold had been succeeded by a few days of milder weather, and over all the trees the frost had thrown a fairy garb of white that sparkled brightly in the morning sun. The air was just cold enough to be bracing. The spotless snow crunched crisply under my feet as I walked rapidly over it, and my spirits rose with every step.

Soon I had climbed the hill pasture, and with one look backward at my dear old home, nestling among its beeches and poplars in the plain below, I plunged into the dense undergrowth that bordered the vast Canadian forest, which stretched away inland for many a mile.

The snow lay pretty deep in the woods, but my snow-shoes made the walking easy. Everywhere across the white surface ran the interlacing tracks of rabbits and red foxes, with here and there the broader, deeper print of the wild cat; for it had been a long, hard winter, and the wild animals, desperate with hunger, were drawing uncomfortably close to the settled districts.

As I pushed on into the lonely, silent forest, its shadows began to cool my ardour, and the inclination to turn back strengthened every moment, so that my pride had hard work to keep my courage up to the mark.

Presently I came to an open glade, almost circular, and about fifty yards across, walled in on all sides by tall, dark pines and sombre hemlocks.

It was so pleasant to be in full view of the sun again, that I halted on the verge of this glade to rest a little, leaning against a huge pine, and letting the sunshine pour down upon me, although my long walk had started the perspiration from every pore.

Tiger, who had been carefully scrutinizing every paw-print, but following up none, as he saw I evidently was not after small game that day, now bounded off along the edge of the forest, and I watched him proudly as, with nose close to the snow and tail high in the air, he ran hither and thither, the very picture of canine beauty and intelligence.

Suddenly he stopped short, snuffed fiercely at a track in the snow, and then, with sharp, eager barks that sounded like a succession of pistol-shots, and startled every nerve and fibre in my body into intense excitement, sprang over the snow with mad haste, until he brought up at the foot of a tree just opposite me on the other side of the glade.

For some moments I stood as if spell-bound. I felt that nothing less than a bear-trail could have put Tiger in such a quiver. Perhaps he had struck the track of *the* bear, about whose immense size father and the boys had talked so much.

I confess that at the thought my knees trembled, my tongue parched as though with hot thirst, and I stood there utterly irresolute, until all at once, like a great wave, my courage came back to me, the hunter instinct rose supreme over human weakness, and grasping my gun tightly, I hurried across to where the dog was still barking furiously.

A bare, blasted tree-trunk stood out gaunt and gray, in marked contrast to the dark masses of the pine and hemlock around. It was plainly the ruin of a magnificent pine, which once had towered high above its fellows, and then paid the penalty of its pre-eminence by being first selected as a target for the lightning.

Only some twenty feet of its former grandeur remained,

and this poor, decapitated stub was evidently hollow and rotten to the roots, for deeply scored upon its barkless sides were the signs of its being nothing more or less than a bear's den—the admirably chosen hiding-place of some sagacious Bruin.

My gun was loaded with an extra charge of powder and two good bullets. I put on a fresh cap, made sure everything was in good order, and took my stand a few yards off from the tree to await the result of Tiger's audacious challenge.

Minute after minute crept slowly by, but not a sound came from the tree. The tension of nerve was extreme.

At length I could stand it no longer. If the bear was really inside the tree-trunk, I must know it immediately.

Looking up, I noticed that an adjoining hemlock sent out a long arm right over the hollow trunk, while a little above was another branch by which I could steady myself.

Taking off my snow-shoes, and laying my gun at the hemlock's foot, I climbed quickly up, Tiger for a time suspending his barking in order to look inquiringly after me.

Reaching the branch, which seemed strong enough for anything, I walked out on it carefully, balancing myself by the one above, my moccasined feet giving me a good foothold, until I was right over the deep, mysterious cavity.

I peered eagerly in, but of course saw nothing save darkness as of Egypt, and, half laughing at my own folly, had turned to retrace my steps, when suddenly, without the slightest warning, the bough on which I stood snapped short off a few feet from the trunk.

For one harrowing instant I clung to the slender branch above, and then, it slipping swiftly through my fingers, with a wild shriek of terror I plunged feet foremost into the awful abyss beneath.

Just grazing the rim of the tree's open mouth, I fell sheer to the bottom, bringing up with such a shock that the fright and fall combined rendered me insensible.

How long I lay there I cannot say. When I did come to myself, my first impulse was to stand up. And words cannot express my relief when I found that, although much shaken up, no bones were broken, thanks to the accumulation of rotten wood at the bottom of this strange well.

But oh, what a fearful situation was mine, and how bitterly I reproached myself for my folly! Shut up in the heart of that hollow tree; four long miles from home and help; utterly unable to extricate myself, for the soft decayed sides of my prison forbade all attempts at ascent; only a few biscuits in my pocket; not a drop of water, and already I was suffering with thirst; and, to crown all, the possibility, ay, the certainty, of the bear returning in a few hours, while I had no other weapon of defence than the hunter's knife which hung at my belt.

Although it was mid-day now, intense darkness filled my prison cell, and the air was close and foul, for Bruin had evidently been tenant of the place all winter.

For some time I could do nothing but gaze at the little

patch of blue sky above me that seemed so hopelessly far away, as if rescue must soon come from thence. I could faintly hear poor Tiger's barking still, and fearing he might go off in search of me, I kicked and pounded against the sides of the tree, shouting at the top of my voice.

I don't know whether he could hear me, but he did not go away at all events. It would have been far better for him, poor fellow, if he had.

After some minutes the first bewildering paroxysm of fright abated, and I set myself seriously to consider what was to be done. I could not give up all hope of escape, desperate as my case seemed, and I felt sure I would lose my mind if I did not keep myself constantly employed in some way.

There seemed but one thing to do, and to that I forthwith applied myself. In my belt hung my strong, keen-edged hunting-knife. Since I could not climb out of my prison, perhaps I could cut my way out. So drawing the knife, I set to work with tremendous vigour.

At first it was easy enough, for the soft decayed wood offered little opposition to my keen blade, and I felt encouraged. But presently I reached the hard rind, and then had to go warily for fear of snapping the steel off short.

The close confinement, the heavy, poisonous air, and the constrained position the work required, all told hard upon me; but I toiled away with the determination of despair.

I must have spent at least an hour thus, when, to my

delight, a hard blow sent the knife-blade clean through the wood, and on drawing it back a blessed little bit of daylight peeped through, which made a new man of me.

At it I went again, and paused not this time until I had a jagged hole chipped out through which I could put my hand. If the bear did not come for a couple of hours more I would be free.

The moment I put out my hand Tiger caught sight of it, and came leaping up against the tree, wild with delight at finding me again, for now of course I could easily make him hear my voice.

A few minutes' rest and the breathing of the pure, fresh air that streamed in through the opening, and chip, chip, chip, I cut away at the hard wood until a hole as big as my face was made.

Another brief rest, for I was getting very tired, when— ah, what is the matter? Why is Tiger barking so madly? Can it be that the bear is returning? Yes, there he comes!

He was half-way across the glade already, and Tiger, trembling with rage, was right below me at the root of the tree, ready to defend me to the death.

Growling fiercely, the huge brute shambled rapidly toward us. Another minute, and Tiger the dauntless sprang at his throat.

But the bear was too quick for him, and with one sweep of his great fore-paw sent his puny opponent rolling over on the snow.

Little hurt, and much wiser for this rebuff, the dog attacked from behind, and bit so sharp and quick that

"IN A FEW SECONDS WE WERE AT THE TOP."

Page 22

Bruin in self-defence, reared up on his hind legs, ready to wheel round and drop on the dog at the first opportunity.

For minutes (which seemed hours) the unequal contest went on before my straining eyes. More than once the bear, in sheer disgust at his inability to crush his agile adversary, attempted to climb the tree, and my heart seemed to stand still as his claws rattled against the wood. But the instant he turned his back Tiger had his sharp fangs deep into his hams, and with a fierce snarl down he dropped to renew the conflict.

The afternoon shades were lengthening now, and a new hope dawned within me. My mother had ere this grown anxious at my long absence from home, and perhaps my father and brothers were even then tracing me through the forest by my snow-shoe track. They would hear Tiger's furious yelps if they were anywhere within a mile of us. If my noble dog could hold out long enough we should both be saved.

Full of this hope I cheered him vigorously, and seeming to be as tireless as fearless, the little hero kept up the fight. They were both before me now in full view, and I could watch every movement. The scene would have been ludicrous if my life had not hung upon its issue—the bear was so clumsy and awkward, the dog so quick and clever.

As it was, I almost forgot my anxiety in my excitement, when, with a thrill of horror, I saw that Tiger's sharp teeth had caught in the bear's shaggy fur, and he could not free himself. The bear wheeled swiftly round upon him.   One instant more, and the huge, pitiless jaws had him in their grasp at last.

There was an awful moment of silence, then a quick half-smothered cry, a harsh exultant roar, and out of that fatal embrace my brave, faithful dog dropped to the ground, a limp, lifeless mass.

I could think of nothing but my dog at first; and in frantic, futile rage I beat against the obdurate walls of my prison, while the bear sniffed curiously at his victim, turned him about with his great paws, and seemed to be exulting over the brave spirit he had conquered. But when, having satisfied his pride, the brute turned to climb the tree, all my thoughts centred upon myself, for I felt that my hour had come.   I could feel his claws scraping against the outside as, wearied with his exertion, he climbed slowly up. There was nothing for me but to wait his coming, and then sell my life as dearly as possible.

Firmly grasping my knife, whose keenness had, alas, been spent upon the tough wood, and feeling as though the bitterness of death were already past, I stood awaiting my fate.   Watching closely the narrow opening at the top, I noticed that the bear was descending tail foremost. Foot by foot he came slowly down, striking his long, sharp claws deep into the spongy wood, his huge bulk completely filling the passage.

Not a movement or a sound did I make.   All at once, as if by inspiration—was it in answer to my poor prayer? —an idea flashed into my brain, at which I grasped as a drowning man might grasp at a straw.

The bear was now close at my head. I waited until he had descended one step more, then reaching up both hands, and taking a firm grip of his soft, yielding fur, I shouted at the top of my voice.

For one harrowing moment the bear paused, as though paralyzed. Heaven help me if he drops, I thought. Then, with a wild spring, he started upward, dragging me after him. Putting forth all his vast strength he scrambled with incredible speed straight up that hollow shaft, I holding on like grim death, and giving all the help I could.

In a few seconds we were at the top, and with a joy beyond all describing I emerged into daylight. No sooner did the bear reach the rim than he swung himself over, and plunged headlong downwards without an instant's pause. At that moment I let go, and tried to make the descent more slowly; but the reaction was too great. My senses deserted me, and I tumbled in a heap at the foot of the tree. In that condition my father found me just before sunset; and although the deep snow had rendered my fall harmless, the strain and shock told so heavily upon me that many weeks passed before I was myself again, and I am not likely to ever forget the very strange way in which I was rescued by a bear.

A BLESSING IN STERN DISGUISE

BRUNO PERRY'S home was in about as lonely and unattractive a spot as one could well imagine; an unpleasant fact, the force of which nobody felt more keenly than did Bruno himself, for he was of a very sociable disposition and delighted in companionship But, besides his father and mother, companions he had none, except his half-bred collie, Steeltrap, who had been given that name because of his sharpness, and who recognized no other master than Bruno, to whom he was unflaggingly devoted.

To find the Perry house was no easy task, for it lay away off from the main road on a little road of its own that was hardly better than a wood-path. Donald Perry was a very strange man. He was moody and taciturn by nature, and much given to brooding over real or fancied wrongs. Some years ago he had owned a fine farm not far from Riverton, but owing to a succession of disputes with his neighbours, about boundary-lines and other matters, he had in a fit of anger disposed of his farm and banished himself and his family to the wilderness, where he had purchased for a mere trifle the abandoned clearing of a timber-jobber.

Poor little Bruno, at that time only ten years old, cried bitterly as they turned their backs upon the pleasant home which he had come to love so dearly, and his mother joined her tears with his. But his father was not to be moved from his purpose. He had not much faith in or sympathy for other people's feelings, or "notions," as he contemptuously called them. The only notice he took of his wife and son in the matter was to gruffly bid them "stop blubbering;" and they both knew him too well not to do their best to obey.

That was full five years ago, and in all this time neither Bruno nor his mother had had any other society than their own, except an occasional deer-hunter or wood-ranger who might beg the favour of a night's lodging if he happened to find the farm-house after sundown.

"Oh, mother, are we always to live in this dreadful place?" exclaimed Bruno one day, when he knew his father to be well out of hearing. "I'm sure I'll go clean crazy if I don't get out of it soon. Father will have it that I must learn to run the farm, so as to take hold when he gives up. But I'll never be a backwoods farmer; I'd rather die first!"

"Hush, hush, my boy," said Mrs. Perry, in gentle reproof "You must not talk that way. You don't mean what you say."

"Yes, I do, mother—mean every word of it," replied Bruno vehemently. "I'll run away if father won't let me go with his consent."

"And what would mother do without the light of her life?" asked Mrs. Perry tenderly, taking her son's curly head in both her hands and giving him a fond kiss on the forehead.

Bruno was silent for a moment, and then exclaimed petulantly,—

"Why couldn't you come too, mother?"

"Ah, no, boy," was the gentle response. "I will never leave my husband, even though my boy should leave me. But be patient yet a little while; be patient, Bruno. I don't think God intended you for a backwoods farmer, and if we only wait he will no doubt open a way for you somehow or other."

"Waiting's precious poor fun, mother," replied Bruno ruefully, yet in a tone that re-assured his mother, who, indeed, was always dreading lest her son's longing for the stir and bustle of city life should lead him to run away from the farm he so cordially disliked, leaving her to bear the double burden of unshared troubles and anxiety for her darling's welfare.

Bruno Perry was not a common country boy, rough, rude, and uncultivated. His mother had enjoyed a good education in her youth, and possessed besides a refined, gentle spirit that fitted her far better for the cultured life of the city than the rough-and-tumble existence to which the eccentricity of her husband had doomed her. Bruno had inherited much of her fine spirit, together with no small share of his father's deep, strong nature; and, thanks to his mother's faithful teaching and the wise use of the few books they had brought with them into the wilderness, was a fairly well educated lad. Every Saturday his father drove all alone to the nearest settlement and brought back with him a newspaper, which Bruno awaited with hungry eyes and eagerly devoured when at last it fell into his hands. By this means he knew a little, at all events, of the great world beyond the forest, and this knowledge maintained at fever-heat his desire to be in the midst of it. Only his deep affection for his mother kept him at home.

The summer just past had been an especially restless, uneasy time for Bruno. His blood seemed fairly on fire with impatience at his lot, and even the cool dark days of autumn brought no chill to his ardour. If anything, they made the matter worse; for the summer, with its bright sunny mornings, its delicious afternoon baths in the clear deep pool beyond the barn, and its long serene evenings, was not so hard to bear, even in the wilderness. Neither was the autumn, with its nutting forays, its partridge and woodcock shooting, and its fruit and berry expeditions, by any means intolerable. But the winter—the long, dreary, monotonous Canadian winter, when for week after week the mercury sank down below zero and rarely rose above it, when the cattle had to be fed and watered though the hands stiffened and the feet stung with bitter biting cold, while ears and cheek and nose were constantly being nipped by pitiless Jack Frost!—well, the long and short of it was that one night after Mr. Perry had gone off grimly to bed, looking much as if he were going to his tomb, leaving his wife and son sitting beside the big wood fire in the kitchen, Bruno drew his chair close to Mrs. Perry's, and, slipping his hand into hers, looked up into her sweet face with a determined expression she had never observed in him before.

"Mother," said Bruno, in low, earnest tones, "it's no use. This is the last winter I shall ever spend in this place. I can't and won't stand it any longer. Father may say what he likes, but he'll never make a farmer of me."

"What will you do, Bruno dear?" asked his mother gently, seeing clearly enough that it was no time for argument or opposition.

"Why, I'll go right into town and do something. I don't care what it is, so long as it's honest and it brings me bread and butter. I'd rather be a bootblack in town than stay out in this hateful place."

"But you hope to be something better than a bootblack, don't you, dearest?" questioned Mrs. Perry, with a sad smile, for she felt that the crisis in her boy's life had come, and that his whole future might depend upon the way she dealt with him now.

"Of course I do, mother," he answered, smiling in his turn. "But that will be better than nothing for a beginning, and something better will turn up after a while."

"Very well, Bruno, so be it. Of course it's no use beginning business as a bootblack in winter-time, when everybody is wearing overshoes. But when the spring mud comes then will be your chance, and perhaps before spring-time a better opening may present itself."

Bruno felt the force of his mother's clever reasoning, and with a quiet laugh replied,—

"All right, mother; I'il wait until spring as patiently as I can."

The afternoon following this conversation Bruno thought he would go into the forest and see if he could not get a shot at something, he hardly knew what. The snow lay deep upon the ground, so he strapped on his snow-shoes, and, with gun on shoulder and hatchet at belt, strode off into the woods. He was in rather an unhappy frame of mind, and hoped that a good long walk and the excitement of hunting would do him good. His father's clearing was not very large, and beyond its edge the great forest stretched away unbroken for uncounted leagues. Close at Bruno's heels ran the faithful Steeltrap, full of joy at the prospect of an afternoon's outing. The air was very cold, but not a breath of wind broke its stillness, and the only interruptions of the perfect silence were the crushing of the crisp snow beneath Bruno's broad shoes and the occasional impatient barks of his canine companion.

Climbing the hill that rose half a mile to the north from his home, Bruno descended the other side, crossed the intervening valley, where a brook ran gurgling underneath its icy covering, and ascended the ridge beyond, pushing further and further into the forest until he had gone several miles from the house. Then he halted and sat down upon a log for a rest. He had not been there many minutes before a sudden stir on the part of Steeltrap attracted his attention, and, looking up, he caught sight of a fine black fox gazing at him curiously for an instant ere it bounded away. As quick as a flash Bruno threw his gun to his shoulder, fired almost without taking aim, and to his vast delight the shot evidently took effect, for the fox, after one spasmodic leap into the air, went limping off, dragging a hind leg in a way that told clearly enough it was broken.

"After him, Steeltrap, after him!" shouted Bruno.

The dog needed no urging on. With eager bark he dashed after the wounded fox, Bruno following as fast as he could. Away went the three of them at the top of their speed, the boy just able to keep his quarry in sight, while Steeltrap was doing his best to get a good grip of his hindquarters so as to bring him to the ground. In this fashion they must have gone a good half mile when they came to a bear-trap, into which the fox vanished like a shadow, while Steeltrap, afraid to follow, contented himself with staying outside and barking vigorously.

On Bruno coming up he hardly knew what to do at first. Telling Steeltrap to watch the door, he examined the trap all round, and satisfied himself that there was no other way for the fox to get out. Then he made up his mind how to act.

"Ha, ha, my black beauty! You're not going to get off so easily as that," he said. And, kneeling down, he slipped off his snow-shoes and stood in his moccasined feet. Then, leaning his gun against the wall of the trap (which, I might explain, is built like a tiny log hut, having a heavy log suspended from the roof in such a way that on a bear attempting to enter it falls upon his back and makes him a prisoner). Bruno took his hatchet from his belt and proceeded to crawl into the trap, carefully avoiding the central stick which held up the loose log. It was very dark, but he could see the bright eyes of the fox as it crouched in the far corner. Holding his hatchet ready for a blow he approached the fox, and was just about to strike when, with a sudden desperate dart, it sprang past him

"BRUNO STRUCK WITH ALL HIS MIGHT AT HIS LEG."

toward the door. With an exclamation of anger Bruno turned to follow it, and in his hasty movement brushed against the supporting-post.

The mischief was done. In an instant the heavy log fell, and, although by a quick dodge to the left Bruno saved his shoulder, the ponderous thing descended upon his thigh, and, rolling down, pinned his right foot to the ground as firmly as if he had been the bear it was intended to capture.

Here, indeed, was a perilous situation for poor Bruno. Flat upon his back, with a huge log across his ankle, what was he to do? Sitting up he strove with all his might to push the log off, but he might as well have tried to move a mountain. He was fastened down beyond all hope of release without outside help.

But what hope was there of outside help? No one knew where he was, for he had not said anything to his mother when setting out, and his father had gone up the road some miles and would not return until dark. The one chance was that his father, on returning home, would miss him, and perhaps come in search of him, following the track made by his snow-shoes. But, even if he did, that could not be for hours yet, and in the meantime he would freeze to death; for the cold was intense, the thermometer being many degrees below zero.

An hour passed, an hour of pain and fruitless conjecture as to the possibility of rescue. As the evening drew near Bruno became desperate. He gave up all hope of his father reaching him in time, and came to the conclusion that he must either free himself or die; and he saw but one way of getting free. The log lay across his leg just above the ankle. His hatchet was near him. To chop the log away was utterly impossible, but it would be an easy thing to chop off the foot that it held so fast. Grasping the hatchet firmly in his right hand, Bruno hesitated for a moment, and then struck with all his might at his leg. A pang of awful agony shot through him, numbed as his nerves were with the cold. But, setting his teeth in grim determination, he struck blow after blow, heeding not the terrible suffering, until at length the bone snapped and Bruno was free.

Well-nigh fainting with pain and weakness, the poor boy, on hands and knees, began the long and terrible journey homeward. His sufferings were beyond description; but life was very precious, and so long as he retained consciousness he would not give up the struggle.

Fortunately for him he had not gone more than a hundred yards over the cold hard snow before a bark from Steeltrap announced somebody's approach, and, just as Bruno fainted dead away, an Indian trapper, who, by the merest chance, had come to see if the trap had taken anything, came striding through the forest already dusky with the shadows of night. With a grunt of surprise he approached Bruno, turned him over gently, while Steeltrap sniffed doubtfully at his leggings; and then, recognizing the boy's face, and not waiting to investigate into the causes of his injury, he bound his sash about the bleeding stump, and throwing the senseless form over his broad shoulders, set out for the Perry house as fast as he could travel.

Not sparing himself the utmost exertion, he arrived there just as night closed in, and, pushing into the kitchen, deposited his burden upon the table, saying to Mrs. Perry, who came forward with frightened face,—

"Your boy, eh? Me find him 'most dead. Took him up right away, eh?"

When Mr. Perry returned, and beheld his son's pitiful and perilous condition, for once in his life he seemed moved.

"I must take him in to the hospital in the city the first thing in the morning," said he. "He'll die if we keep him here."

And so it came about that, watched over by his parents, Bruno was next day carefully driven to the city, where by evening he was snugly ensconced in a comfortable cot in the big bright ward of the hospital.

He got well again, of course. So sturdy a lad was not going to succumb even to such injuries as he had suffered. But his foot was gone, and there was no replacing that. And yet in time he learned to look upon that lost foot as a blessing, for through it came the realization of all his desires. A boy with only one foot could not, of course, be a farmer, but he could be a clerk or something of that sort. Accordingly, through the influence of a relative in the city, Bruno, when thoroughly recovered, obtained a position in a lawyer's office as copying clerk. Some years later he was able to enter upon the study of the law. In due time he began to practise upon his own account, and with such success that he was ultimately honoured with a seat upon the bench as judge of the Supreme Court

IN PERIL AT BLACK RUN.

THERE were four of them—Hugh, the eldest, tall, dark, and sinewy, bespeaking his Highland descent in every line of face and figure; Archie, the second, short and sturdy, fair of hair and blue of eye, the mother's boy, as one could see at a glance; and then the twins, Jim and Charlie, the joy of the family, so much alike that only their mother could tell them apart without making a mistake—two of the chubbiest, merriest, and sauciest youngsters in the whole of Nova Scotia.

Squire Stewart was very proud of his boys; and looking at them now as they all came up from the shore together, evidently discussing something very earnestly, his countenance glowed with pride and affection.

When they drew near he hailed them with a cheery "Hallo, boys! what are you talking about there?"

Archie's face was somewhat clouded as he answered, in quiet, respectful tones, "Hugh and I were talking about going over to Black Run for a day's fishing, and Jim and Charlie want us to take them too."

"What do you think about it, Hugh?" asked the squire, turning to his eldest son.

"Well, it's just this way, sir," answered Hugh. "The little chaps will only be a bother to us, and perhaps get themselves into trouble. We can't watch them and watch our lines at the same time, that's certain."

"No, we won't," pleaded Jim, while Charlie seconded him with eager eyes. "We'll be *so* good."

"Oh, let them come," interposed Archie. "I'll look after them."

Hugh still seemed inclined to hold back ; but the squire settled the matter by saying,—

"Take them with you this time, Hugh, and if they prove to be a bother they need not go again until they are old enough to take care of themselves."

"All right, sir! We'll take them.—But mind you, youngsters"—turning to the twins—"you must behave just as if you were at church."

Black Run was the chief outlet of the lake on which Maplebank, the Stewart house, was situated. Here its superabundance poured out through a long deep channel leading to a tumultuous rapid that foamed fiercely over dangerous rocks before settling down into good behaviour again. The largest and finest fish were sure to be found in or about Black Run. But then it was full six miles away from Maplebank, and an expedition there required a whole day to be done properly, so that the Stewart boys did not get there very often.

The Saturday to which all four boys were looking eagerly forward proved as fine as heart could wish, and after an early breakfast they started off. Hugh and

Archie took the oars, the twins curled up on the stern-sheets, where their elder brother could keep his eye upon them, and away they went at a long steady stroke that in two hours brought them to their destination.

"Where'll be the best place to anchor, Hugh?" asked Archie, as he drew in his oars, and prepared to throw over the big stone that was to serve them as a mooring.

"Out there, I guess," answered Hugh, pointing to a spot about fifty yards above the head of the run.

"Oh, that's too far away; we won't catch any fish there," objected Archie, who was not at all of a cautious temperament. "Let's anchor just off that point."

Hugh shook his head. "Too close, I'm afraid, Archie. The current's awfully strong, you know, and we'd be sure to drift."

"Not a bit of it," persisted Archie. "Our anchor'll hold us all right."

But Hugh was not to be persuaded, and so they took up their position where he had indicated. They fished away busily for some time, the two elder boys using rods, and the twins simply hand-lines, until a goodly number of fine fish flapping about the bottom of the boat gave proof of their success. Still, Archie was not content. His heart was set upon fishing right at the mouth of the run, for he had a notion that some extra big fellows were to be caught there, and he continued harping upon the subject until at last Hugh gave way.

"All right, Archie. Do as you please. Here! I'll take the oars, and you stand on the bow, and let the anchor go when you're at the spot."

Delighted at thus gaining his point, Archie did as he was bidden, and with a few strong strokes Hugh directed the boat toward the run. So soon as they approached she began to feel the influence of the current, and Hugh let her drift with it. Archie was so engrossed in picking out the very best place that he did not notice how the boat was gathering speed until Hugh shouted,—

"Drop the anchor, Archie! What are you thinking about?"

Archie was standing in the bow, balancing the big stone on the gunwale, and the instant Hugh called he tumbled it over. The strong line to which it was attached ran swiftly out as the boat slipped down the run. Then it stopped with a sharp sudden jerk, for the end was reached, and the stone had caught fast between the big stones on the bottom.

When the jerk came, Archie, suspecting nothing, was standing upright on the bow thwart, and at once, like a stone from a catapult, he went flying head-first through the air, striking the water with a loud splash, and disappearing into its dark embrace.

Hugh's first impulse was to burst out laughing, for he knew Archie could swim like a seal; and when, a moment later, his head appeared above the water, he hailed him gaily: "Well done, Arch! That was splendid! Come back and try it again, won't you?" while the twins laughed and crowed over their brother's amusing performance.

Archie was not disposed to take a serious view of the

matter either, and shouted back, "Try it yourself. Come along; I'll wait for you."

When, however, he sought to regain the boat, he found the current too strong for him, and despite his utmost exertions, could make little or no headway against it. This would not have been a cause for much alarm, however, had not the banks of the run been lined with a dense growth of huge rushes through which Samson himself could hardly have effected a passage, while at their edge the water ran deep and swift. Moreover, it still had plenty of the winter chill in it, for the time was mid-spring.

Beginning to feel a good deal frightened, Archie called out, " You'll have to come and help me, Hugh. I can't get back to you."

Now unquestionably the proper thing for Hugh to have done was to take up the anchor, and letting the boat drift down to where Archie was, haul him on board. But strange to say, cool, cautious Hugh for once lost his head. His brother's pale, frightened face startled him, and without pausing to think, he threw off his coat and boots and leaped into the water, where a few strenuous strokes brought him to his brother's side.

The twins, in guileless innocence of any danger, thought all this great sport. Here were their two elder brothers having a swim without first taking off their clothes. They had never seen anything quite so funny before. They kneeled upon the stern-sheets, and leaned over the gunwale, and clapped their hands in childish ecstasy over what seemed to them so intensely diverting.

But to the two elder brothers it was very far from being diverting. When Hugh reached Archie he found him already half exhausted, and when, grasping him with his left hand, he strove to force him upward against the current, he realized that ere long he would be in the same condition himself. The strength of the current was appalling. The best that he could do, thus encumbered by Archie, was to keep from slipping downward. To make any headway was utterly impossible. Hoping that there might be, perhaps, a helpful eddy on the other side of the run, he made his way across, only to find the current no less powerful there. The situation grew more and more serious. The dense rushes defied all efforts to pierce them, and the boys were fain to grasp a handful of the tough stems, and thereby keep themselves from being swept away by the relentless current into the grasp of the fatal rapids, whose roar they could distinctly hear but a little distance below.

Hugh says that the memory of those harrowing moments will never lose its vividness. Blissfully unconscious of their brothers' peril, the twins laughed and chattered in the stern of the boat, their chubby faces beaming upon the two boys struggling desperately for life in the rushing water. Even in the midst of that struggle Hugh was thrilled with anxiety as he looked back at them lest they should lose their balance and topple over into the water, and he shouted earnestly to them,--

"Take care, Jim! Take care, Charlie!" whereat they both nodded their curly heads and laughed again.

Hugh was now well-nigh exhausted, and sorely divided in his mind as to whether he should stay by his brother and, perhaps, go down to death with him, or, leaving him in his desperate plight, struggle back to the boat, if that were possible, to prevent a like catastrophe to the twins. Poor fellow! it was a terrible dilemma for a mere lad.

Happily, however, he was spared the necessity of choosing either alternative. Suddenly and swiftly a boat shot out from the northern side of the run's mouth, and in it sat a brawny farmer, whose quick ear caught at once Hugh's faint though frantic shout for help.

"Hold on there, my lads; I'll get you in a minute," he shouted back. Sending his boat alongside that of the Stewarts', he quickly fastened his painter to it, and then dropped down the current until he reached the endangered boys. "Just in time, my hearties," said he cheerily. "Now, then, let me give you a hand on board;" and grasping them one after the other in his mighty arms, he lifted them over the side into his own boat.

Neither Hugh nor Archie was any the worse for their wetting, and the twins thought them even more funny-looking in their wet, bedraggled condition than they were in the water; but neither of them is nevertheless at all likely to forget, live as long as they may, the time they were in such peril at Black Run.

TOUCH AND GO.

ALL the oldest inhabitants of Halifax were of one mind as to its being the very coldest winter in their recollection. It really seemed as if some rash fellow had challenged Jack Frost to do his best (or worst) in the matter of cold, and Jack had accepted the challenge, with the result of making the poor Haligonians wish with all their hearts that they were inhabitants of Central Africa instead of the Atlantic coast of British America.

One reason why they felt the cold so keenly was that, owing to the situation of their city right on the edge of the ocean, with the great Gulf Stream not so very far off, their winters were usually more or less mild and broken.

But this particular winter was neither mild nor broken; on the contrary, it was both steady and severe. One frosty day followed another, each one dragging the thermometer down a few degrees lower, until at last a wonderful thing happened—so wonderful, indeed, that the already mentioned oldest inhabitants again were unanimous in assuring inquirers that it had happened only once before in their lives—and this was that the broad, beautiful harbour, after hiding its bosom for several days beneath a cloud of mist, called by seafaring folk the "barber," surrendered one night to the embrace of the Ice King, and froze over solidly from shore to shore.

Such a splendid sight as it made wearing this sparkling breastplate! Not a flake of snow fell upon it. From away down below George's Island, up through the Narrows, and into the Basin, as far as the eye could reach, lay a vast expanse of glistening ice, upon which the boys soon ventured with their skates and sleds, followed quickly by the men, and a day or two later horses and sleighs were driving merrily to and fro between Halifax and Dartmouth, as though they had been accustomed to it all their life The whole town went wild over this wonderful event. No—not quite the whole town, after all, for there were some unfortunate individuals who had ships at their wharves that they wanted to send to sea, or expected ships from the sea to come in to their wharves, and they quite failed to see any fun in sleighing or skating where there ought to have been dancing waves.

If, however, some of the business men thought a frozen harbour an unmitigated nuisance, none of the boys who attended Dr. Longstrap's famous school were of the same mind. To them it was an unmixed blessing, and they were so carried away by its taking place that they actually had the hardihood to present a petition to the stern doctor begging for a week's holiday in its honour. And what is still more extraordinary, they carried their point to the extent of one whole day, with which unwonted boon they were fain to be content.

It was on this little anticipated holiday that the event took place which it is the business of this story to relate. Two of the most delighted boys at Dr. Longstrap's school were Harvey Silver and Andy Martin. They were great chums, being as much attached to each other as they were unlike one another in appearance. They lived in the same neighbourhood, were pretty much of the same age— namely, fourteen last birthday—went to the same school, learned the same lessons, and were fond of the same sports. But there the resemblance between them stopped. Andy was hasty, impetuous, and daring; Harvey was quiet, slow, and cautious. In fact, one was both the contrast and the complement of the other, and it was this, no doubt, more than anything else, which made them so attached to each other. Had their mutual likeness been greater, their mutual liking would perhaps have been less.

"Isn't it just splendid having a whole holiday to-morrow?" cried Harvey, enthusiastically, to his chum, as the crowd of boys poured tumultuously out of school for their morning recess, Dr. Longstrap having, with a grim smile, just announced that in view of the freezing of the harbour being such an extremely rare event, he had decided to grant them one day's liberty.

"We must put in the whole day on the harbour," responded Andy heartily. "Couldn't we take some lunch with us, and then we needn't go home in the middle of the day?"

"What a big head you have, to be sure!" exclaimed Harvey, with a look of mock admiration. "That's a great idea. We'll do it."

The following day was Thursday, and when the two boys opened their eyes after such a sleep as only tired healthy schoolboys can secure, they were delighted to find every promise of a fine day. The sun shone brightly, the air was clear, the wind was hushed, and everything in their favour. As Harvey, in the highest spirits, took his seat at the breakfast table, he pointed out the window, from which a full view of the harbour could be obtained. "Look, father," said he, "if there isn't the English mail steamer just coming round the lighthouse! There'll be no getting to the wharf for her to-day. What do you think they'll do?"

"Come up the harbour as far as they can, and then land the mails and passengers on the ice, I suppose," answered Mr. Silver.

"But how can she come up when it's all frozen?" queried Harvey.

"Easily enough. Ram her way through until it is thick enough to stop her."

"Oh, what fun that will be!" exclaimed Harvey. "How glad I am that we have a holiday to-day, so we can see it all!"

"Well, take good care of yourself, my boy, and be sure and be back before dark," said Mr. Silver.

When, according to promise, Andy Martin called for him soon after breakfast, Harvey dragged him to the dining-room window, and pointing out the steamer, now coming into the harbour at a good rate of speed, said gleefully,—

"There's the English mail steamer, Andy, and father

says she'll ram her way up through the ice as far as she possibly can.   Won't that be grand?"

Shortly after, the two boys left the house, and hastened off down Water Street until they reached a wharf from which they could easily get out upon the ice.   They were both good skaters for their age, strong, sure, and speedy, and their first proceeding was to dart away across the harbour, spurting against one another in the first freshness of their youthful vigour, until they had reached the outer edge of the Dartmouth wharves.   They then thought it was about time to rest a bit and regain their breath.

"What perfect ice!" gasped Andy.   "It's ever so much better than fresh-water ice, isn't it?"

Harvey, being very much out of breath, simply nodded.

Andy was right, too.   Whatever be the reason, the finest ice a skater can have is that which forms upon salt water.   It has good qualities in which fresh-water ice is altogether lacking.

"Hallo, Andy! there's the steamer," cried Harvey suddenly, having quite recovered his wind.

Sure enough, just beyond George's Island the great dark hull of the ocean greyhound was discernible, as with superb majesty she solemnly pushed her way through the thin, ragged ice which marked where the current had been too strong for the breastplate to form properly.   Full of impatience to watch the steamer's doings, the two boys hurried toward her at their best pace, so that in a few minutes they were not far from her bows, and as far out upon the ice as they thought it safe to venture.

No doubt it was a rare and thrilling sight, and not only the boys, but all who were upon the harbour at the time, gathered to witness it. The steamer was now in the thick, well-knitted ice, and could no longer force her way onward steadily, so she had to resort to ramming. Her course lay parallel to the wharves, and about one hundred yards or more from them. Reversing her engines, she would back slowly down the long narrow canal made in her onward progress until some hundreds of yards away; then coming to a halt for a moment, she would begin to go ahead, at first very slowly, almost imperceptibly, then gradually gathering speed as the huge screw spun round, sending waves from side to side of the ice-walled lane; faster and still faster, while the spectators, thrilling with excitement, held their breath in expectation; faster and still faster, until at last, with a crash that made even the steamer's vast frame tremble from stem to stern, the sharp steel bow struck the icy barrier, and with splintering sound bored its way fiercely through, but losing a little impetus with every yard gained, so that by the time the steamer had made her own length her onset was at an end, and sullenly withdrawing, she had to renew the attack.

As at the beginning, so at the end of the steamer's charge, there was a moment when she stood perfectly still. This was when all her impetus was exhausted, and for a brief second she paused before rebounding and backing away. During this almost imperceptible instant it was just possible for a swift skater to dart up and touch the bow as it towered above the ice hard pressed against it.

There was absolutely nothing in such a feat except its daring. Yet—and perhaps for that very reason—there were those present rash enough to attempt it. Big Ben Hill, the champion speed skater, was the first, and he succeeded so admirably that others soon followed his example. Harvey and Andy were intensely interested spectators as one after another, darting up just at the right moment, touched with outstretched finger-tips the steamer's

bow, and then, with skilful turn, swung safely out of the way.

"I'm going to try it too," said Andy, under his breath.

"You'll do nothing of the kind, Andy," answered Harvey. "It's just touch and go every time."

"Yes, I will. Buntie Boggs just did it, and if he can do it, I can," returned Andy eagerly.

As he spoke, the steamer came gliding on for another

charge. With eyes flashing, nerves tingling, muscles tense, and heart beating like a trip-hammer, Andy awaited her onset. Crash, crack, splinter; then pause—and like an arrow he flew at her bow. Harvey tried to hold him back, but in vain. Over the smooth ice he shot, and right up to the big black bow. With a smile of triumph he stretched out his hand, when—crash! the ice opened suddenly beneath his very feet, and he pitched headlong into the dark swirling water.

A cry of horror went up from the crowd, and with one impulse they moved as closely as they dared to the edge of the open water. There was a moment of agonized silence, then a shout of joy as a fur cap, followed by a dark body, emerged from the water, and presently Andy's frightened face was turned imploringly toward them. He could swim well enough, and keep himself afloat all right; but the steamer retreating along the narrow canal created a strong current, which bore him after her, and he was in no slight danger.

"Save him! oh, save him, won't you?" cried Harvey, grasping Ben Hill's arm imploringly.

"I will that, my lad; never fear."

But how was it to be done? All along the edge of the canal in which Andy was struggling for life, and for some yards from it, the ice was cracked and broken into jagged fragments, making it impossible for any one to approach near enough to the boy to help him out, and for the same reason he was unable to climb out by himself.

"A rope! a rope! I must have a rope!" shouted Ben

Hill, looking eagerly around him. His quick eye fell upon a schooner lying at the head of a wharf near by.

"Cheer him up, boys," cried Ben; "I'll be back in a second;" and like a flash he sped off toward the schooner.

Almost in less time than it takes to tell it he reached her side, sprang over the low bulwarks on to the deck, snatched up a coil of rope that lay upon the cabin poop, leaped back to the ice, and with mighty strides came down toward the water, amid the cheers of the onlookers.

"Look out for yourself, Andy!" Ben shouted, as he drew close to the canal's edge, coiling the rope for a throw. "Now, then, catch!" and the long rope went swirling through the air

A cry of disappointment from the crowd announced that it had fallen short.

"All right, Andy—better luck next time," called Ben, as he rapidly recovered the rope for another fling. Venturing a little nearer, and taking more pains, he flung it out with all his strength, and this time a shout of joy proclaimed that his aim had been true.

"Put it under your arms," called out Ben.

Letting go the cake of ice to which he had been clinging, Andy slipped the rope under his arms.

"Now, then, hold tight." And slowly, carefully, hand over hand, big Ben, with feet braced firmly and muscles straining, drew Andy through the broken cakes and up upon the firm safe ice. The moment he was out of danger a shout burst forth from the relieved spectators, and they crowded eagerly round rescued and rescuer.

"Out of the way there, please! out of the way!" cried Ben, as he gathered Andy's dripping form up in his arms. "This lad must be beside a fire as soon as possible."

Fortunately the crew were still on board the schooner from which the precious rope had been borrowed, and they had a fine fire in the cabin. Into this warm nook Andy was borne without delay. His wet clothes were soon stripped off, and he was turned into a bunk until dry ones could be procured. A messenger was despatched with the news to his home, and before long his mother, with feelings strangely divided between smiles and tears, drove down for the boy who had come so near to being lost to her for ever.

That evening, as Harvey and Andy were sitting by the fireside recounting for the tenth time the stirring incidents of the day, and voicing together the praises of big Ben Hill, Andy, with a sly twinkle of the eye, turned to Harvey, saying, "Do you remember saying to me that it was a touch and go every time?"

"Yes, Andy; what of it?"

"Well, I was just thinking that in my case I didn't touch, but I went—under the water, and I won't be in a hurry to try it again."

THE CAVE IN THE CLIFF.

"SAY, Bruce, don't you think we could manage to put in a whole week up among the hills this autumn?" asked Fred Harris of Bruce Borden, as the two friends strolled along together one September afternoon through the main street of Shelburne, one of the prettiest towns upon the Nova Scotian sea-board.

"I guess so, Fred," responded Bruce promptly. "Father promised me a week's holiday to spend any way I chose if I stuck to the shop all summer, and I've been thinking for some time what I would do. That's a grand idea of yours. When would we go?"

"About the first of next month would be the best time, wouldn't it? We could shoot partridges then, you know, and there won't be any mosquitoes or black flies to bother us."

"All right, Fred. Count me in. I'm just dying for a shot at the partridges; and, besides, I know of a lake 'way up in the hills where there are more trout than we could catch in a year, and splendid big fellows, too! Archie Mack was telling me about it the other day."

"Why, that's the very place I wanted to go to; and it was Archie who told me about it, too," said Fred. "I'll tell you what, Bruce, we must get Archie to come with us, and then we'll have a fine time for sure."

"Hooray! You've got the notion now," cried Bruce with delight. "Archie's a splendid fellow for the woods, and he's such a good shot; he hardly ever misses. Why, I wouldn't mind meeting a bear if Archie was present."

"Ah, wouldn't you though, Mr. Bruce!" laughed Fred. "I guess if either you or I were to come across a bear he'd see more of our heels than our face. I know I wouldn't stop to make his acquaintance."

"I'll warrant Archie wouldn't run from any bear," said Bruce, "and I'm not so sure that I would either. However, there's small chance of our seeing one, so it's not much good talking about it. But I must run back to the shop now. Won't you come in after tea to-night, and we'll make our plans?"

Fred promised he would, and went on down the street, while Bruce returned to his place behind the counter; and if he was a little absent-minded in attending to the customers, so that he gave Mrs. White pepper instead of salt, and Mrs. M'Coy tea instead of coffee, we must not be too hard upon him.

Bruce Borden was the son of one of the most thriving shopkeepers in Shelburne, and his father, after letting him go to school and the academy until he was sixteen years of age, had then put an apron on him and installed him behind the counter, there to learn the management of the business, which he promised him would be Robert Borden and Son in due time if Bruce took hold of it in the right way. And Bruce did take hold. He was a bright, active, energetic lad, with a pleasant manner, and made an excellent clerk, pleasing his father so well that as the first year's apprenticeship was drawing to a close, Mr. Borden, quite of his own accord, made glad Bruce's heart by saying that he might soon have a whole week's holiday to do what he liked with, before settling down to the winter's work.

Bruce's friend, Fred Harris, as the son of a wealthy mill-owner who held mortgages on half the farms in the neighbourhood, did not need to go behind a counter, but, on the contrary, went to college about the same time that Bruce put on his apron. He was now at home for the vacation, which would not end until the last of October. He was a lazy, luxurious kind of a chap, although not lacking either in mind or muscle, as he had shown more than once when the occasion demanded it. Bruce and he had been playmates from the days of short frocks, and were very strongly attached to one another. They rarely disagreed, and when they did, made it up again as soon as possible.

In accordance with his promise, Fred Harris came to Mr. Borden's shop that same evening just before they were closing up, bringing Archie Mack with him; and after the shutters had been put on and everything arranged for the night, the three boys sat down to perfect their plans for the proposed hunting excursion to the hills.

Archie Mack bore quite a different appearance from his companions. He was older, to begin with, and much taller, his long sinewy frame betokening a more than usual amount of strength and activity. He had only of late come to Shelburne, the early part of his life having been spent on one of the pioneer farms among the hills, where he had become almost as good a woodsman as an Indian, seeming to be able to find his way without difficulty through what looked like trackless wilderness, and to know everything about the birds in the air, the beasts on the ground, or the fish in the waters. This knowledge, of course, made him a good deal of a hero among the town boys, and they regarded acquaintance with him as quite a privilege, particularly as, being of a reserved, retiring nature, like all true backwoodsmen, it was not easy to get on intimate terms with him. He was now employed at Mr. Harris's big lumber-mill, and was in high favour with his master because of the energy and fidelity with which he attended to his work.

"Now then, Fred, let's to business," said Bruce, as they took possession of the chairs in the back office. "When shall we start, and what shall we take?"

"Archie's the man to answer these questions," answered Fred. "I move that we appoint him commander-in-chief of the expedition, with full power to settle everything."

"You'd better make sure that I can go first," said Archie. "It won't do to be counting your chickens before they're hatched."

"Oh, there's no fear of that," replied Fred. "Father

promised me he'd give you a week's holiday so that we could go hunting together some time this autumn, and he never fails to keep his promises."

"All right then, Fred, if you say so. I'm only too willing to go with you, you may be sure. So let us proceed to business," said Archie. And for the next hour or more the three tongues wagged very busily as all sorts of plans were proposed, discussed, accepted, or rejected, Archie, of course, taking the lead in the consultation, and usually having the final say.

At length everything was settled so far as it could be then, and, very well satisfied with the result of their deliberations, the boys parted for the night. As soon as he got home, Fred Harris told his father all about it, and readily obtained his consent to giving Archie a week's leave. There was, therefore, nothing more to be done than to get their guns and other things ready, and await the coming of the 1st of October with all the patience at their command.

October is a glorious month in Nova Scotia. The sun shines down day after day from an almost cloudless sky; the air is clear, cool, and bracing without being keen; the ground is dry and firm; the forests are decked in a wonderful garb of gold and flame interwoven with green whose richness and beauty defy description, and beneath which a wealth of wild fruit and berries, cherries, plums, Indian pears, blackberries, huckleberries, blueberries, and pigeonberries tempts you at every step by its luscious largess. But for the sportsman there are still greater attractions in the partridges which fly in flocks among the trees, and the trout and salmon which flash through the streams, ready victims for rod or gun.

Early in the morning of the last day in September the three boys set out for the hills. It would be a whole day's drive, for their waggon was pretty heavily loaded with tent, stove, provisions, bedding, ammunition, and other things, and, moreover, the road went up-hill all the way. So steep, indeed, were some of the ascents that they found it necessary to relieve the waggon of their weight, or the horse could hardly have reached the top. But all this was fun to them. They rode or walked as the case required; talked till their tongues were tired about what they hoped to do; laughed at Prince and Oscar, their two dogs—one a fine English setter, the other a nondescript kind of hound —as they scoured the woods on either side of the road with great airs of importance; scared the squirrels that stopped for a peep at the travellers by snapping caps at them; and altogether enjoyed themselves greatly.

Just as the evening shadows were beginning to fall they reached the farm on which Archie Mack's father lived, where they were to spend the night, and to leave their waggon until their return from camp. Mr. Mack gave them a hearty welcome and a bountiful backwoods supper of fried chicken, corn-cake, butter-milk, and so forth, for which they had most appreciative appetites; and soon after, thoroughly tired out, they tumbled into bed to sleep like tops until the morning.

"Cock-a-doodle-doo! Time to get up! Out of bed

with you!" rang through the house the next morning, as Archie Mack, who was the first to waken, proceeded to waken everybody else.

"Oh dear, how sleepy I am!" groaned Fred Harris, rubbing his eyes, and feeling as though he had been asleep only a few minutes.

"Up, everybody, no time to waste!" shouted Archie again; and with great reluctance the other two boys, dragging themselves out on the floor, got into their clothes as quickly as they could.

Breakfast was hurriedly despatched, and soon after, with all their belongings packed on an old two-wheeled cart drawn by a patient sure-footed ox, and driven by Mr. Mack himself, the little party made their way through the woods to their camping-ground, which was to be on the shore of the lake Archie had been telling them about. Without much difficulty they found a capital spot for their tent. Mr. Mack helped them to put it up and get everything in order, and then bade them good-bye, promising to return in six days to take them all back again.

The first four days passed away without anything of special note happening. They had glorious weather, fine fishing, and very successful shooting. They waded in the water, tramped through the woods, ate like Eskimos, and slept like stones, getting browner and fatter every day, as nothing occurred to mar the pleasure of their camp out. On the afternoon of the fourth day they all went off in different directions, Fred taking Prince the setter with him, Bruce the hound Oscar, and Archie going alone.

When they got back to camp that evening Bruce had a wonderful story to tell. Here it is in his own words :—

"Tell you what it is, fellows, we've a big contract on hand for to-morrow. You know that run which comes into the lake at the upper end. Well, I thought I'd follow it up and see where it leads to; so on I went for at least a couple of miles till I came to a big cliff. I felt a little tired, and sat down on a boulder to rest a bit. Oscar kept running around with his nose at the ground as if he suspected something. All of a sudden he stopped short, sniffed very hard, and then with a loud, long howl rushed off to the cliff, and began to climb a kind of ledge that gave him a foothold. I followed him as best I could ; but it wasn't easy work, I can tell you. Up he went, and up I scrambled after him, till at last he stopped where there was a sort of shelf, and at the end of it a big hole in the rock that looked very much like a cave. He ran right up to the hole and began to bark with all his might. I went up pretty close, too, wondering what on earth Oscar was so excited about, when, the first thing I knew, one bear's head and then another poked out of the hole, and snarled fiercely at Oscar. I tell you, boys, it just made me creep, and I didn't wait for another look, but tumbled down that ledge again as fast as I could and made for camp on the dead run. It was not my day for bears."

" You're a wise chap, Bruce," said Archie, clapping him on the back. " You couldn't have done much damage with that shot-gun, even if you had stayed to introduce yourself. I'm awfully glad you've found the cave. Father told me about these bears, and said he'd give a sovereign for their tails. There's an old she-bear and two half-grown cubs. I guess it was the cubs you saw. The old woman must have been out visiting."

"If I'd known that they were only cubs I might have tried a dose of small shot on them," said Bruce regretfully.

"It's just as well you didn't," answered Archie. "We'll pay our respects to them to-morrow. I'll take my rifle, and you two load up with ball in both barrels, and then we'll be ready for business."

So it was all arranged in that way, and then, almost too excited to sleep, the three lads settled down for the night, which could not be too short to please them.

They were up bright and early the next morning, bolted a hasty breakfast, and then proceeded to clean and load their guns with the utmost care. Fred and Bruce each had fine double-barrelled guns, in one barrel of which they put a bullet, and in the other a heavy load of buckshot. Archie had his father's rifle, and a very good one it was, which he well knew how to use. Besides this each carried a keen-bladed hunting-knife in his belt.

Thus armed and accoutred they set forth full of courage and in high spirits. They had no difficulty in finding and following Bruce's course the day before, for Oscar, who seemed to thoroughly understand what they were about, led them straight to the foot of the cliff, and would have rushed right up to the cave again if Archie had not caught him and tied him to a boulder. Then they sat down to study the situation. For them to go straight up the ledge with the chance of the old bear charging down upon them any moment would be foolhardy in the extreme. They must find out some better way than that of besieging the bears' stronghold.

"Hurrah!" exclaimed Archie, after studying the face of the cliff earnestly. "I have it! Do you see that ledge over there to the left? If we go round to the other side of the cliff we can get on that ledge most likely, and it'll take us to right over the shelf where the cave is. We'll try it, anyway."

Holding Oscar tight, they crept cautiously around the foot of the cliff, and up at the left, until they reached the point Archie meant. There, sure enough, they found the ledge two sharp eyes had discovered, and it evidently led over toward the cave just as he hoped. Once more tying the dog, who looked up at them in surprised protest, but was too well trained to make any noise, the boys made their way slowly along the narrow ledge, until at last they came to a kind of niche from which they could look straight down upon the shelf, now only about fifteen feet below them.

"Splendid, boys!" whispered Archie, gripping Fred's arm. "We're as safe as a church-mouse here, and they can't poke their noses out of the cave without our seeing them."

Keeping very still and quiet, the boys waited patiently for what would happen. Then, getting tired of the in-action, Bruce picked up a fragment of rock and threw it down upon the ledge below, where it rattled noisily.

"ARCHIE AIMED STRAIGHT AT THE BEAR'S HEART."

Immediately a deep, fierce growl came from the cave, and a moment afterwards the old bear herself rolled out into the sunshine.

"The top of the morning to you, missus!" called out Archie saucily. "And how may your ladyship be feeling this morning?"

At the sound of his voice the bear turned quickly, and catching sight of the three boys in such close proximity to the privacy of her home, uttered a terrible roar of rage, and rearing up on her hind legs, strove to climb the piece of cliff that separated them from her.

Bruce and Fred, who had never seen a wild bear before, shrank terror-stricken into the corner, but Archie, looking as cool as a cucumber, stood his ground, rifle in hand.

"No, no, my lady; not this morning," said he, with an ironical bow. "You're quite near enough already."

Foiled in her first attempt, the great creature gathered herself together for another spring, and once more came toward them with a savage roar. As she did so her broad, black breast was fully exposed. Without a tremor of fear or excitement Archie lifted his rifle to his shoulder and aimed straight at the bear's heart; a sharp report rang out through the clear morning air, followed close by a hideous howl of mingled rage and pain; and when the smoke cleared away the boys, with throbbing hearts, looked down upon a huge black shape that writhed and struggled in the agonies of death. A simultaneous shout of victory burst from their lips and gave relief to their excited emotions.

"Hurrah, Archie! You've done for her," cried Fred, clapping him vigorously on the back.

"Yes. I reckon she won't have any more mutton at father's expense," said Archie with a triumphant smile. "Just look at her now. Isn't she a monster?"

In truth she was a monster; and even though the life

seemed to have completely left her, the boys thought it well to wait a good many minutes before going any nearer. After some time, when there could be no longer any doubt, they scrambled down the way they came, and, unloosing Oscar, approached the cave from the front. Oscar bounded on ahead with eager leaps, and catching sight of the big black body, rushed furiously at it. But the moment he reached it he stopped, smelled the body suspiciously, and then gave vent to a strange, long howl that sounded curiously like a death lament. After that there could be nothing more to fear; so the three boys climbed up on the shelf and proceeded to examine their quarry. She was very large, and in splendid condition, having been feasting upon unlimited berries for weeks past.

"Now for the cubs," said Archie. "The job's only half done if we leave these young rascals alone. I'm sorry they're too big to take alive. Ha, ha! Oscar says they're at home."

Sure enough the hound was barking furiously at the mouth of the cave, which he appeared none too anxious to enter.

"Bruce, suppose you try what damage your buckshot would do in there," suggested Archie.

"All right," assented Bruce, and, going up to the mouth, he peered in. Two pairs of gleaming eyes that were much nearer than he expected made him start back with an exclamation of surprise. But, quickly recovering himself, he raised his gun and fired right at the little round balls of light. Following upon the report came a series of queer cries, half-growls, half-whimpers, and presently all was still.

"I guess that did the business," said Bruce.

"Why don't you go in and see?" asked Archie.

"Thank you. I'd rather not; but you can, if you like," replied Bruce.

"Very well, I will," said Archie promptly, laying down his gun. And, drawing his hunting-knife, he crawled cautiously into the cave. Not a move or sound was there inside. A little distance from the mouth he touched one soft, furry body from which life had fled, and just behind it another. The buckshot had done its work. The cubs were as dead as their mother. The next thing was to get them out. The cave was very low and narrow, and the cubs pretty big fellows. Archie crawled out again for a consultation with the others. Various plans were suggested but rejected, until at length Archie called out,—

"I have it! I'll crawl in there and get a good grip of one of the cubs, and then you fellows will catch hold of my legs and haul us both out together."

And so that was the way they managed it, pulling and puffing and toiling away until, finally, after tremendous exertion, they had the two cubs lying beside their mother on the ledge.

"Phew! That's quite enough work for me to-day," said Fred, wiping the perspiration from his forehead.

"For me too!" chorused the others.

"I move we go back to camp and wait there until

father comes with his cart, and then come up here for the bears," said Archie.

" Carried unanimously !" cried the others, and with that they all betook themselves back to camp.

The rest of the story is soon told. Mr. Mack came along that afternoon, praised the boys highly for their pluck, and with experienced hands skinned and cut up the bears. To Archie, as of right, fell the skin of the old bear, while the others got a cub-pelt apiece, with which they went triumphantly home to be the heroes of the town for the next nine days at least.

TOBOGGANING.

IF skating be the poetry of motion—and who shall say no?—tobogganing is certainly the perfection of motion. There is nothing of the kind to surpass it in the world; for coasting, however good, is not to be mentioned in the same breath with this glorious sport. No previous acquaintance with fast going—speeding along behind a fast trotter, or over the shining rails at the tail of a lightning locomotive—would prepare you for the first shoot down a regular toboggan slide.

The effect upon a beginner is brightly illustrated by the replies of a fair American who made her first venture at the Montreal Carnival. Arriving safely at the bottom after a particularly swift descent, she was asked how she liked it.

"Perfectly splendid!" she gasped, as soon as she recovered her breath. "I wouldn't have missed it for the world."

"Then, of course, you'll take another?"

"Oh no, indeed! Not for the entire universe."

But she did, all the same, and soon became as enthusiastic over the fun as any of her Canadian cousins.

All ages and all sorts and conditions of people toboggan in Canada. Indeed, if you were to ask what is the national winter sport of the New Dominion, the answer would infallibly be tobogganing. In no other country was it ever known until within the past few years, when such accounts of its delights have gone forth that it bids fair to come into common use wherever there is snow enough to permit it. While it can be enjoyed to perfection only at the slides specially prepared for the purpose, any smooth sharp slope with a bit of level plain at its foot, well covered with snow having a good hard crust, affords the means for fine sport.

The advantage of the artificial slide is that it can be kept constantly in order, and therefore may be in first-class condition for sliding when the snow is altogether too soft and deep upon the hills. These slides are to be seen in every part of Canada, their gaunt framework rising up tall and stiff out of some level field, or, better still, upon a hill-top, thus securing a double elevation. They are roughly yet strongly constructed of beams and boards, and comprise one, or sometimes two, long troughs placed side by side, with a flight of stairs adjoining. These troughs are curved in the shape of a cycloid, and are from three to five feet wide, the length, of course, varying with the height of the structure. When winter has finally set in they are paved with big blocks of ice from bottom to top, over which loose snow is scattered, and then abundance of water poured on, until, Jack Frost kindly assisting, the whole is welded together into one solid substantial mass.

A slide once properly prepared, and kept in order by the addition of a little more snow and water now and then, will last all winter; and the more it is used, the faster and truer it becomes. In the grounds of Rideau Hall, the official residence of the Governor-General of Canada, there are two immense slides, and tobogganing may there be enjoyed in full perfection.

Let us suppose we have been invited to one of those brilliant torchlight fêtes which form so popular an item in the programme of the viceroy's winter hospitality. A more beautiful scene than that which lies all around and underneath us, when we have accomplished the toilsome ascent of the steep, slippery stairs of the toboggan slide, can hardly be imagined. Stretching away from the narrow platform upon which we stand, two long double lines of flaring torches mark out the slides, slanting sharply downward until they reach the level far below, and then run

off to hide their endings somewhere in the dusky recesses
of the forest. At our left another line of torches, interspersed with Chinese lanterns, encircles a gleaming mirror,
upon whose surface the skaters glide smoothly this way
and that, while from its centre—looking oddly out of season, it must be confessed—a Maypole flaunts its rainbow
ribbons.

A little further on, the long, low curling rink, gaily
decorated, proclaims good cheer from every lighted window.
Turning to our left, we catch through the trees a glimpse
of the other skating pond, with its ice palace for the band
and quaint log hut for tired skaters. Right in front of us
a huge bonfire blazes up, making music with its merry
crackling.

But we have lingered too long in taking all this in. We
are stopping the way, and an impatient crowd is pressing
hard upon us. Let us place our toboggan, then, carefully
in the centre of the groove, adjust the cushions, coil up the
cord, and seat ourselves securely, with stout grasp upon
the hand-rail.

"All ready?" cries the steerer.

"Ay, ay!" we reply.

Giving the toboggan a strong shove, he springs on behind,
with foot outstretched for rudder, and the next instant—
well, the only way to describe what follows is that we just
drop into space. We don't simply coast, for so steep, so
smooth is the descent that we are not conscious of having
any connection whatever with the solid earth for at least
twenty-five yards, and then, with a bump and rattle and

scrape of hard wood against still harder ice, we speed like an arrow through lines of flashing light and rows of open-eyed onlookers, until full four hundred yards away we come gently to a stop in the soft, deep snow amid the trees.

The ordinary toboggan is made in the following fashion: Three strips of birch or basswood, a quarter of an inch thick and from four to eight feet long by eight or nine inches broad, are put side by side and held in position by cross-pieces placed about two feet apart, the whole being bound tightly together by lashings of gut, for which grooves are cut in the bottom so that they may not be chafed by the snow. The thin end of the strips is then turned up and over, like the dashboard of a sleigh, and secured by strong pieces of gut tied under the first cross-piece. A long thin pole on either side, made fast by loops to the cross-pieces, for a hand-rail; a comfortable cushion, stuffed with straw, shavings, or wool, and a long cord, are then added, and behold your toboggan is complete.

As may be guessed from the use of gut for fastenings, the toboggan is an Indian invention, and was in use among the red men as a means of winter conveyance for centuries before the white man saw in it a source of delightful amusement. It is doubtful if the Indian way of making toboggans can be much improved upon, although within the past few years pale-face ingenuity has been exerted toward that end. The peculiarity of the new toboggans consists in narrow hard-wood slats being used instead of the broad, thin boards, and screws in place of gut lashings.

For my own part, I prefer the old-fashioned kind.. The new-fangled affairs are no faster, are a good bit heavier, more liable to break, and being much stiffer, have not that springy motion which forms so attractive a feature of the others.

A third kind, just now making its appearance, has the hand-rail held some inches high by means of metal sockets, and the front is gathered into a peak, while it too is put together with screws. The higher hand-rail is unquestionably an advantage, and if it prove durable, will probably render this last style very popular.

In choosing a toboggan you must be careful to select one whose wood is straight-grained, and as free from knots as possible, precisely as a cricketer would choose his bat. The cross-pieces should be closely examined, for they have to endure severe strains, and will be sure to snap if there is a weak spot in them. Then the gut lashings ought to have close inspection, especial care being taken to see that they are well sunk into the wood along the bottom, so as to be safe from chafing. Where the gut has given way I have substituted strong brass wire with very good results, after once it was drawn tight enough; but this I found no easy matter.

Having selected a toboggan to your satisfaction, the next thing is to cushion it. The cushion should run the whole length, and be not less than two inches thick. Good stout furniture rep, stuffed with "excelsior," makes a capital cushion, although some prefer heavy rug material, and extravagant folk even go the length of fur trappings. The cushion must be well secured to the hand-rail, or it will give trouble by slipping off at the first bump.

As to the management of a toboggan, it is not easy to say much more than that it requires a quick eye, a good nerve, and strength enough to steer.

There are several ways of steering. One is to sit with feet turned up in front, and guide the machine by means of sticks held in the hands. Another is to kneel, and employ the hands in the same way. Then some very daring and reckless fellows will venture to stand up, and using the cord as reins, go careering down the slope, with the danger of a tremendous tumble every moment. The most sensible and effective way of all, however, is to sit sideways, having one leg curled up underneath you, and the other stretched out behind, like the steering oar of a whale-boat, " Yankee fashion," as it is called in Canada. This mode not only gives you perfect control of your toboggan, but has the further and very important advantage of making it easy for you to roll off, and acting as a drag, bring the whole affair to a speedy stop in the event of danger appearing ahead. More than once have I escaped what might possibly have been serious injury at the cost of a little rough scraping over the snow.

From two to six people can sit comfortably on a toboggan, according to its length. The perfect number is four —a man at the front to bear the brunt of danger, and ward off the blinding spray of snow, two ladies next, and then the steerer bringing up the rear, and responsible for the safety of all. Ah me! but what a grand thing it is to be young enough to thoroughly enjoy the tobogganing season.

The toboggan has many advantages over the sled such as is used for coasting. Wherever a sled can go, a toboggan can go also, while on many a hill that offers splendid tobogganing, a sled would be quite useless. Again, it is much lighter than the sled, which means that you do not have to work half so hard for your fun. A third advantage is its safety, more especially in the hands of children. It has no sharp iron-shod ends to make ugly gashes in little legs. Tobogganing has its perils, of course, and I might, if I chose, tell some experiences that would perhaps cause a nervous thrill; but what sport is absolutely free from danger? And since Mark Twain has earned the gratitude of us all by proving that more people die in their beds than anywhere else, why should the most timid be deterred by the faint possibility of peril from enjoying one of the finest and most healthful winter amusements in the world?

A MIC-MAC CINDERELLA.

THE dear old stories that delighted us in our nurseries as mother or sister lured the lingering dustman to our eyes by telling them over and over, do not by any means belong to us alone. They are the common property of mankind. Even the most rude and ignorant peoples have them in some form or other, and the study of these myths and the folk-lore associated with them is one of the most interesting branches of modern philology. "Jack the Giant-Killer," "Puss in Boots," "Aladdin and his Wonderful Lamp," and all the rest of them, have their parallels in the farthest corners of the globe. They are to be found, too, among the dusky race whose mothers told them to their children long before pale-face eyes looked covetously upon American shores and pale-face powder sent terror into the hearts of brown-skinned braves. Take this pretty legend of Tee-am and Oo-chig-e-asque as it was told to an unforgetful listener beside a Mic-Mac camp-fire in Nova Scotia, and, comparing with our own familiar fable of Cinderella, see if the two are not alike in so many points as to make it easy to believe they had a common origin.

In the heart of one of those vast forests that used to cover the Acadian land with billowy seas of verdure as boundless seemingly as the ocean itself, lay a large, long lake, at one end of which an Indian village of more than usual size had grown up. It was a capital place for a settlement, because the lake abounded with fish, the surrounding forest with game, and near at hand were sunny glades and bits of open upon which sufficient corn, beans, and pumpkins could be raised for the needs of the inhabitants. So highly did these village folk value their good fortune that they would allow no other Indians to share it, and any attempt to settle near that lake meant the massacre or flight of the rash intruders. A little way from the village the lake shore rose up into a kind of eminence having a clump of trees upon its crown, and in the midst of this clump stood a wigwam that had more interest for the maidens of the place than any other. They would often watch the smoke-wreaths curling up through the trees, and wish that in some mysterious way they could get into the interior of that wigwam without the occupants having any warning; and many times they would, quite by chance, you know, wander off in that direction, or along the beach below, where the owner's canoe would be drawn up when he was at home, looking out very eagerly and very hopefully from their brown eyes, but always returning from their quest disappointed.

Now what was the reason of their curious conduct? Well, I'll tell you in a few words. In this wigwam, which was larger and finer than any in the village, lived a young chief named Tee-am (the Moose), who was not only very handsome and very rich, but who—most aggravatingly attractive quality of all—possessed the power of making himself invisible at will, so that he could be seen only by those to whom he was pleased to reveal himself. Taking these three things into account, and adding a fourth—to wit, that Tee-am was generally understood to be meditating matrimony—is it any wonder that the dusky lasses with seal-brown eyes and ebon locks took a particularly lively interest in the wigwam on the Point?

As was very natural under the circumstances, the possessions, merits, and designs of Tee-am formed the most important item of village gossip, especially as he had made it known that he would select his wife after so curious, not to say ungallant, a fashion; for instead of his going awooing among the girls, he proposed that the girls should come awooing to him. Adorned in their bravest attire, and looking their very prettiest, the maidens were to present themselves before him, and the first one that could see him plainly enough to describe what he had on, he would marry. The way they went about it was as follows:—They washed their faces, anointed their heads, bedecked themselves with their brightest ornaments, and then directed their steps to the wigwam of Tee-am, arranging it so as to arrive there a little before the hour of the young chief's return from his daily hunting foray. Tee-am's sister, who kept house for him, and of whom he was very fond, would receive them graciously, and together they would go down to the shore to await the hunter's coming. Presently a fine canoe would be seen gliding swiftly over the lake's calm surface. Eagerly the maidens peer through the gathering shadows; but the canoe seems impelled by magic, for no human hand is visible. As it nears the shore the sister asks,—

"Nemeeyok richigunum?" (Do you see my brother?)

Every eye is strained in the direction of the canoe, and some over-eager maiden—imagination coming to the aid of desire—would perhaps pretend she could see its mysterious occupant.

"Coo-goo-way wisko-book-sich?" (Of what is his carrying-strap made?) is then asked.

This was a poser. But a lucky guess might possibly hit the mark; so the aspirant for the chief's hand would make answer that it was a piece of raw hide, or withe, or something else that had been known to be applied to such a use.

"Oh, no!" the sister would reply softly, but crushing out all hope. "Let us go home. You have not seen my brother."

And so they would go back to the wigwam, where, a little later, they would be tantalized by seeing the sister taking a load of game apparently from the air, and a pair of moccasins from feet that obstinately refused to be visible. Thus they were convinced that there was no deception—that Tee-am was really present, although they could not see him. One after another the village maidens had tried their luck "Moose-hunting," as they called it; but all had failed alike to catch even a glimpse of the provoking master of the wigwam on the Point.

Matters had gone on in this unsatisfactory fashion for some time, and the fastidious Tee-am bid fair to be an old bachelor, when he was saved from so sad a fate in the way I shall now proceed to relate. Near the centre of the village stood a large wigwam, in which dwelt a widower who had three daughters, the eldest of whom was a tall, fine-looking girl; the second a medium-sized, rather plain girl; and the youngest a short, slight, delicate little creature, with a pretty, pleading face, who was despised by her big sister, and very cruelly treated by her, because she seemed so weak and useless. In fact, poor Oo-chig-e-asque led a wretched life of it; for her sister, who was of course mistress of the tent, would lay far heavier tasks upon her than she could possibly perform, and then if they were not done, would beat her most unmercifully, and sometimes even burn her with brands from the fire. When her father, who, to tell the truth, was but an indifferent sort of a parent, would find her covered with burns and bruises, and ask the meaning of it, the elder sister would reply that she had fallen into the fire, or tripped over a tree root, or something of that kind; and neither Oo-chig-e-asque nor the second sister dared contradict her, they were both so much afraid of her strong hands. So this shameful state of affairs continued until the poor girl's condition was most pitiable; for her hair was singed off close to her head, her face and body scarred with burns and bruises, and her back bent with toil it was not strong enough to bear.

Of course the two elder sisters had been among the can-

didates for Tee-am's hand; and, proud as they were of their
good looks and of their finery, both had failed utterly to

see the mysterious chief.   Their despised little sister knew
of their going only too well, for her persecutor gave her a
wicked beating when she came home disappointed, by way

of working off her ill-humour. One day, when Oo-chig-e-asque was sitting alone in the wigwam weeping over her hard fate, the thought suddenly flashed into her mind—why should *she* not try her fortune at Moose-hunting? It seemed absurd, of course, but it could hardly make things any worse; and even though Tee-am would not think her worth marrying, he might in some way not very clear to the poor girl's troubled mind shield her from her sister's cruelty.

Oo-chig-e-asque had no fine clothes to put on. A few beads given her by a compassionate squaw were her only ornaments. But this did not deter her. Gathering a quantity of birch-bark, she fashioned for herself an odd, misshapen gown, that was ill-fitting enough to give even an Indian *modiste* "a turn;" an old pair of her father's moccasins were soaked to soften them, and drawn over her bruised feet; and then, with a queer head-dress to hide her singed poll, and her scanty beads arranged to the best advantage, she set off quietly one afternoon toward the camp on the Point. Her big sister, seeing the direction she was taking, screamed after her to come back; but she only hastened her steps forward. The people of the village stared rudely at her as she passed, and, divining her purpose, hooted derisively after her; but she kept steadily on, and paid no heed to them. Her whole heart was in her enterprise, and she felt as though she would die rather than turn back. At length she reaches Tee-am's lodge. Tee-am's sister comes to the door, and receives her pleasantly. At the proper time she conducts her to the landing-place, where they await the hunter's return, the sister soothing her visitor's throbbing pulse by gentle inquiries as to her life and kindly sympathy for her woes. Just at dusk a canoe comes toward them, shooting swiftly over the water, and the sister says,—

"That's my brother's canoe. Can you see him?"

"Yes," murmurs Oo-chig-e-asque, her heart beating high with hope.

"Of what, then, is his carrying-strap made?"

"Munewan," is the quick reply. "It is a piece of rainbow."

"Very good," responds the sister, with a brilliant smile. "You have indeed seen my brother. Let us go home and prepare for him."

So they hasten back to the wigwam, Oo-chig-e-asque's heart palpitating betwixt delight at her success and anxiety lest Tee-am, when he found what an insignificant little creature she really was, might refuse to keep his promise to marry the girl who should first be able to see him. As soon as they reach the tent the sister proceeds to prepare her visitor for the nuptial ceremony, and the young girl gives herself unhesitatingly into her hands. The uncouth birch-bark dress is stripped off and flung into the fire, and a handsome robe, richly adorned with beads, takes its place. Pure spring water is brought, and as the kind sister dashes it over the girl's face, and rubs the scarred features softly with her hands, lo! every scar and spot and blemish vanishes, and the face comes out fair and beautiful as it never was before. Realizing the wondrous change, the young girl utters an exclamation of delight; then checks herself, and puts her hand to her head.

"Ah!" she says sadly, "I have no hair. Tee-am will despise me when he sees I have no hair."

"Never fear, little one," the sister answers reassuringly, and, passing her hands over the singed and frizzled hair, behold another marvel! for it springs out in richer profusion than ever before, and falls in long thick tresses down the back of Oo-chig-e-asque, now too happy to speak. Catching it up, the sister coils it deftly round the young girl's head; and then, just as the toilet is complete, and radiant with joy, hope, and beauty Oo-chig-e-asque stands in the centre of the lodge, Tee-am comes bounding in with his load of game. At sight of the charming girl before him he stops short, and looks inquiringly at his sister. Then the situation dawns upon him.

"Way-jool-koos" (We are discovered at last), he says, with a bright smile, taking the young girl's hand.

"Yes, brother, your wife has come at last," replies the sister, "and is she not a beauty?"

So Tee-am and Oo-chig-e-asque were married, and, like the heroes and heroines of all true fairy tales, lived happily ever after.

BLUE-NOSE FISHER FOLK.

SCATTERED up and down the rocky, foam-fringed shore of Nova Scotia, sometimes standing out bravely upon a promontory that projects into the very midst of the breakers, sometimes nestling away cosily in the curve of a quiet bay, the white cottages of the hardy fisher folk give touches of warmth and life to a scene that would otherwise be one of unredeemed desolation.

They are not very imposing edifices, and viewed from the respectful distance which the dangers of that inhospitable coast compel the passing ship to keep, they seem still smaller than is really the case; but they are all homes, and in their two or three cramped rooms boys and girls have been born and bred, the young people made love and mated, and the old people closed their eyes in the last long sleep, as generation has succeeded generation.

So it is no wonder that the lads who thence go forth into distant parts of the world, as many of them do, find their hearts turning longingly back to the little cottage by the sea, and that they often return to spend their last years in the old place.

Voyaging along the coast some lovely summer afternoon, and from your comfortable chair on the steamer's deck watching these pretty cottages with their black roofs and white sides coming into view as point after point is opened out, and noting how trim and secure they seem, and the glorious prospect they command from the windows which look out from either side the central door, like sleepless eyes, it is easy to imagine that the fishermen's sons must have a fine, free, healthy life of it, and be far better off than the boys in the dusty, noisy, over-crowded cities.

Well, no doubt they are better off in some respects. They have plenty of fresh air and sunshine, and room to grow in, while nothing could be more wholesome than their food of fish and potatoes. But their life is a hard one, nevertheless, and I doubt if many city-bred lads would be eager to exchange with them, could they first have a year's experience of it.

If the mackerel, herring, cod, and haddock upon which

the fisher folk depend for their living, were more regular in their habits, and turned up at the same place at the same time every year, so that the men with the nets and hooks could count upon their harvests as the men with the scythes and hoes can upon theirs, the fisherman's lot would be a fairly comfortable one.

But there is nothing in this world more uncertain than fish. Not the slightest reliance can be placed upon them. They are here to-day, and off somewhere else to-morrow. One season, school after school of mackerel will pour into the little bay where Norman Hays and John Mackesey and George Brown have their fishing "berths," as the area assigned to each man is called, and fill the seines of these lucky fellows to repletion again and again as fast as they can spread them.

Then perhaps one, two, three seasons will pass without enough fish putting in an appearance to make one good haul.

The mackerel catching is the most interesting as it is the most profitable phase of the fisherman's toil, and for both reasons the boys like it the best, although from its being at the same time the most uncertain in its results, they know very well it cannot be depended upon for a living.

The season for these beautiful and delicious fish begins about the end of June, and so soon as it is time for them to appear, the highest points along the coast are taken possession of by men and boys, who stay there all day long watching intently the surface of the sea below them for the first sign of the silver scales which, when caught, can be turned into silver coins.

It is often long and weary work this watching. Day succeeds day without bringing anything; but through scorching sun or soaking rain, fine weather or foggy weather, the look-outs patiently persevere. At last some bright morning, when the sea seems still asleep, Jack Hays' keen young eyes descry a curious ripple on the water far beneath his eyrie.

His heart gives a throb, and his pulses beat like trip-hammers, but he is afraid at first to shout, for fear it is only a morning zephyr. Shading his eyes with his hand, and fairly quivering with excitement, he gazes intently for one moment more, and then shouting, " A school! a school!" at the top of his strong young voice, he goes bounding down the hill-side like a loosened boulder, till he reaches the cluster of cottages far below.

In an instant all is activity and bustle. The men spring into the boats lying ready at the little wharves, the boys tumble in pell-mell after them, the wives and daughters fling their aprons over their heads to keep off the sun, and run out to the end of the wharves, or climb up on the flakes, so that they may see as much as possible.

In a minute more the boats are heading for the mackerel as fast as brawny arms can drive them. Half a mile away the calm blue water is dark and disturbed for a space about the size of an ordinary tennis-court; it looks, in fact, as if it were boiling and bubbling just there, though all around is still and smooth.

Toward this spot the boats are hurried. Presently they reach it. Then they stop. One of the smaller boats goes up to the long flat-bottomed, high-stemmed craft that carries the seine, and takes one end of the net on board. Everything is done quietly, for the fish are easily frightened, and if alarmed will sink right down into the deep water, where they cannot be got at.

As quickly as sinewy arms can send her along, the small boat describes a circle round the fish, that continue to frisk about, all unconscious of their peril.

At length a shout of joy announces that connection has been made. The two ends of the seine are joined, and, if it be a purse-seine, the bottom is drawn together also, and then the tired, excited fishermen can take a little rest, and they try to guess how many barrels this "stop" of mackerel will make. Jack Hays and the rest of the boys can hardly contain themselves with delight, for won't they all have a trip up to the city so soon as the fish are ready to be sold, and these trips are the great events of their life.

Having got the fish nicely caught inside the seine, the next thing is to get them out again. The big net with its precious load is drawn as near the shore as possible, the boats crowd round it, and a busy scene ensues, as the blue-backed, silver-bellied beauties are taken from the meshes, and piled up in the boats until these little craft can hold no more.

In a little while all the fish are safely on shore, and then comes the splitting and salting, in which not only the boys, but the girls and their mothers too, take a hand, for the more quickly it is done the better.

The dexterity shown by the workers is astonishing. Holding a sharp knife in their right hand, they stand before a pile of glistening mackerel. With one motion they seize a fine fat fellow, with another they split him open from head to tail, with a third they despoil him of his entire digestive apparatus, with a fourth they put in its place a handful of salt, with a fifth fling him upon a pile beside them, and the whole operation is done in the twinkling of an eye.

To see the girls at this—and none are more expert than they—takes a good deal of the romance out of one's ideas of fisher-maidens; but it cannot be helped. They cannot afford to be romantic, or look picturesque. Their life is too hard for that kind of amusement.

In the catching of mackerel and herring there is not much danger, and the fishermen need not go far from home. But it is different with the cod and haddock and hake. To get these big fellows you must go out upon the Banks, as those strange, shallow areas in the Atlantic Ocean are called; and going out upon the Banks means being away for long weeks at a time, and exposed to many dangers.

Storms are frequent there, and the waves run mountain high, so that stanch and trim as the fishing craft are, and thoroughly expert their masters, hardly a season passes without the loss of a *Nancy Bell* or *Cod-Seeker* with all on board. Often, alas! do

> " The women go weeping and wringing their hands,
> For those who will never come back to the town."

Another danger ever present, ever indeed growing greater, is that of being run down some foggy night by the great ocean steamers that are thronging past in increasing numbers.

Picture to yourself a dense, dark night, when you can hardly see your hand before your face; a little schooner tossing at anchor on the Banks, all but one of her crew asleep in their bunks. Suddenly there falls upon the solitary watcher's ear a sound that thrills him with terror: it is the throbbing of mighty engines and the onward rush of an ocean greyhound as she spurns the foaming water from her bows.

Springing upon the poop he shouts with all his might, the crew below leap from their berths, and though only half awake join him in the cry.

But it is of no avail. The mast-head light is seen by the steamer's look-out too late to change her course. There is a splintering crash, the iron monster feels a slight shock, hardly enough to waken the lightest sleeper in her state-rooms, and the sharp prow cuts through the little schooner as though it were but another wave.

Then the frenzied shrieks of strong men in their agony ring out upon the midnight air; then all is silent again, and the steamer speeds on to her destination, while to another home in Herring Cove comes the dreadful experience of which the poet says,—

> " How much of manhood's wasted strength,
>   Of woman's misery, —
> What breaking hearts might swell the cry,
>   They're dear fish to me."

Yet it is the ambition of every boy at Herring Cove

or Shad Bay to have a share in a *Banker*, or, better still, to own one all by himself; and to this he looks forward, just as city boys do to being bank presidents or judges or editors of newspapers.

Hard work, much danger, a little schooling, and still less playing is the summary of a fisher-boy's life. It makes him very healthy, brown, and strong, but it never makes him rich. The most he can do is to earn enough to build and furnish a cottage when he marries, and provide plain food and coarse clothing for the family that soon springs up around him.

Now and then—that is, whenever he has fish to sell—he goes up to the city; and this is his only holiday. While still a boy he generally behaves himself well enough on these visits, but, growing older, he does not always grow wiser, I am sorry to say, and I have often seen sad-faced wives rowing the heavy boat wearily home, while their husbands lay in the stern-sheets in a drunken stupor.

LOST ON THE LIMITS.

(A CHRISTMAS STORY.)

"I WISH you had taken my advice and stayed at the shanty, Harry."

The speaker was a stalwart young man, so closely wrapped in a blue blanket capote that only a portion of his face showed itself, and the one addressed was a boy of sixteen, similarly accoutred.

"I felt more than half-afraid of this storm overtaking us," the young man continued; "and now we're in a pretty fix. I can't imagine how we'll ever reach the depot."

There was something so despondent in his tone that one might have expected his words to exercise a dispiriting effect upon his companion; but, instead of that, Harry answered brightly,—

"Reach the depot! Of course we will; and in good time for our Christmas dinner, too! You mustn't worry on my account, Mr. Maynard. If anything should happen, it would be all my own fault, you know. You wouldn't be the least bit to blame."

Mr. Maynard shook his head negatively.

"It's very good of you to say so, Harry, but I can't help feeling responsible all the same. Oh!" he cried, with a gesture of irritated protest against the situation, "what a plague this snow is! Surely we had enough of it already, and didn't need this storm."

John Maynard was the bush superintendent on one of the great timber limits of Booth and Bronson, the millionaire lumbermen of Canada.

The duty devolved upon him of driving about from one "shanty" (as the permanent camps of the log-cutters are called) to another, taking account of the work done, and giving directions as to the bunches of timber next to be attacked.

This was a very arduous occupation, entailing as it did long and lonely drives through forest roads, passable only in winter, across the broad bosoms of frozen lakes, and along the winding courses of ice-bound rivers. For this purpose he had a pair of powerful horses and a low, strong sleigh, made altogether of wood, that had accommodation for just two persons and some baggage.

As a rule he made these journeys alone, but this winter he had been favoured with a companion in Harry Bronson. the eldest son of a member of the firm, who had asked permission to spend the winter at the "shanties."

His request had been readily granted, for he would have to take his father's place in the business in due time, and the more thoroughly he knew its details the better. Consequently Mr. Bronson was very glad to let him go, while Harry rejoiced at getting away from the confinement of the office, and at the prospect of having some exciting experiences before he returned.

So far he had been having a very good time. John Maynard was as pleasant a companion as he was a competent bush superintendent, and, while going the round of the shanties, there were many chances for shots at partridges or rabbits, and always the exciting possibility of encountering a bear.

Then at the shanties their welcome was always so warm, and the French-Canadian shantymen were so amusing with their exhaustless fund of song and dance and story, that Harry never knew what it was to feel dull for a moment.

Christmas week found him at the shanty on the Opeongo—the one that stood farthest away of all from the depot at which Maynard made his headquarters, and to which it was his intention to return in time to celebrate Christmas there.

The superintendent was particularly anxious to get back by that time, because, having completed a round of the shanties, he could leave them unvisited for a fortnight or so, and he proposed to spend Christmas week in Montreal, where he had many friends.

Harry on his part was hardly less anxious to get to the depot; for, although he did not intend going any further, he had been promised lots of fun there by the clerk in charge, and a first-class Christmas dinner into the bargain.

Accordingly, when certain infallible signs of a change for the worse in the weather, which had hitherto been almost perfect, made their appearance, and Maynard, willing to take any risk himself, but reluctant to expose Harry to danger, suggested that the boy should remain at the Opeongo shanty until the threatened storm passed, and then get back to the depot by one of the ordinary teams, Harry would not hear of it.

"No, no, Mr. Maynard," said he stoutly. "If you can stand the storm, I can too. I'm going with you."

Clearly enough the superintendent would have to either allow Harry to accompany him or stay at the shanty himself. He could not accept the latter alternative, so he replied,

"Very well then, my boy, we'll start ; and if bad weather catches us, we'll have to do the best we can."

The distance between the Opeongo shanty and the depot, as the crow flies, was fifty miles ; but the circuitous route that was necessary in order to avoid ranges of rocky hills and impassable gullies made it full half as long again, and, in view of the state of the road, Maynard calculated that two days might be required to make their destination. Accordingly they set out in the morning of the second day before Christmas.

It hardly needed the practised eye of a wood-ranger to foretell a coming change in the weather.

The sun's bright face was hidden behind a dense veil of sullen clouds ; the air, that had been so crisp and clear, seemed dank and heavy like a dungeon's ; and both man and beast moved about in a listless way, as if every movement was an effort.

More than once the superintendent's mind misgave him ere they had gone many miles. He was naturally a cautious, far-seeing man, not disposed to run unnecessary risks, although utterly regardless of personal peril in any matter of duty.

Not that he felt any concern on his own account; but he would have felt much easier in his mind had Harry been persuaded to stay at the shanty.

Yet how could he reasonably expect that, when he himself was pushing on to the depot?

Harry's argument, that if the superintendent could stand the storm he could also, was not easy to answer, and it prevailed.

"If this confounded road was only in better shape, we might get there to-night," said Maynard impatiently that afternoon as the sleigh slowly toiled up a steep ascent, the horses sinking above their fetlocks in the fine dry snow at every step.

Had their way been as well broken as a city street they might indeed have accomplished this feat, but under the circumstances the best they could hope for was to reach the depot early on Christmas eve.

Harry, understanding that he was the chief object of the superintendent's concern, felt it incumbent upon him to take as hopeful a view of matters as possible, so he responded in his cheeriest tone,—

"Oh, we'll get there to-morrow afternoon right enough! We're more than half way to Wolf Hollow now, aren't we?"

" Yes, a good bit more ; but there's the snow beginning. We must drive ahead as fast as we can.   It'll soon be dark."

The horses accordingly were urged to the utmost speed possible, and, by dint of some rather reckless driving, Wolf Hollow was safely reached in the face of a blinding snowstorm ere the darkness fell.

At this place there stood a shanty which had been abandoned some years before, all the timber being cut in the neighbourhood, and here Mr. Maynard proposed to spend the night.

The building was found to be in good condition—quite storm-proof, in fact—and it did not take long to gather an abundant supply of firewood wherewith to expel the cold, damp air that filled it.

The horses could not be left out, of course, exposed to the pitiless storm, so they were allotted the farthest corner of the long, low room.   The sleigh, too, was brought inside with all its contents.

A substantial supper was prepared and enjoyed, the horses were given a good feed of oats, and then both the travellers being thoroughly tired, they fitted up one of the bunks with the sleigh robes, and, so as to waste no heat, lay down side by side, and were soon sound asleep.

At daybreak the superintendent got up and hastened to see how matters looked outside.   The prospect was anything but cheering.

Snow had been falling heavily all night, and there seemed no sign of its ceasing.   All marks of the road were completely obliterated, and it would evidently test to the utmost his knowledge of woodcraft to keep in the right track.

Such was the condition of affairs that called forth the exclamation reported at the beginning of this story.

However, there was nothing to gain by delay, so hardly waiting to snatch a bite of food and to allow their horses to finish their portion of oats, they harnessed up and drove forth into the storm.

Even had the track been easily distinguishable, they could not have made rapid progress, for the snow came in big, blinding flakes that were very bewildering, and had already covered the ground to a depth of nearly a foot.

By the aid of familiar landmarks, Mr. Maynard was able for a time to direct their course accurately enough; but about mid-day they reached a wide lake which they had to cross, and here their real difficulties began.

The broad expanse of Loon Lake had presented a fine playground for the wind, and upon it the snow was heaped in vast drifts, far surpassing anything met with in the woods, where the trees afforded protection.

In these drifts the horses and sleigh soon stuck so fast that their extrication was evidently quite beyond the power of the passengers.

There seemed no alternative but to abandon them to their fate, and to continue the journey on snow-shoes, which, fortunately, were lashed to the back of the sleigh.

Mr. Maynard felt sorely reluctant to desert his faithful horses, but no time could be spared for unavailing regrets.

"There's no help for it, Harry," he said resolutely.

"We'll have to leave them where they are. We cannot get them out, and we've enough to do to look after ourselves."

The poor creatures whinnied appealingly as their human companions moved off, and made frantic efforts to follow, but the remorseless snow-drift held them fast.

It was certainly a pity to leave two such fine animals to perish, but yet what could be done?

Striding along on the snow-shoes, in the use of which they were both expert, the superintendent and Harry made better progress than they had been doing in the sleigh, and now the chief anxiety was to hit the right spot on the other side of the lake, where the road continued through the woods.

On a clear day Mr. Maynard would have found little difficulty in doing this, but in the midst of a blinding snowstorm it was no easy task; yet their very lives depended upon its successful accomplishment.

When they reached the middle of the lake they were dismayed to discover that the heavily - falling snow shrouded not only the shore for which they were making, but the one which they had left. They were absolutely without a mark to guide them.

Here was an unexpected peril. Mr. Maynard halted and strove to peer through the ominous obscurity of white, but on every side it was the same.

"What are we to do now, Harry?" he cried in a tone of deep concern. "I can't make out our way at all."

By this time Harry's spirits, which had hitherto

"THE POOR CREATURES WHINNIED APPEALINGLY."

been keeping up bravely, were beginning to fall, for he was growing weary of the long struggle with the storm.

"I'm sure I don't know," he responded ruefully. "I suppose there is nothing else to do but to push ahead and take our chances of hitting the shore somewhere."

"That's about all, Harry," was the superintendent's reply. "Just rest a minute to get your breath, and then we'll make a dash for it."

For a little space they stood still and silent, the mind of each absorbed in anxious thought, and then Mr. Maynard called out,—

"Come along now, Harry. Keep right in my tracks, and I'll see if I can't make the shore all right."

For half-an-hour they toiled steadily onward, and well it was for both that they had such skill in the use of snow-shoes. Without them they could not have made a hundred yards' headway, so heavy was the snow. Even as it was, the hard work told upon Harry, and presently he had to call to his companion,—

"Hold on a minute, Mr. Maynard; I'm out of breath."

The superintendent stopped short and came back to him.

"Not played out already, are you, Harry?" he asked, peering anxiously into his face.

"Oh, no!" and the boy made a gallant effort at a re-assuring smile. "I just want to get my wind; that's all. This abominable storm nearly suffocates me."

As they rested again for a few minutes, the wind

suddenly shifted, parting the whirling snow to right and left, and through the rift thus made, Mr. Maynard's keen eyes caught a glimpse of a dark mass rising dimly into the air a little more than a mile away.

With a shout of joy he slapped his companion upon the back, crying,—

"Eagle Rock, Harry. See!" and he pointed with a quivering finger to the spectral appearance. "Once we make that, I can find the road all right enough. Come along!"

Cheered by the sight, which the next moment the snow-curtain again hid from them, they pushed forward with renewed energy.

It was terribly hard walking. Their snow-shoes sank deep into the drifts at every step, and it was an effort each time to release them. The afternoon was also waning fast, and they had not more than an hour of daylight left at best. Truly they were in desperate straits.

On they went over the drifts that seemed to be determined to bar their way, the superintendent straining his eyes for another glimpse of Eagle Rock. At last, as Harry was about once more to cry halt, his companion exclaimed joyfully,—

"There's Eagle Rock, Harry! I see it. We're making straight for it. A few minutes more will take us there."

The cheering announcement revived the boy's failing energies for another effort. He shut his lips upon the request for a rest, and doggedly tramped on after his guide.

Ten minutes more and they were at the foot of the lofty crag called Eagle Rock, in a friendly recess of which they found welcome shelter from the furious wind.

"Thank goodness!" ejaculated Harry, throwing himself wearily down upon a snow-bank, "we've got thus far anyway. How many miles more, Mr. Maynard?"

"About ten, Harry," was the answer, given in quite a matter-of-fact tone.

"Ten!" echoed Harry in dismay. "I hoped it would only be about five. I'll never do it in the world."

"Oh yes, you will, my boy!" replied Mr. Maynard. "I'll help you you know."

To their vast relief the snow now began to abate, and presently ceased falling altogether.

"That's something to be thankful for," said the superintendent. "Are you ready to start again?"

"Go ahead," was the response.

But no sooner had one danger passed than another presented itself. The light began to fail, for night was at hand.

A ten-mile tramp on snow-shoes through a desolate forest was not much to be desired under any circumstances. To accomplish it in the dark, tired as they both felt already, was a feat the achieving of which seemed more than doubtful.

Mr. Maynard had his misgivings, but he carefully concealed them from his companion, and even started whistling a lively march as he led the way along the faintly discernible road.

Never will either of them ever forget that awful tramp.

The night soon enfolded them, leaving only the scant light of the glimmering stars for guidance. Every step they took had to be carefully considered, lest they should stray from the track and be hopelessly lost.

Again and again the silence through which they marched was broken by the blood-curdling cry of the lynx or the dismal howl of the wolf, seeking what they might devour.

The superintendent's rifle hung at his back, and Harry had a good revolver; but they prayed in their hearts that they might have no occasion to use them.

Every little while they had to pause that the boy might take a brief rest. Then on they went again.

Mile after mile of the dreary, toilsome way was slowly yet steadily overcome, each one adding to poor Harry's weariness, until he felt as if he must give up the struggle and throw himself down in the snow to die.

But Mr. Maynard cheered him up and helped him, and kept him going, knowing well that to give up really meant death.

At last the exhausted boy sank down with a piteous wail,—

"It's no use, Mr. Maynard, I can't take another step."

"Oh yes, you can, Harry!" said the superintendent soothingly; "just take a little rest, and then you'll be all right."

While Harry rested he went on ahead a short distance, for it seemed to him that they could not be very far from the depot.

Presently there came from him a glad hurrah, and running back he put his arm around his companion, and helped him to his feet, exclaiming joyfully,—

"I can see a light, Harry. We're safe now. It's the depot."

And he was right. They were within half a mile of their haven. Forgetting all their weariness, they put on a gallant spurt, and in less than ten minutes were in the midst of their friends, telling the story of their thrilling experience.

All's well that ends well. The superintendent kept his appointments in the city; Harry had a royal Christmas time with the clerks in the depot; and, happy to relate, the horses were not lost, for a relief party that went out the following morning with a big sledge found them still alive, and brought them and the sleigh back to the depot, little the worse for the long imprisonment in the snow-drift.

"THERE'S nothing for it, Maggie, but to let the place go. I've tried my best to raise the money, but those that are willing to help a fellow haven't it to lend, and those that have it ain't willing to help. It's mighty hard lines, I tell you," and, with a groan of despair, Alec M'Leod buried his head in his hands, as he leaned heavily upon the table.

Hard lines it was, indeed, as no one knew better than Moses Shearer, the money-lender, to whose conduct was due Alec the miller's anguish of mind. He had chosen that particular time for enforcing satisfaction of his claim, because he understood that it could not be done without a sale of the mill property; and this was just what he desired, as he intended to bid it in for himself.

It did seem a cruel thing for Mr. M'Leod to be sold out of the snug, well-equipped mill that represented his whole fortune; and all for a debt of one hundred pounds, incurred under special circumstances for which he was in no wise to blame.

No wonder that he was sorely cast down, and that gloom reigned in his household, which consisted of a devoted wife and two children—Robert, the elder, a sturdy, enterprising lad of fourteen, and Jessie, a sweet, fair-haired lassie two years younger. They were all in the room when the miller gave voice to his despair, and Rob, full of sympathy, hastened to say something comforting, with all the hopefulness of youth.

"Don't give up yet, father," said he. "The sale is more than a week off, and you may be able to get the money somehow before then."

Mr. M'Leod shook his head without raising it from his hands. He had exhausted every available resource, and saw no way in which help could come. He was not a religious man, although of unblemished integrity of character, and had no faith to sustain him in his grievous trial; nor did his wife know how to lay hold upon God, and claim the fulfilment of his promises.

In this they both had much to learn from their own children, for, thanks to sound teaching in Sunday school, Rob and Jessie believed in the prayer of faith. They believed God was always ready and willing to respond in his wisdom to the petitions of his children, and when they learned of their father's trouble, their thoughts took the same direction.

That night, when Rob went up to his room, he found Jessie there.

"O Rob!" she hastened to say, "I've been waiting for you to come."

"What do you want to do, Jessie?" inquired Rob.

"Why, Rob, you know when father told us of his

trouble, I made up my mind to ask God to help him out of it. What is that in the Bible about God doing anything that two of his people agree to ask for?"

Proud of his memory, Rob promptly repeated the verse: "If two of you shall agree on earth as touching anything that they shall ask, it shall be done for them."

"Yes, that's it!" exclaimed Jessie. "Now then, Rob, can't we agree to ask God to help father to pay off that dreadful Mr. Shearer?"

"Of course we can," responded Rob heartily; "and we'll do it right away."

So down on their knees they went, and each in turn presented an earnest, simple petition to God that aid should be granted their father in the present emergency. When they rose their faces were radiant.

"It will be all right now, won't it, Rob?" said Jessie, as she went to her own room.

The following day passed without any sign of an answer, and so did the next. Rob, boy-like, began to grow impatient, but Jessie was more trustful. Each night they renewed their united requests.

On the third night Rob, the window of whose room overlooked the mill-pond, happening to awake about midnight, thought he heard a most unusual splashing noise coming from the pond. Sitting up in bed, and listening attentively, he asked himself :--

"What can it be? Has somebody fallen into the pond? No, it can't be that, or there would be cries for help. Oh! it's only some old cow that's fooling around."

He was about to accept this explanation and settle down to sleep again, when there was added to the frantic splashing a hoarse bellow such as no domestic animal ever uttered.

"I must see what that is," said he to himself. So out of bed he jumped, hurried on his clothes, and slipping quietly out of the house, hastened across the yard to the mill-platform, from which he could command a view of the whole pond.

It was a bright, clear night, with the moon at the full, and the still waters of the pond reflected its silver rays like a huge mirror. At first the boy could see nothing to account for the strange noises he had heard, but presently he discovered a big creature, whose exact nature he could not make out, in the deepest part of the pond, where, surrounded by the floating logs which had rendered futile all its efforts to extricate itself, it was, for the moment, resting quietly as though exhausted.

Rob's appearance upon the platform evidently aroused the creature to fresh exertions, and it proceeded to fling itself about with reckless fury, in the course of which its head emerged from the shadow into a broad band of light, and with a cry of astonishment Rob, who had been bending over the edge of the platform, sprang to his feet.

"Why, it's a moose!" he exclaimed; "and a monster one, too. And I'm going to catch him." Then looking down at the imprisoned animal, he added: "Just stay there, my beauty; I'll be back in a jiffy to look after you."

Darting over to the house he quickly aroused his father, who, as soon as he had assured himself that his son's story was correct, hastened to call up some of the neighbours. He did not stop to think what he would do with the moose when he had him safely secured. He was merely glad of a diversion that would help him to forget his troubles for a while.

But Rob already had a scheme worked out in his mind, of which, however, he intended to say nothing until the capture had been successfully accomplished. Then he would let it be known.

The neighbours responded readily to Mr. M'Leod's summons, and in a quarter of an hour half-a-dozen men were upon the scene, some armed with pitchforks, others with stakes, and all eager to have a share in the honours of the capture.

Many and various were the suggestions as to the best plan for getting the animal out of the pond uninjured, but no sooner had Mr. M'Leod offered his than it was unanimously adopted as the best.

By pushing away the logs a clear space could be made leading to the incline up which the logs were drawn to meet their fate at the saw's teeth, and the miller's idea was to lasso the moose by the antlers, drag the creature through the water to the foot of the incline, then attach the rope to the chain for drawing up the logs, and turn on the water-power.

The strongest animal that ever stood on four legs could not resist the tug of the chain, and thus the moose would be drawn up on the platform, and kept there, a safe prisoner, until he could be removed to the barn.

Mr. M'Leod had little difficulty in getting the rope fastened to the big branching antlers, and not much more in towing his captive around to the foot of the incline.

CAPTURING THE MOOSE.

But then came the rub. The monarch of the forest fought frantically against being drawn out of the water, and it seemed as if he might kill himself in his desperate efforts for freedom.

There was no resisting the inexorable strain of the log-chain, however, and foot by foot he was compelled to ascend the incline until he reached the platform.   Then the power was shut off, and Mr. M'Leod decided that it was best to allow the great creature to stay where he was until daylight.

The men all went back to their beds, but Rob remained. He did not want to leave the prize which had thus strangely fallen into his hands, and which he hoped to make signally helpful in his father's trouble.   So he chose a corner of the platform where he could keep the moose in full view, and composed himself to wait for the morning.

As he sat there his heart went up in gratitude to God, for right before him had he not the answer to the prayer he and Jessie had united in offering?

With the dawn Mr. M'Leod and the other men returned, and by dint of much shouting, flourishing of pitchforks, and tugging of ropes, the moose, after many furious attempts at breaking away, was at length safely conveyed to the barn, and securely fastened up in such a manner that he could do himself no hurt, struggle and kick as he might.

"Hip, hip, hurrah!" shouted Rob as the big door closed with a bang, and he flung himself against it to make sure that it was shut tight.   "We've got him all right enough. He can't get out of there until we want him."

"And now that you have got him, Robby," said the miller, laying his hand affectionately on the boy's shoulder, "perhaps you'll tell us what you are going to do with him."

Up to this point Rob had kept his own counsel, because his Scotch shrewdness told him it would be best to do so until the capture was successfully effected. But now there was no longer need for reserve.

"You remember that gentleman who was here hunting last winter, don't you, father?" said he, looking up eagerly into Mr. M'Leod's face.

"You mean Professor Owen from New York."

"Yes. Well, you know he said he'd give a hundred pounds for a full-grown moose alive; and now you must write and tell him you've got a beauty for him, and to come along and get it."

The miller's face became radiant as his son spoke. He now understood what had been in Rob's mind, and why he had shown such intense anxiety to secure the moose uninjured.

"God bless you, my boy!" he exclaimed, throwing his arms around his neck, for the revulsion of feeling broke down his characteristic reserve. "I see what you've been driving at. You always were a bright lad, and now, maybe, you're going to save me from ruin. I won't wait to write Professor Owen; I'll telegraph him. He left me his address so that I might let him know when the hunting was good."

Mounting his best horse, Mr. M'Leod hastened to the village, and sent this despatch to the professor: "Have a splendid live moose in my barn. Do you want him?"

Before many hours the reply came: "Am coming for him by first train."

The following evening Professor Owen appeared. When he saw the moose he fairly shouted with delight.

"A perfect specimen, and in the very prime of life," he cried. "I'll give you a hundred pounds for him on the spot. Will that be right?"

The offer was gladly accepted; and as soon as the necessary arrangements could be made, the moose was taken away to become the chief attraction in a famous zoological garden.

On the day before the sheriff's sale Mr. M'Leod, greatly to the money-lender's chagrin, paid his claim in full, and cleared his property from all encumbrance.

That night they had a praise-meeting at the mill; for when Mr. M'Leod was told about Rob and Jessie praying together for his deliverance from the grasp of Moses Shearer his heart was deeply stirred, and he joined in thanking God who had thus signally answered the children's petitions. Not only so, but both he and his wife were moved to withhold no longer from God's service, and they became active, happy members of the church.

As for Rob and Jessie, their faith was wonderfully strengthened, and often afterwards the recollection of this incident helped them to be trustful in the midst of many difficulties.

THE Canadian Pacific train, speeding swiftly on toward Winnipeg, had just dashed over an iron bridge which threw its audacious spider-web across a foaming torrent. Pointing down at the tumbling water beneath, one of the men in the smoking compartment of a palace car exclaimed,—

"I'd like to try that rapid in my *Rice Lake*."

"Are you so fond of a wetting as all that?" asked Charlie Hall with a smile.

"Oh, I'd risk the wetting. I've been through worse rapids than that without so much as being sprinkled." He proceeded to support his assertion by relating some of his adventures.

When Jack Fleming came to the end of his tether, the others had their say, for they had not been without experiences of a similar nature. Meanwhile, the fourth member of the group had been listening with interested attention, as if their stories were so novel that he did not wish to lose a word of them. He was merely a chance acquaintance, who had fallen into conversation with his fellow-travellers through the freemasonry of the pipe. They knew his name, Ronald Cameron, but they knew nothing more about him.

It was more for the sake of saying something courteous than with any idea of drawing the stranger out that Fleming turned to him and said, "Perhaps you know something about running rapids too?"

The stranger's bronzed face broke out into a smile, which meant unmistakably, "As well ask Grant if he knew something about fighting battles;" but there was not the faintest trace of boastfulness in his tone as he replied, "I have run a few rapids in my time."

"Well, it's your turn now; tell us your experience," said Fleming, and without much urging Cameron began.

"I must explain that I am in the employ of the Hudson Bay Company, and have spent many years in the North-west districts. My duties have required frequent long trips by York boat and bark canoe, in the course of which I have had my full share of tussles with rapids of all kinds. I could tell you half-a-dozen rather exciting little episodes, but I'll give you only one just now, namely, my passage of the Long Cañon of the Liard in a canvas boat."

"In a canvas boat?" broke out Fleming, half incredulously.

"Yes, in a canvas boat," repeated Cameron. "Not a particularly seaworthy craft, I must confess. But it was a notion of my own in order to get over the difficulty in which I was placed. I had been over in British Columbia, and was on my way back to Athabasca. The season was growing late, and I had only two men with me—an Indian and a half-breed. The Indian was a splendid canoe-man, but the half-breed was not of much account. The first part of the journey could be made by boat easily enough, but for us three men to drag a heavy boat over Grizzly Portage, which is about six miles long, and has a portage-path that climbs a thousand feet up the mountain side, was quite out of the question.

"So before I started I had a boat made out of tent canvas, which would be no trouble to carry. The wooden boat was to be left at the head of Grizzly Portage to take care of itself.

"Well, we got on smoothly until we passed the portage, and the Long Cañon opened out before us. As I looked at its wild rush of water, and realized that this was only the beginning, and far from the worst of it, I confess I felt tempted to turn back. But my pride soon banished that thought, and I set about getting my frail craft ready for the trip. Dennazee, the Indian, did not show the slightest concern; but Machard, the half-breed, was evidently much frightened.

"Assuming a cheery indifference I by no means felt, I went about the work in the most matter-of-fact way, and, with Dennazee helping heartily, the canvas boat was put together and set afloat.

"But it became evident immediately that she was not minded to stay afloat long. Although I had taken the precaution to give the canvas a good coat of oil, no sooner were we on board than the treacherous stuff leaked through every pore. Clearly this must be remedied before we could attempt the passage.

"Bidding the men gather all the gum and balsam they could find, I put the whole of our bacon, some ten pounds at least, half-a-dozen candles, and the gum and balsam into our pot, set it over a brisk fire, and produced the most extraordinary compound you can imagine.

"With this we thickly daubed the outside of the boat from stem to stern, and then left her for the night. The next morning she was as tight as a drum, and we started off, the poor half-breed muttering prayers in full expectation of a watery grave, the Indian as stolid as a statue, and myself much more anxious at heart than I cared to have either man know.

"The cañon is about forty miles long, and in that distance the river falls quite five hundred feet. Old Lepine, who has piloted boats up and down the Liard for thirty years or more, asserts that once, when the water was unusually high, he went through the whole length of the cañon in a York boat in two hours. The old man may be a few minutes short of the record, but there is no doubt that in the spring, when the snow is melting on the mountain slopes, the river runs at a fearful rate. I had hoped for low water, but, as luck would have it, a sudden spell of intensely hot weather had set the snow going, and the Liard was just high enough to be a very ugly customer.

"Well, we paddled out into the current, and then there was nothing to do but steer. I had the stern, and Denmazee the bow, while Machard clung tightly to the centre thwart, and was useful only as ballast. Like an arrow our little boat sped down stream, darting this way and that, dipping and dancing about like a cork, doing exactly what the water willed.

"At the very first swirl I found out something that gave me an additional shiver. This was that the boat could bear very little pressure from the paddle. If the water pulled one way and the paddle the other, the frail thing squirmed and twisted like a snake instead of obeying the steersman, so that it was quite impossible to make her respond readily or to effect a sharp turn. No doubt Dennazee discovered this as soon as I did, but he gave no hint of it, as with intent face and skilful arm he did his part of the work to perfection.

"The first few miles were not very bad, but we soon came to a place where whirlpool followed whirlpool in fearfully quick succession, and I no sooner caught my breath after escaping one than we were struggling with another. Our canvas cockle-shell appeared to undulate over the frothing waves rather than cut through them. I seemed to feel every motion of the water through her thin skin. In the very thick of it I could not help admiring the wonderful skill of the Indian in the bow. Again and again he saved us from dashing against a rock, or whirling around broadside to the current.

"For mile after mile we were tumbled about, and tossed from wave to wave like a chip of bark. My heart was in my mouth. I could scarcely breathe. My knees quaked, though my hand was firm, as, with eyes fixed upon Denazee, I instantly obeyed every motion of his paddle.

"In this fashion, one hairbreadth escape succeeding another, we did half the distance unscathed, and made the shore by the aid of an eddy at the head of the Rapids of the Drowned. These rapids got their forbidding name from the fate of eight voyagers, who lost their lives while attempting to run them in a large canoe. Being studded with rocks, these rapids are extremely dangerous. As the cañon widens out sufficiently to leave a narrow beach at this point, we preferred portaging our canvas boat to impaling her on one of the rocks.

"It was a strange thing that our sudden appearance should have so startled two moose who were standing on the shore that, instead of retreating up the hill, they plunged boldly into the river, of whose pitiless power they evidently knew nothing, and were borne helplessly away to destruction. A little later we saw their bodies stranded on a shoal, and the sight gave me a chill as I thought that that perhaps would be our fate, too, before we escaped from the Long Cañon.

"We had hard work getting the boat and ourselves over the broken, boulder-strown beach beside the Rapids of the Drowned, and the boat had more than one 'close call' as we slipped and stumbled about. I've no doubt Machard would have been glad to see it perforated with a hole beyond repair. But by dint of great care and hard work we did manage to bring it through uninjured, and then we halted for a rest and a bit of dinner.

"When it came to starting again, Machard vowed he would not get aboard. He pleaded to be allowed to follow us on foot; but I would not listen to him. I needed him for ballast in the first place, and moreover, if we did get

SHOOTING A FALL.

through alive, I could not afford to waste half a day waiting for him to overtake us. Drawing my revolver, I ordered him to get on board. He obeyed, trembling, and we started again, Dennazee as imperturbable as ever.

"We had the worst part of the passage still before us. The sides of the cañon drew close together until they became lofty walls, between which the river shot downward like a mill-race. The great black cliffs to right and left frowned upon us as if indignantly, and at every turn in the cañon a whirlpool yawned, ready to engulf us. Again and again I thought we were caught in a whirl, but in some marvellous manner Dennazee extricated us, and we darted on to try our fate with another.

"Extreme as our peril was, it had a wonderful thrill and excitement about it, and in the midst of it I found myself thinking that were I only in a big York boat I would be shouting for joy instead of filled with apprehension.

"The great difficulty was to keep our boat straight with the stream, for, as I have already told you, she was so pliant that she bent and twisted instead of keeping stiff, and more than once I felt sure she would cave in under the tremendous pressure upon her thin sides. To make matters worse she began to leak again, and although I commanded Machard to bail her out with a pannikin, he did it so clumsily in his terror that I was afraid he would upset us, and had to order him to stop.

"We must have had an hour or more of this, when for the first time Dennazee spoke. Turning round just for a moment he pointed ahead, and exclaimed, ' Hell Gate !'

"I knew at once what he meant. We had almost reached the end of the cañon. There remained only Hell Gate, and our perils would be over. *Only Hell Gate !*

I've not been much of a hand at praying, but I'm not ashamed to confess that I imitated poor Machard's example then. As for him, the moment he heard what Dennazee said, he fell on his knees in the bottom, and, clinging to the thwart, set to praying with all his might and main.

"With a thrilling rush we swept around the curve and plunged into Hell Gate. It is an awful place. The walls of the cañon are two hundred feet high, and not more than a hundred feet apart. The deep water spins along at the rate of twenty miles an hour, while at the end is a sort of drop into a black, dreadful pool, where the whirls are the worst of all.

"We got through the narrow passage all right, and then, with a dive that made my heart stand still, entered the whirlpools. There were three of them, and we struck the centre one. In spite of our desperate efforts, it got its grip full upon us, and round and round we went like a teetotum.

"It is not at all likely that I shall ever forget that experience. Our flimsy craft seemed to be trying to collapse every moment. It writhed and squirmed like a living thing, and at every turn of the awful circle we drew nearer to its centre, which yawned to engulf us.

"I had given up all hope, and was about to throw away my paddle and prepare for the last struggle, when suddenly there came a great rush of water down the cañon. The whirlpools all filled up and levelled over; for one brief minute the river was on our side.

"With a whoop of delight Dennazee dug his paddle deep into the water, and put all his strength upon it. I seconded his efforts as well as I could. The boat hesitated, then obeyed, and moved slowly but surely forward; and after some moments of harrowing suspense we found ourselves floating swiftly but safely onward, with no more dangers ahead."

Cameron ceased speaking, and picked up his pipe. There was a moment of silence, and then Fleming, drawing a deep breath, said with a quizzical smile, "Perhaps you *do* know something about running rapids."

THE CANADIAN CHILDREN OF THE COLD.

AFTER centuries of seclusion and neglect, broken only by the infrequent visits of ambitious seekers for the north pole, or mercenary hunters for the right whale, and by the semi-religious, semi-commercial ministrations of the Moravian missionaries, the Eskimos of the Labrador and Hudson Bay region suddenly had the eyes of the world turned inquiringly upon them.

The shocking story was published far and wide that a winter that did not change to spring in the usual way had cut off their supply of food, and that in consequence they were devouring one another with the ghastly relish of a Fiji cannibal. Although this report proved untrue, happily, the Eskimos are sufficiently interesting to attract attention at all times, and are little enough known to furnish an adequate excuse at this time for a brief paper upon them.

I.

To aid me in presenting the earliest glimpses of the Eskimos, I am fortunate in having before me a manuscript prepared by the late Robert Morrow of Halifax, Nova Scotia, an accomplished student of the literatures of Iceland and Denmark.

That to the Norsemen and not to the Spaniards rightfully belongs the credit of first discovering America is now settled, and that when the Norsemen first touched American soil they found the Eskimos already in possession is also certain. Yet it was not these bold adventurers that gave these curious people the name by which they are most commonly known. In the expressive Norse tongue they were described as "Skraelings"—that is, the "chips, parings." The intention was not, of course, to convey the idea that they were cordially accepted as "chips of the old block," but, on the contrary, to show that they were regarded by their handsome and stalwart discoverers as little better than mere fragments of humanity—a view which, however unflattering, their squat stature, ugly countenances, and filthy habits went far to justify.

The name "Eskimo" was given to them by the Abenaki, a tribe of Indians in southern Labrador. It is an abbreviation of "Eskimautsik," which means "eating raw fish," in allusion to their repulsive custom of eating both fish and flesh without taking the preliminary trouble of cooking it. The Eskimos themselves assert very emphatically that they are "Innuit"—that is, "the people"—just as though they were the only people in the world (and, by the way, it is worth noticing that each particular tribe of these "Huskies" thinks itself the entire population of the globe until undeceived by the advent of visitors). Their national name, if they have one at all, is "Karalit," the plural of "Karalik," meaning "those that stayed behind."

With reference to this latter title, Mr. Morrow points out a curious fact, which is suggestive. Strahlenburg, in his description of the northern part of Asia, states, on the authority of the Tartar writer Abulgazi Chan, that Og, or Ogus Chan, who reigned in Tartary long before the birth of Christ, made an inroad into the southern Asiatic countries, and as some of his tribes stayed behind, they were called in reproach "Kall-atzi," and also "Karalik." Now this "Karalik," with its plural "Karalit," is the very name that the Eskimos give themselves. So striking a resemblance, amounting in fact to identity, can surely be accounted for in no other way (and for this suggestion I must assume all responsibility) than that those who stayed behind in Tartary subsequently moved over to the American continent.

When Eric the Red sailed across from Iceland to Greenland (somewhere about the year 985), he found many traces of the Eskimos there; and when Thorvald, some twenty years later, ventured as far south as Vinland, identified as the present Martha's Vineyard (with which he was so delighted that he exclaimed, "Here is a beautiful land, and here I wish to raise my dwelling"), the unexpected discovery of three skin boats upon the beach affected him and his followers much as the imprint of a human foot did Robinson Crusoe. They found more than the boats, however, for each boat held three men, all but one of whom they caught and summarily despatched, for reasons that the saga discreetly forbears to state.

But retribution followed fast. No sooner had the invaders returned to their ships than the Skraelings attacked them in great force, and although the Norsemen came out best in the fighting, their leader, Thorvald, received a mortal wound. He charged his men to bury him upon the cape "at which he had thought it best to dwell;" for, as he pathetically added, "it may happen that it was a true word that fell from my mouth that I should dwell here for a time." His men did as they were bid. They set up two crosses over his grave, whose site is now known as Summit Point. They then hastened homeward.

After the lapse of two years, one Thorfinn Karlsifori,

fired by what he heard in Iceland of the wonderful discoveries made by the hardy sons of Eric the Red, fitted out an imposing expedition, his boats carrying one hundred and sixty men, besides women, cattle, etc., and set sail for Vinland. He reached his destination in safety, and remaining there for some time, improved upon his predecessor's method of treating the Skraelings. Instead of aimlessly killing them, he cheerfully cheated them, getting huge packs of furs in exchange for bits of red cloth. He has thus described his customers' chief characteristics: "These men were black and ill-favoured, and had straight hair on their heads. They had large eyes and broad cheeks." All of which shows that although the Eskimos have changed their habitat since then, they have not altered much in their appearance.

After two years of prosperous trading, the relations between the Norsemen and the Skraelings became strained from a cause too amusing not to be related. As already stated, the visitors brought a few of their cattle with them, and it happened one day that a huge bull had his feelings excited some way or other, perhaps by a piece of red cloth thoughtlessly paraded in his view; at all events he bellowed very loud, and charging upon the terrified Eskimos, tossed them about in the most lively fashion. They incontinently tumbled into their boats, and, without a word of farewell, rowed off, to the vast amusement of the bull's owners. But the latter's laughter vanished when presently the runaways returned "in whole ranks, like a rushing stream," and began an attack in which the Norsemen were vanquished by sheer force of numbers, and deemed it prudent to make off without standing upon the order of their going.

II.

With the departure of the Norsemen, the curtain of obscurity falls upon the Eskimos, and is not lifted again until we find them, not luxuriating amid the vine-entangled forests of Vinland, but scattered far and wide over the hideous desolation of the far north, and engaged in a ceaseless struggle with hunger and cold. Just when they thus moved northward, and why, does not yet appear. If their innate and intense hatred of the Red Indian be of any service as a clue, it is, however, within the bounds of reason to believe that they were driven from their comfortable quarters by their more active and warlike fellow-aborigines, and given no rest until they found it amidst the icebergs and glaciers of Labrador and Hudson Bay, where they may now be met with in bands numbering from a dozen to a hundred or more. Throughout the whole of this Arctic region they fearlessly range in search of food.

The Eskimos are, in fact, the only inhabitants of a vast territory, which includes the shores of Arctic America, the whole of Greenland, and a tract about four hundred miles long on the Asiatic coast beyond Behring Strait, thus extending over a distance of five thousand miles from east to west, and three thousand two hundred miles from north to south. Notwithstanding this wide distribution, there is a remarkable uniformity, not only in the physical features of the Eskimos, but also in their manners, traditions, and language. Consequently very much that may be said of the Canadian Children of the Cold (that is, the Eskimos of Labrador and Hudson Bay) would be equally true of the other branches of the race.

For a great deal of interesting information concerning them we are indebted to the writings of such men as Ribbach and Herzeburg, Moravian missionaries, who, with a heroic zeal that only those familiar with their lot can adequately appreciate, have devoted themselves to "the cure of souls" among the Eskimos. There are six of these Moravian missions scattered along the eastern coast of Labrador. Nain, the chief one, was established as far back as 1771, Okkak in 1776, Hopedale in 1782, and Hebron, Zoar, and Ramah more recently.

The bestowal of so attractive Biblical names helps very little, however, to mitigate the unfavourable impression produced by the forbidding surroundings of these tiny oases almost lost in a seemingly illimitable desert. Sheer from the sea, except where broken by frequent gulf and fiord, the coast line towers up in tremendous and unpitying sternness, and at its base the breakers thunder with a force and fury that knows little pause throughout the year. From end to end the shore is jagged like a gigantic saw with innumerable bays and inlets, sprinkled thick with islands and underlaid with hidden reefs, which makes these waters difficult to find and dangerous to navigate.

The interior of the country is equally repellent. Although toward the west it becomes less mountainous and slightly undulating, like the American prairie, it presents nothing but an inhospitable and savage wilderness, covered with immense forests, broken by numerous swamps and lakes, and untouched by human foot, save when now and then a band of Red Indians venture thither, lured by the hope of food and fur.

The Eskimos upon the eastern coast of Labrador are, as a rule, small of stature, not much exceeding five feet. Those upon the western shore, however, are taller and more robust; they are quite strongly built, with hair and beard sweeping down over the shoulders and chest. When the good seed sown by the patient missionary finds lodging in a Husky's heart, he usually signalizes his adoption of Christianity by indulging in a clean shave, or at least by cutting his beard short with a pair of scissors, in deference perhaps to the judgment of St. Paul that " if a man have long hair, it is a shame unto him."

They have small, soft hands, broad shoulders, big flat faces, large, round heads, and short, stubby noses,

" Tip-tilted, like the petals of a flower,"

and very generous mouths, which, being nearly always on the broad grin, make free display of fine rows of sharp, white teeth. In complexion they are tawny and ruddy, and the face is of a much darker shade than the body. At spring-time, when the sun's burning rays are reflected from glistening banks of snow, they become almost as black in the face as negroes; but new-born babes may be seen as fair as any English child. Their eyes are small and almost uniformly black, and peep brightly out at you from underneath a perfect forest of brow and lash. Their hair is black, also, and very thick and coarse.

Their ordinary food is the flesh of the seal, with its attendant blubber, and the fish that abound along the shore. They are not particular whether their dinner is cooked or not, and I seriously question whether a professional pugilist in the height of his training could swallow his beef-steak as "rare" as the Eskimos will their seal cutlets. They are also very partial to tallow, soap, fish oil, and such things, which they look upon as great delicacies, a big tallow candle being rather more of a treat to an Eskimo youngster than a stick of candy to a civilized small boy.

That these peculiar and decidedly repulsive tastes are, after all, bottomed on the laws of nature, is clearly shown by the fact that when the natives around a mission station adopt a European diet (and they soon become passionately fond of bread and biscuits) they inevitably grow weak and incapable of standing the intense cold. When Joe, that heroic Eskimo who supported Hall's expedition by his hunting, after Hall himself had died, was transplanted to America and thence to England, he soon languished and grew consumptive, despite every effort to preserve his health. On joining Captain Young in the *Pandora*, his only remark, uttered with a depth of eager, confident hope that was very touching, was, "By-and-by get little seal meat; then all right,"—a prediction that was fulfilled to the very letter when he regained his native ice. As soon as they killed their first seal Joe was given free rein, and he began to revive at once. His hollow cheeks resumed their old-time chubbiness (and smeariness too, no doubt), his languor left him, and he was, in short, another man.

The seal is, in fact, everything to the Eskimo. What the buffalo was to the American Indian, what the reindeer is to the European Laplander, all that, and still more, is the seal to these Children of the Cold. Upon its meat and blubber they feed. With its fur they are clothed. By its oil they are warmed and lighted. Stretched upon appropriate framework, its skin makes them sea-worthy boats and weather-proof tents. While, unkindest use of all, with its bladder they float the fatal harpoon that wrought its own undoing. To sum it all up in one sentence, take away the seal, and the Eskimo could not exist for a month.

There is not much room for fashion's imperious sway in Labrador. Seal-skin from scalp to toe is the invariable rule; and there would be no small difficulty in distinguishing between the sexes, if the women did not indulge in a certain amount of ornamentation upon their garments, and further indicate their feminity by appending to their sacques a curious tail reaching almost to the ground, which they renew whenever it becomes so dirty as to shock even their sluggish sensibilities. Still another distinguishing mark, permissible, however, only to those who have attained the dignity of motherhood, is the amook, a capacious hood hung between the shoulders, which forms the safest

and snuggest of all carrying places for babies that otherwise would be " in arms."

SEAL-HUNTING.

III.

In addition to the records of the Moravian missionaries,
the reports of the Arctic explorers and the stories brought
back by whalers concerning the Eskimos, much information
has been gained of late through the measures taken by the
Canadian Government to determine the practicability of
Hudson Bay as a commercial highway. For three successive years expeditions on an extensive scale have been

despatched to that little-known region, and observing stations have been maintained throughout the year at different points along the coast of Labrador and the shores of that great inland sea which has not inappropriately been termed the " Mediterranean " of Canada.   As one result of these expeditions, much attention has been drawn to the natives.   Lieutenant Gordon, who has commanded all three, has many kind words for them.   He finds them docile, amiable, and willing to work, and apparently much pleased with the prospect of increased intercourse with the white man.   Occasionally one is met that has been sufficiently enterprising to acquire the English language, while many others understand well enough what is said to them in that language, although they cannot be persuaded to speak it.

They are wildly fond of any article of civilized clothing, and the head-man at one settlement exhibited no little pride in the possession of a stand-up linen collar, almost worthy to be placed beside one of Mr. Gladstone's. Although he displayed it to the utmost advantage, he did not, like the Fiji chieftain, consider all other clothing superfluous.

When stores were being landed at the stations, the Eskimos would gather about and offer their services, which were always accepted, and then all day long they would toil cheerfully side by side with their white brethren, requiring no other remuneration than biscuits.   When so much has been written by Arctic explorers about the incorrigible kleptomania of the natives, it is no less a matter for surprise than for gratification that Lieutenant Gordon can bear this testimony as to the moral status of the Eskimos at Hudson Bay : " One word may be said in regard to their honesty. Although scraps of iron and wood possess a value to them which we can hardly appreciate, they would take nothing without first asking leave. Not even a chip or broken nail was taken without their first coming to ask permission of the officer who was on duty !"

No doubt the fact that practical prohibition prevails has something to do with this highly commendable showing. The law, aided and abetted by the vigilant missionaries, shuts out everything stronger than lime-juice, and the path of the Eskimo is free from the most seductive and destructive of all temptations, except when some unprincipled whaler offers him a pull out of his flask. This, however, is a rare occurrence, and there is no record of any such disturbance ever having been raised as would in more highly civilized communities call for the interference of the police. Although the simplicity of their life and their freedom from many modern vices conduce to longevity, these advantages are more than counterbalanced by the strain put upon their constitutions by the severity of the climate and the incessant struggle for food. Consequently they soon age, and seldom live beyond sixty years.

The doctrine that cleanliness is next to godliness finds few adherents in Eskimo land. The rule seems to be to eschew washing throughout the year, and many a mighty hunter goes through life innocent of a bath, unless, indeed, he should happen to be tumbled out of his kayak by some irate walrus with other than sanitary designs in mind. Mr. Tuttle, the historian of the first Hudson Bay expedition, is authority for the statement that the children, when very young, are sometimes cleaned by being licked with their mother's tongue before being put into the bag of feathers that serves them as bed, cradle, and blanket; but one cannot help thinking that this particular version of "a lick and a promise" is rather too laborious to have extensive vogue.

So familiar has the world been made through the medium of Arctic exploration literature with the igloos (huts), kayaks and umiaks (boats), sledges, dogs, harpoons, and other possessions of these people, which are precisely the same wherever they may be found, that reference to them seems unnecessary, especially as the Canadian Eskimos offer nothing peculiar. But, before concluding, a few words must be added as to the intellectual and moral characteristics of the race. Their intelligence is considerable. In some instances they display not only a taste but a talent for music, chart-making, and drawing. One case is mentioned where a mere lad drew an excellent outline of the coast for over a hundred miles, indicating its many irregularities with astonishing accuracy. They are capital mimics, and are apt at learning the songs and dances of their white visitors. But they are poor men of business. They generally leave to the purchaser the fixing of the price of anything they have to sell.

It is said that in their private lives their state of

morality is low, although they avoid indecency calculated to give public offence. Stealing and lying were unknown among them until these "black arts" were introduced by the whites as products of civilization, and, unhappily, the natives are proving apt pupils. They are also somewhat given to gambling. Although by no means without courage, they seldom quarrel, and never go to war with one another.

As to religion, the Eskimos, before they accepted Christianity, had little or none that was worthy of the name. They believe in the immortality of the soul, but liberally extend this doctrine to the lower animals also, which they endow with souls. They hold, also, that human souls can pass into the bodies of these very animals.

With respect to the higher powers, their creed is that the world is ruled by supernatural beings whom they call "owners;" and as almost every object has its owner, this would seem to be a kind of Pantheism. After death human souls go either up or down; but in curious contrast to the belief of all other races, the good, in their opinion, go to the nether world, where they bask in a land, not of milk and honey, but of inexhaustible seal meat and blubber. The bad, on the other hand, go to the upper world, where they suffer what a fashionable preacher euphemized as "eternal uneasiness," not from excess of heat but from frost and famine. There they are permitted to lighten their misery by playing ball with a walrus head, which diversion, by the way, in some inexplicable fashion, gives rise to the aurora borealis.

Like all aborigines they have their own legend of the deluge, and to this day they proudly point out a large island lying between Okkak and Hebron, rising to the height of nearly seven thousand feet, which they claim was the only spot left uncovered by the flood, and upon which a select party of their antediluvian ancestors survived the otherwise all-embracing catastrophe..

The future destiny of this interesting race may be readily forecast. In common with the Red Indian of the plains, the swarthy Eskimo may adopt with reference to the white man those words of fathomless pathos uttered by John the Baptist in reference to the Messiah, " He must increase, but I must decrease." It is merely a question of time. All over the vast region he inhabits are signs showing that his numbers were far greater once than they are at present. The insatiable greed of his white brothers is rendering his existence increasingly difficult. The seal and the walrus are ever being driven farther north, and that means a sterner and shorter struggle for life. As the Indian will not long survive the buffalo, so the Eskimo will not long survive the seal. There are, perhaps, fifteen thousand of them now scattered far and wide over the tremendous spaces between Labrador and Alaska. Each year their numbers are growing less, and ere long the last remnant of the race will have vanished, and the great lone North will return to the state of appalling solitude and silence that only the Canadian Children of the Cold had the fortitude to alleviate by their presence.

FACE TO FACE WITH AN "INDIAN DEVIL."

THERE were three of us, and we were all untiring explorers of the forests and streams within reach of our homes in quest of such possessors of fur, fin, or feather as our guns and rods could overcome.

Plenty of luck did we have too, for we lived in a sparsely-settled part of Nova Scotia, and the trout and partridges and rabbits had not had their ranks thinned by too much hunting. It was no uncommon thing for us to bring back, as the result of an afternoon's whipping of the brooks, two or three dozen speckled trout weighing from half-a-pound to three pounds each, while less than a dozen brace of plump partridges or bob-tailed rabbits was looked on as a very poor bag for a day's shooting.

Adventurous and enterprising as we were, however, one stream of which we had knowledge remained undisturbed by our lines. It was known among the Mic-Macs, a band of whom roamed about the neighbourhood, as Indian Devil Run, being so called because of their belief that the dense dark forest in which it took its rise was the fastness of a family of panthers, of which they stood in great dread.

Nor was the name without good foundation, for one autumn a hunter with gun and trap ventured into this place, and returned with the body of a panther, stating that he believed others still remained.

Indian Devil Run began somewhere in the North Forest, ran through its heavy shadows for several miles, and then appeared to add its contribution to the Digdequash River, at which point we made its acquaintance.

We often talked about following it up into the depths of the forest, but the Indian stories made us pause, until at last one evening in September, Jack Johnston, craving some fresh excitement, dared us to make the attempt, and we rashly accepted the challenge.

The following morning we set off, letting no one know the object of our expedition. We were armed in this fashion: Charlie Peters bore an ancient Dutch musket, warranted when properly loaded to kill at both ends; Johnston had a keen tomahawk, which the Indians had taught him to use like one of themselves; and I carried an old-fashioned smooth-bore shot-gun, dangerous only to small game.

"Now, if we come across an Indian devil, Charlie," said Johnston, "you give him a broadside from 'Dutchie,' and I'll finish him with my tomahawk."

"And where do I come in?" I asked, with a smile.

"*You?* Oh, you blaze away at him with your pepper-pot; you might perhaps put his eyes out, you know," Jack laughingly responded, and so our order of battle was settled upon.

We crossed the Digdequash in a canoe, hid our craft in the underbrush, and in high feather entered upon the exploration of Indian Devil Run.

It proved to be a succession of falls and rapids, overshadowed by huge trees for several miles, and we had hard work making our way up its course. But we toiled steadily on, and just before mid-day were rewarded for our pains by reaching a lovely spot, where the banks of the stream widened to form an enchanting pond encircled by a meadow, and offering every inducement to stay and rest.

Glad were we to do so. The pond evidently swarmed with trout. Quickly adjusting our fishing-tackle, we got to work. Shade of Izaak Walton! what a paradise for anglers! The water fairly boiled as the hungry trout fought for the privilege of being hooked. In one hour we landed as many as we could carry home, and they were fine fellows every one of them.

"The greatest place for trout I ever struck!" exclaimed Charlie Peters, throwing down his rod. "I positively haven't the heart to catch any more. It seems like taking a mean advantage of them."

So we stopped the slaughter—apparently much to the disappointment of our prey, who hung about asking to be made victims—and proceeded to dispose of the ample lunch with which our thoughtful mothers had provided us. Then we had a refreshing plunge in the clear water, scaring the trout nearly out of their skins, and by this time it was necessary that we should retrace our steps.

On our way up I had brought down a fine brace of birds, and to save carrying them to and fro had hung them to a high branch, intending to pick them up on the return journey.

"Don't forget your partridges, Hal," said Jack to me, as we shouldered our bags heavy with trout.

"No fear of that," I replied. "I know exactly where I left them."

Hitherto we had seen and heard nothing to justify the Indians' superstitious dread of the locality. No signs of wild animals were visible, and in high spirits at having discovered so rich a fishing-ground we hastened homeward.

"I guess the Indian devils have got tired of this place and left," remarked Charlie Peters. "But don't let us give it away all the same. We must keep this run all to ourselves as long as we can."

Hardly had he spoken when an appalling shriek pierced the silence of the woods, and brought us to a sudden stop, while we looked into one another's faces with an apprehension we made no attempt to conceal. We were close to the tree where the partridges had been hung.

"It's the Indian devil!" exclaimed Jack Johnston, under his breath. "He's eaten the partridges, and now he wants to eat us."

We fully realized our danger, and after the first shock of fright braced ourselves to meet it with a determined front. Johnston, as the eldest and coolest of the three, took command.

'Charlie," said he, "you must let him have Dutchie full in the face the moment we sight him.—Hal, you blaze

"JOHNSTON SENT HIS TOMAHAWK WHIZZING THROUGH THE AIR."

away with your shot-gun, and I'll stand by to finish him with my tomahawk.'

Nodding assent to these directions, we stood side by side, gazing eagerly into the forest gloom.

"There he is!" said Johnston.   "See! on that big limb."

We followed the direction of his finger, and saw the brute clearly enough, stretched upon a limb not twelve yards away, his great green eyes glaring horribly at us.

"Quick, Charlie!" cried Jack.   "He's going to spring. Rest your gun on my shoulder, and aim for his chest."

Charlie did as he was bid, and pulled the trigger. Bang went the old musket with a tremendous report. Over went Charlie on his back, his shoulder well-nigh dislocated by the kick of his weapon; and down came the panther to the ground, badly wounded in his neck and breast.   The instant he touched ground I let him have the contents of my shot-gun.   But they only served to bother him for a moment, and looking terrible in his fury, he was just gathering himself for a spring into our midst, when Johnston, stepping forward, sent his tomahawk whizzing through the air with all the force of his strong right arm.

It was a perfect throw.   No Mic-Mac could have done it better.   Like a flash of lightning the bright steel blade went straight to its mark, and buried itself in the panther's forehead right between those awful eyes, whose malignant gleam it extinguished for ever.

Lifting Charlie to his feet we rushed forward, and stood in triumph over our fallen foe, shaking hands across his mighty body.   How our hearts swelled with pride at the thought of the sensation our exploit would make!

With a twisted withe for a rope we laboriously dragged our prize to the canoe, and so got it across the river. Here we met the Indian who had been Johnston's teacher in the art of tomahawk-throwing. He seemed immensely relieved at seeing us.

" Me see you boys go over this morning, then hear devil scream this afternoon, and hear you go bang. Me 'fraid you all deaded this time."

Then as he discovered the fatal gash in the brute's head, his face lit up with pride.

" Johnston, you do that!" he cried. " Ah! smart boy. Me learn you how throw tomahawk like that."

Jack blushingly acknowledged the fact, and gave his Indian instructor due meed of praise for having taught him so well.

It was too big a job to get the heavy carcass of the panther any further, so the Indian took off the head and skin for us, and we presented him with the body, which he said was good to eat, and would " make Indian strong."

Our arrival at home with the trophies of our triumph over the terror of the forest caused great rejoicing. We were the heroes of the hour, and Charlie quite forgot his bruised shoulder in the pleasant excitement of the occasion.

We often revisited Indian Devil Run after that, and took many a fine fare of fish from its well-stocked waters, but we never saw another panther. We had apparently killed the last of the brood.

IN THE NICK OF TIME.

"WILL you be out to practice this evening, Charlie?" asked Rob M‘Kenzie of his friend Kent, as the two, who had been walking home from the high school together, parted at a corner.

"Indeed, that I will," was the reply; "and every evening, too, until the match comes off. It'll take all the practice we can put in to beat those Riverside chaps, I can tell you."

"Pshaw! What makes you think they'll be so hard to beat this time?" returned Rob. "We've always had our fair share of the games so far."

"So we have; but they didn't have Sam Massie playing with them."

"Sam Massie! who's Sam Massie?" exclaimed Rob, in surprise.

"Don't you know who Sam Massie is? Why, he's one of the first twelve of the Torontos," replied Charlie, looking somewhat astonished at his friend's ignorance.

"Then how on earth can he play with the Riversides?" asked Rob. "Can't we protest?"

"Oh, that's all right enough. His uncle lives in Riverside, and he is staying with him for a while, so we can't object to his playing."

"Humph!" growled Rob. "It's a pity we can't. We've got nobody to match him."

"I don't think it's a pity at all," returned Charlie cheerfully. "I'd a good deal rather see a crack player like Sam Massie, and get some points from him, than object to his playing, even if he gains the match for the other fellows. We'll do our best to give him a good day's work, any way. So let's practise hard." And Charlie went off whistling.

There was an intense rivalry between the villages of Riverside and Heatherton in the matter of lacrosse. Each village had a good club, in which not only the players but the people also took a hearty interest, and the matches that were played once a month alternately in each village during the season never failed to draw out to see them everybody in the population that could possibly manage to be present. They were always played on Saturday, because then the farmers from round about came in to the village to do their week's business early in the morning, and by rushing things a little could easily get through by three o'clock, and then they and the shopkeepers and the rest of the village folk would adjourn to the lacrosse-field and have a lively time of it, shouting, and cheering, and laughing as the game went on before them.

Charlie Kent and Rob M'Kenzie were the two youngest members of the Heatherton lacrosse twelve, and they naturally felt very proud of their position, which they had won by proving themselves the best players in the high school, and thereby attracting the attention of the Heather-ton captain quite early in the season. The day when big Tom Brown called them both aside and invited them to play with the first twelve was one of the proudest in their lives; and Tom had had no reason to regret his invitation on any game that summer, for the two "young cubs," as he called them, proved themselves very useful additions, being quick, careful, plucky, and, best of all, thoroughly obedient, always doing exactly what he told them.

The next match with Riverside was of special import-ance, because it would be the final and decisive one of five which the two clubs were playing for a fine set of silk flags, which had been offered as a trophy by some generous friends of lacrosse in both villages. Each club had won two matches, and now on the approaching Saturday the fifth and final match would take place, rain or shine.

The rumour of Sam Massie being with the Riversides had reached Heatherton early in the week, and caused no little concern, some of the players being disposed to make a protest if he appeared on the field, and even a refusal to play. But Tom Brown would not listen to them. Sam Massie was, for the time being at least, a resident in River-side, and to object to his playing would be acting in a way he did not approve of, so the dissatisfied ones were fain to hold their tongues.

The eventful Saturday came, and was as fine as heart could wish. It was Heatherton's turn to have the match, and the home team rejoiced at this, because it would in some measure compensate them for the advantage their opponents undoubtedly possessed in having Sam Massie with them.

Never before had so large a crowd assembled to watch the match. It really seemed as if half the population of Riverside and three-fourths of the population of Heatherton had turned out. The whole field was surrounded with a fringe of spectators, ready to applaud every good point in the game.

In due time the Riverside team made their appearance, looking very jaunty in their blue jerseys, caps, and stockings, and white knickerbockers, and all eyes were turned upon them to discover the redoubtable Sam Massie. It was easy to distinguish him from the others, and he certainly was a dangerous-looking player.

He was not of more than medium size, but the perfection of his condition, the graceful ease and quickness of his movements, and the unfailing accuracy of his catching and throwing, as the team indulged in the usual preliminary exercise, impressed everybody with the idea that he fully merited his reputation.

Charlie Kent's place was centre-field, his quickness and steadiness entitling him to that important position, while Rob M'Kenzie was the next man between him and the opponent's goal. Charlie was very anxious to see where the Riversides would put Massie, and was not at all sorry when that player took his place at cover-point, for now he would be certain to cross sticks with him more than once during the match, and find out just how strong a man he was.

Amid the breathless suspense of the spectators the two teams lined up, were briefly adjured by the referee to indulge in no rough play or fouls, and then in pairs departed to their places, the white and blue of the Riversides contrasting picturesquely with the white and crimson of the Heathertons as the players strung out from goal to goal.

"Are you all ready?" cried the referee.

The captains nodded their heads, the two centre-fields kneeled opposite one another for the face, the ball was placed between the lacrosse sticks, and with a shout of "Play" the referee sprang aside, and the struggle began.

There was a second's scuffle between the two centres, and then the Heathertons raised a shout; for Charlie had got the ball away from his opponent, tipped it cleverly to Rob, who, after a short run, had thrown it to "outside home," and the Riverside goal was in danger.

But before outside home could do anything, Massie was down upon him with the swoop of an eagle. With a sharp check he knocked the ball off his stick, then picked it up at once, and dashed away down the field, dodging in and out between his two opponents like a veritable eel. Not until he reached the Heatherton cover-point was he obliged to stop, and then he took a shot at goal, which, but for the plucky goalkeeper putting his broad chest squarely in the way, would certainly have scored.

Back the ball went, however, to the other goal, and continued thus to travel up and down for fully fifteen minutes before some skilful passing and sharp dodging on the part of the Heathertons brought it in front of the Riverside goal, when, after a hard tussle, it was swiped through by a lucky stroke from Charlie Kent.

Great was the elation of the Heathertons at scoring the first game.

" Guess they're not invincible, after all, if they have Sam Massie," said Charlie to Captain Brown.

" Mustn't crow too soon, Charlie," replied Brown cautiously. " We've got the afternoon before us yet."

When the Riversides, thanks to a brilliant run of Massie's, won the next game in five minutes, Charlie felt somewhat less confident ; and when, after a severe struggle, they by a pure piece of luck took the third game in twenty minutes, he began to feel a little down in the mouth.

But the winning of the fourth game by the Heathertons braced him up again, and he went into the fifth and final struggle with a brave and determined heart.

The excitement had now become intense. It had been agreed before play commenced that the game should be called at six o'clock, and if not then finished, played over again at Riverside the following Saturday.

The Heathertons fully appreciated the advantage of playing on their own ground, and were determined to settle the fate of the flags before six o'clock if at all possible.

The Riversides were equally determined to play out the time if they could do nothing better. Accordingly they concentrated all their strength upon the defence, and surrounded the redoubtable Sam Massie with the best men in the team.

Once more Charlie Kent won the face, and again tipped to Rob, who did not fail to send it well down towards the goal, but the stone-wall defence quickly sent it back. Again and again the rubber sphere went flying through the air or bounding along the ground towards the Riverside goal, and again and again it returned, not even being permitted to stay there a moment.

The minutes passed quickly, and six o'clock drew near.

"Charlie, can't you and Rob manage to get that ball down between you? Never mind your places; just play for the goal," said Captain Brown earnestly to Charlie.

"All right, captain, we'll do our best," replied Charlie, as he passed the word to Rob.

As luck would have it, the Riversides, grown bold by their success, opened out their defence just then, and moved nearer the Heatherton goal. Charlie's quick eye noted the change of tactics instantly.

"Look sharp now, Rob," he called, and Rob nodded meaningly.

A moment later the ball came flying his way, and springing high he caught it cleverly, amid a howl of applause from the spectators. Then signalling Rob to keep parallel with him, he dashed off at full speed towards the Riverside goal.

Charlie was lightly built and long-winded, and constant practice had made him the fastest "sprinter" in Heatherton. But he had never run before as he had then

The onlookers held their breath to watch him as he sped on. One, two, three opponents were safely passed by brilliant dodging, and now only Sam Massie stood between him and the goal.

He knew it would be useless to try to dodge Sam. But there was a better play. Before Sam could reach him he tipped the rubber over to Rob. Instantly Sam turned upon Rob, and brought his stick down upon Rob's with a resounding whack. But the ball was not there. Already it was rolling towards Charlie. who had continued straight on, and scooping it up from the ground, with a straight, swift overhand throw he sent it flying through the goal-posts just in time to allow the cry of "Goal! goal!" to be triumphantly raised ere the six-o'clock whistle sounded the hour for calling the game.

Charlie Kent was, of course, the hero of the day. Sam Massie, brilliantly as he had played, was quite forgotten. But he did not forget to come up and clap Charlie warmly on the back, saying,—

"Bravo, my boy! You'll make a championship player some day. You must come up to Toronto. We want your kind up there."

SNOW-SHOEING.

THREE things have the "red children of the forest" given to the white children of the cities which are so perfect in their way that it is hardly possible there will ever be an invention filed in the pigeon-holes of the patent-office that will surpass them. The canoe for shallow water and what might be called cross-country navigation, the toboggan, and the snow-shoe for deep snow, seem to be the very crown of human ingenuity, even though they are only the devices of ignorant Indians. One cannot help a feeling of hearty admiration when looking at them, and noting how perfectly they fulfil the purpose for which they were designed, and are at the same time as light, graceful, and artistic in form and fashion as the most finished work of highly-civilized folk. They all follow the line of beauty so closely that it is no wonder the ladies love to decorate their drawing-rooms and boudoirs with them, or to have their pins and brooches modelled after them.

To the Indian the canoe, snow-shoe, and toboggan were quite as important implements as the spade, the plough, and the rake are to the farmer. Without them he could

SNOW-SHOEING.

not in winter-time have roamed the snow-buried forests, whose recesses supplied his table, or voyaged in the summer-time upon the broad rivers and swift-running streams, whose bountiful waters furnished him their ready toll of fish. His white brother has in adopting them put them to a different use. He had no particular need for them in his work, but he was quick to see how they would help him in his play, and erelong they had all three become favourite means of sport and recreation.

Snow-shoeing disputes with tobogganing the honour of being Canada's national winter sport; for although snow-shoes have been seen in Siberia and Tartary, and are used to some extent in Scandinavia, in none of these places do the people derive much amusement from them. Simple as the snow-shoe seems, I would not advise any one to try to make a pair for himself. Only the Indians can do this really well, and even in Canada the vast majority of shoes are put together by dusky hands.

This is how they make a shoe of three feet six inches, which is a fair average size:—A piece of light ash about half-an-inch thick, and at least ninety inches in length, is bent to a long oval until the two ends touch, when they are lashed strongly together with catgut. Two strips of tough wood about an inch broad are then fitted across this frame, one being placed about five inches from the curving top, the other some twenty inches from the tapering end. The object of these strips is to give both strength and spring to the shoe. The three sections into which the interior of the frame has thus been divided are then woven across with catgut, each having a different degree of fineness in the mesh, the top section being very fine, the middle section, upon which almost the whole strain comes, coarse and strong, and the end section a medium grade between the other two. The gut in the middle section is wound right around the framework for the sake of greater strength, but in the other two is threaded through holes bored at intervals of an inch or so. Just behind the front cross-bar an opening about four inches square is left in the gut netting, in order to allow free play for the toes in lifting the shoe at each step. Both wood and gut must be thoroughly seasoned, or else the one will warp, and the other stretch and sag until the shoe is altogether useless.

The shoes are made in many shapes and of many sizes, ranging from two to six feet in length, and from ten to twenty inches in breadth. But for all practical purposes a shoe measuring three feet six inches by twelve or fifteen inches is the best. In racing, narrower shoes are used, but they rarely go below ten inches, that being the regulation measurement for club competitions. Then, again, some snow-shoes are turned up in front like tiny toboggans, instead of being flat, this kind being worn principally by ladies.

And now supposing that we have a pair of shoes entirely to our satisfaction, let us constitute ourselves members of a snow-shoe club, and take a tramp with it. Snow-shoeing is immensely popular in Montreal, as all visitors to the winter carnival well know. There are twenty or more organized clubs there, the membership in most cases being rigidly confined to the masculine gender, and every fine night in the week, all winter long, some club or other has a meet. Discipline is pretty strictly enforced at these club tramps, and seeing how earnestly the members go about the business, an onlooker might well be pardoned for thinking that there was quite as much work as play in this particular amusement. The pace set and the distance travelled are both beyond the powers of beginners, so that unless one is willing to stand a good deal of merciless chaffing, and have a pretty hard time of it altogether, it is better to wait until fairly familiar with the use of the *raquet* (the French name for the snow-shoe) before joining a club.

Let us imagine, then, that it is one of those glorious nights in midwinter when this dull old earth of ours seems transformed into fairy-land. The snow lies in white depths upon the ground, dry and firm as ocean sand; Jack Frost has brought the mercury away down some points below zero, and the keen air sets every nerve a-tingle; a superb full-orbed moon swings high in the heavens, flooding the wintry world with her silver splendour, and a hundred active, muscular young fellows have gathered at the rendez-vous, clothed in white blanket coats with rainbow borders, brilliant blue sashes and *tuques* (conical knitted caps sacred to snow-shoeing), knickerbockers of the same material as the coats, and stockings of the same colour as the sashes, while on their feet are soft moccasins skilfully decorated by Indian fingers. Sharp on time the club captain arrives,

THE START.

and in a trice all hands are down upon their knees fastening the raquets to their feet.

"Are you all ready?" shouts the captain. A hearty
chorus of "Ay, ay," rings out on the keen air. "Off, then!"
he answers, striding rapidly away, his followers stringing
out in a long line behind, for the walking is always done
in Indian file, and they set forth to attack the mountain,
which towers up so grandly behind the city, forming one
of the finest parks in the world.

The line of march is made up very simply. The captain, who is selected for that much-coveted position because
of his renown for speed and endurance, as well as his
knowledge of the best routes, takes the lead. The rank
and file follow in any order they please, and the rear is
brought up by the whipper-in. Although the post of
whipper-in is *not* much coveted, that officer ranks next in
importance to the captain, and should be one of the strongest and most experienced members in the club. His really
arduous duties are to quicken up the laggards, assist the
unfortunate, and inspire the despondent, for upon him it
depends to have the club all in together at the end of the
tramp. Wending along the snow-covered tree-bordered
paths, or diving deep into the forest where there are no
paths at all, the long thin line climbs steadily upward,
growing longer as the steep ascent begins to tell upon the
weaker ones, and they lag behind. At length the summit
is reached, and a halt is called for a few minutes, that the
panting, perspiring climbers may get their breath, and
close up the gaps in their ranks.

THE CLOSE.

"All up?" inquires the captain. "All up," is the cheery response. "Then forward!" and off they go again, this time down instead of up, with head thrown back, shoulders braced firmly, muscles at high tension, and eyes alert for dangers in the shape of hidden stumps or treacherous tree branches. Faster and faster grows the pace as the impetus of the decline is more and more felt, the shoes rattle like castanets, and the long line of white-coated, blue-capped figures undulates in and out among the tree clumps, appearing, vanishing, and reappearing like some monstrous serpent in full chase after its prey.

Ha! What's that? A fence right across the path? What is to be done now? The leader soon answers this question, for over the obstacle he goes as lightly as a bird, and his followers imitate him as best they may, some being content to crawl gingerly across by dint of hands and knees. One luckless wight, tripping on the top, takes a sudden header into the snow-bank on the other side, leaving only a pair of legs in sight to mark the place of his downfall. But the whipper-in comes to the rescue, and soon has him on his shoes again. What between fences, hedges, ditches, and other difficulties, the line is far from being well kept up. Gaps are frequent and wide. Some have fallen, and lost time in getting upright; others have been outstripped; but the leaders, like time and tide, wait for no man, and soon the welcome lights of the club-house, nestling in the valley, flash cheeringly across the snow.

Then the captain pauses a few minutes, that those who have been distanced may regain their places: and all being once more together, a final spurt at racing speed brings them, with shouts of joy and sighs of relief, to their goal. Here shoes are slipped off tired feet, coats and tuques thrown gleefully aside, and parched mouths cooled with refreshing drinks. An hour or more is spent in rest and frolic, and then the return journey made by the well-beaten road with the shoes strapped upon the back.

The distance "across the mountain" is nearly three miles, yet it has been done by an amateur in sixteen minutes twenty-eight seconds, which, considering the nature of the course, is remarkably good going. The best amateur time for a hundred yards on the flat is twelve and a half seconds, so that, clumsy and cumbersome as the raquets may seem at first glance, they are really a very slight bar to speed when the wearer is thoroughly expert in their use.

Hare and hounds on snow-shoes is a sport that must commend itself to all strong and vigorous boys who have a taste for cross-country work, if only for the reason that the snow-shoes make the sport possible at a time when it would otherwise be out of the question. The "hare" can be followed by his tracks, thus doing away with the necessity of carrying cumbrous bags of paper "scent."

Snow-shoeing differs from many other sports in being very easy to learn. Once you have mastered the art of sliding one shoe over the other with very much the same motion that you would make in skating, instead of lifting it up high as though you were wading in deep snow, as you are sure to do at first—once you properly understand this your chief difficulty is conquered, and proficiency comes with a little practice.

Throughout the length and breadth of Canada snow-shoeing is popular with young and old Every centre of population has its clubs. Competitions are held every winter, at which tempting prizes are offered to the winners in races at different distances, from one hundred yards up to ten miles.

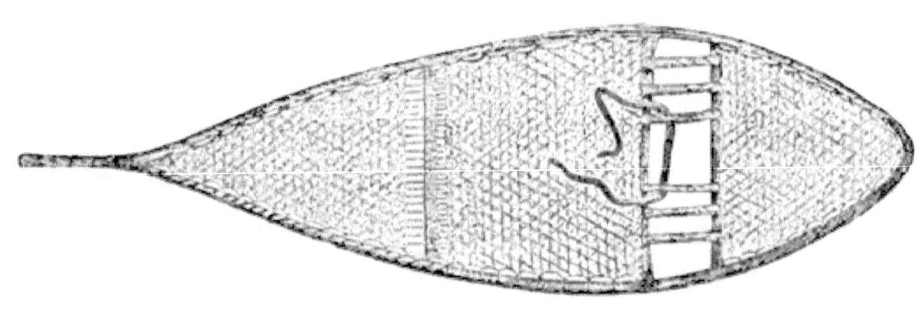

THE SWIMMING MATCH AT THE ARM.

"FRANK, Frank! Hold on there a second," cried Jack Stone breathlessly, as he ran after his friend.

Frank halted until Jack caught up to him.

"Well, Jack, what's your news? You seem to be excited about something," said he.

"So I am," panted Jack, "for I've big news to tell you. Uncle William has offered a sovereign to the fellow that makes the best time swimming across the North-west Arm. What do you think of that?"

"Why, I think it's just splendid of him, and I'm going to try, for one."

"And I, too, you may be sure. And George Murray and Hal Hemming say they're going in. I was telling them about it this morning. Of course we can't all win; but the more the merrier, you know, and I think you and I will stand as good a chance as any of them."

"Just about as good," assented Frank. "That is, if none of the big boys are allowed to try. Did your uncle make any rule about that?"

"Of course he did," replied Jack. "Nobody over fifteen can compete."

"Oh, that's all right! And it's only fair, too," said Frank, evidently much relieved.

"S'pose we go out and have a practice this afternoon," suggested Jack. "It's so hot that the water ought to be as warm as milk."

"All right!" said Frank. "Just wait till I leave this parcel at the house and get a couple of towels, and then I'm with you."

Accordingly, a few minutes later the two boys, with towels in hand, were trudging toward the North-west Arm, impatient to be in the water, for the sun was sending down lots of heat that summer afternoon.

Frank Brookfield and Jack Stone were very great friends; had been so, indeed, almost from their nursery days. They got along about as well together as two boys who had each his own share of spirit and selfishness could; and although they were rivals in a good many of their boyish sports, they had a wise way of looking at the matter, for, next to coming out first himself, each was eager that the other should, and consequently they had no occasion to quarrel over the result.

In the science of swimming they were very evenly matched; what Jack lacked in strength as compared with Frank, who stood an inch taller, being about made up by a superiority in style that was natural to him in everything he did.

Hot as the afternoon was, they were too eager for their dip to walk slowly, and when they reached the projecting rock from which they were accustomed to bathe—Black

Rock it was called, being a mass of dark, rusty iron-stone —they were both very warm and in a high state of perspiration.

This, however, would not have mattered much if they had undressed immediately and plunged right in; but instead of doing so, they laid aside their outer clothes and then sat down to cool off, thus allowing a reaction to set in that came near having serious consequences.

When they thought they had cooled sufficiently, they finished their undressing and were ready for the water.

"I've half a mind to swim clear across," said Frank, as they stood out on the end of the rock, hesitating for a moment, as all swimmers do, before diving into the cool, green depths.

"Better not," said Jack, who was the more cautious of the two. "You might be too tired to swim back."

"Well, then, I'll tell you what we'll do. We'll swim out to the middle and back again, and that'll be just the distance for the race."

"All right! Here goes!" assented Jack.

And with a plump! plump! the two boys, like two gigantic bull-frogs, went head first into the water, coming up again three or four yards away, with dripping heads and blinking eyes, and striking out vigorously toward the centre of the Arm.

"Ah, but it's cold!" exclaimed Frank, half gasping.

"You bet," concurred Jack, very heartily—"cold as ice! What business has the water to be so cold on such a broiling day as this?"

"Oh, it's just a little way it has," said Frank. "But cold or not cold, I'm going out to the middle."

And with a powerful overhand stroke he ploughed his way through the rippled brine, his shoulders gleaming white as he bent to his work.

Jack, using the ordinary breast stroke, kept close up to him, and they worked too hard to do much talking until the centre of the Arm was reached, and they could see the whole beautiful sheet of water from end to end.

Then they paused, and Frank, saying he was beginning to feel tired, turned over on his back for a little rest, Jack forthwith imitating his example.

"Sakes alive, but this water *is* cold!" cried Jack. "If we stay in it much longer we'll be getting the cramps. Let's make for the shore."

"All right! Go ahead; I'm after you," replied Frank.

Jack accordingly turned his face shoreward, and, trying the side stroke now, was making pretty good progress, having got about half-way in, when a cry from Frank, who was a few yards behind, made him stop suddenly and wheel round to see what was the matter.

"Come here, Jack," said Frank, in a troubled voice.

And Jack immediately went back to him.

"What's the matter, old chap?" asked he anxiously.

"Why," answered Frank, "I seem to be losing all my strength. See! I can hardly take a stroke."

And, sure enough, his strength seemed to have left him, and instead of the wide, powerful sweeps he usually made, he could manage to do little more than paddle enough with his hands to keep his head afloat.

The fact of the matter was that he had been seized with muscular cramp, and was in great danger, for there was no boat in sight, and the shore lay nearly fifty yards away, with water deep enough between to swallow an ocean steamer.

Jack fully realized the danger, but was too sensible to say so. Taking a firm grasp of Frank's right shoulder with his left hand, he said cheerily,—

" Come along now ; I'll give you a lift."

Then, putting forth all his strength, he pushed Frank forward ; while the latter could just manage to keep his head above water, and pointed in the right direction.

In this fashion they crept slowly along, Frank growing more helpless and Jack more tired every yard. Frank now could not even keep his mouth above water, for the deadly cramp was drawing him all together, his back being bent like a bow, and his arms and legs contracted until they were almost altogether useless.

Jack, too, began to feel the cruel cold fastening upon him, and his strength departing from him. His heart sank as he looked at the distance still ahead, and felt himself weakening at every stroke.

In his extremity, the temptation to let go of Frank, and strike for the shore alone, even flashed into his mind, only to be contemptuously dismissed with the silent resolution to stay by his friend whatever happened.

At length, by dint of grim determination, Jack got Frank

within ten yards of the shore, and then, feeling as though any further effort on his part were impossible, he gave him a big push forward, saying,—

"Now then, Frank, do the rest yourself."

With a muffled, half-finished cry of "For heaven's sake, Jack!" poor Frank, utterly helpless, went under, half turning over on his back as he did so.

Not for a moment did Jack hesitate. Weak and chilled as he was, the sight of his playmate's peril nerved him to fresh exertions, and summoning all his energies for one supreme final effort, he grasped Frank's shoulder once more, and with desperate spasmodic strokes fought his way through the water.

Never will he forget that wrestle with death. Frank, fortunately, still keeping collected and quiet, could get but an occasional breath, for now nearly his whole face was submerged, and Jack himself seemed to be swimming in some dense fluid that stubbornly opposed the movements of his arms. But foot by foot he struggled on, until at length, just when every atom of strength and hope seemed exhausted, he saw below him the dark, seaweed-covered rock, and putting down his foot, found solid bottom beneath him.

"Thank the merciful Father, we're saved, Frank!" he cried, half sobbingly, as he drew his companion up on to the rock.

"God bless you, Jack! you've saved my life," replied Frank, with a fervour that showed how clearly he understood the magnitude of the peril through which he had passed. "Yes, Jack, you've saved my life, and some day I'll show you how grateful I am."

"Oh, that's all right!" said Jack. "You'd do the same for me if you had the chance."

"I hope I won't have the chance, all the same," answered Frank, "for perhaps I wouldn't keep as cool as you did: and then where would we be?"

Half-an-hour's basking in the hot sun took all the cramp out of the boys' bodies, and they went back home, not a whit the worse for their experience, and a good deal wiser. They kept the matter to themselves, prudently thinking it would only alarm their parents if it came to their ears, and perhaps make them worry, while really there was no occasion for further anxiety.

The following Saturday afternoon was the time fixed for the swimming race, and the two friends practised diligently, determined that the sovereign should fall to one of them at all events, or perhaps be divided between them if they came out a tie.

The eagerly-anticipated day dawned sunnily, and proved as fine, bright, and warm as heart could wish. A great deal of interest was felt in the swimming race, for at least six boys had entered for it, and in the afternoon the Arm, at the place where the swimming would take place, was dotted over with boats, containing the fathers, mothers, sisters, cousins, aunts, and friends of the different contestants.

Uncle William (or, to give him his proper title, Mr. William Cunard) was the judge at the finish, and the six boys, wearing the scantiest possible bathing suits, were rowed across to the other side of the Arm in boats.

"I'm awfully excited," said Jack Stone to Frank Brookfield on the way over, in so low a tone that none of the other boys heard him. "Father says he'll double the prize if I win. But if I don't win, I hope to goodness you will."

"Whoever wins will have a hard fight for it," said Frank. "Both George and Hal can swim like fishes. I don't know about the other two."

Presently the boat touched the shore, and the boys all leaped out and took up their positions upon the ledge of rock from which they were to start.

"Are you ready?" called out the starter. "Then go."

And with a tremendous splash the whole six plunged into the water like one man.

The next moment they were all at the surface again, and cleaving the calm water at the top of their speed.

Frank was using his favourite overhand stroke, Jack the side stroke, and the rest the ordinary breast stroke.

For some distance there was little difference between them. You might have covered them with a handkerchief, so to speak. Then, little by little, Frank and Jack, keeping well together, began to draw away from George and Hal, who in their turn led the other two.

By the time the centre of the Arm was reached, it was plain to all that the race lay between the two friends, and amid cheers and shouts of "Go it, Frank!" "Hit her up,

Jack!" "Pretty work, both of you; keep it up!" they ploughed through the water side by side.

"JACK FELT HIMSELF WEAKENING."

Three-fourths of the distance was now covered, and their positions were unchanged, when with a pang that went right to his heart Jack felt himself weakening.

Inch by inch his stroke shortened, and first Frank's head, then his neck, then his shoulders slipped past him.

Gritting his teeth with fierce determination, and breathing hard, he strained every nerve to recover his lost ground; but all in vain. Frank gained steadily until his heels were in a line with Jack's head.

Already they were raising the shouts of victory, when Frank, turning to see what lead he had, caught sight of Jack's pale face, in which disappointment and despair were already showing themselves, and it brought up in his mind that same face a week before, when, pallid but resolute, just as it was now, it cut the water close beside him, while the boy to whom it belonged struggled so bravely with the death that threatened.

A mist came in his eyes and a lump rose in his throat as he thought of this

"He saved my life," he murmured to himself.

"Hallo! what's up with Frank?" said Mr. Cunard. "He has almost stopped. He must be done out. Just shove out that boat there toward him, will you?"

"Go on and win, old chap," said Frank to Jack, when the latter came up to him. "I'm used up. I'll just paddle in slowly. Oh, I'm all right," he added, as Jack showed signs of stopping to help him. "Tired out, that's all."

Cheer after cheer rang out as Jack, nearly exhausted himself, but undaunted in spirit, swept by Frank, now paddling quite leisurely, and finished the course amidst a general chorus of congratulation.

He felt as proud as Punch, and when Frank came ashore, threw his arms around him affectionately, saying,—

"You're a dear, good fellow to let me beat you."

Not that he had the slightest suspicion as to how it had really happened.

Frank never told him. Indeed he never told anybody except his mother, and she alone of all the people who witnessed it knew the secret of Frank Brookfield's sudden collapse in the swimming match at the Arm.

HAROLD'S LASTING IMPRESSION.

"HAROLD, Harold, Harold!" cried Mrs. Owen, at the top of her clear, strong voice, her anxiety increasing as no answer came back. "Mercy on me! what can have become of that boy? As sure as anything, he has gone down to the wharf again—and after all that I have said to him too. I do wish something would make a lasting impression upon him." And with a feeling of uneasiness she could not shake off, the troubled mother went back to her house-work, sighing over her boy's disobedience.

Now Harold Owen was not really a bad boy. He loved his mother dearly, and always felt sorry when he had grieved her; but he was such a thoughtless little chap. Eight years old last October; stout, cheery, and brave; full to overflowing of animal spirits; eager to do everything he saw the older boys doing, and always wanting to be with them; quite as heedless and forgetful as he was affectionate and obliging, sturdy little Hal was just the kind of boy to make a mother whose only child he was no less anxious than proud about him. And in these lovely summer days, when nobody wanted to be indoors between daylight and dark, except to eat their meals, poor Mrs.

Owen had her hands full in trying to keep track of her son, who would stray off in spite of her orders to stay near home. You see, Harold did not just mean to flatly disobey his mother. For days together he would do exactly what she told him, and make her very happy. But every now and then some of the boys in the neighbourhood—Jack Hardie, perhaps, or Frank Lawson—would come along, and get talking with Hal over the garden fence; and as sure as they did, it ended in the little fellow's forgetting all about his mother's commands, and going off to the wharves, where sometimes he stayed so long as to give his mother quite a fright.

That was exactly what had happened this glorious July morning, when Mrs. Owen, missing her boy's shouts from the front garden, ran out to the door, her bare arms all white with flour, for she had been making a cake, and called "Harold, Harold, Harold!" so loud that you might have heard her half-way down to the wharves. If, indeed, she could have been heard all the way down, perhaps her call might have brought Harold back; and in that case he should not have got his lasting impression, and I would have had no story to tell. But just at this time our little man was altogether too much taken up with what Jack Hardie was telling him to hear anything less noisy than a steam-engine.

"I'll bet my boots, Hal, you never saw such a funny little chap in your life. He is about as big as our baby, but nothing like so fat, and he has long hair all over him—over his face too—and he jumps around, and talks away at the fellows, and sits up on his hind legs to eat nuts and crackers.   Oh, I tell you he's lots of fun!"

This was part of Jack's account of a very interesting monkey belonging to the black cook of a large ship then at the wharf; and it was the promise of showing him this monkey—what eight-year-old boy could resist such a temptation?—that had lured Hal away from home. Down to the wharf they ran as fast as their legs could carry them, and there they found half-a-dozen other youngsters much about their own age, all evidently bent on the same errand.   The stately *Roseneath* lay right across the end of the wharf, and was being fed with long, yellow, sweet-smelling deals that would make houses in England some day.   The boys stood for a while watching the huge planks sliding through the bow-ports into the dark mysterious hold, and then there was a general rush for the stern, where they expected to find the rope-ladder by which they would climb on board.   But, much to their disappointment, no ladder could they see, and no way of climbing up except a thick rope that dangled over the side, reaching quite down to the wharf; the truth of the matter being that the sailors, getting rather tired of the boys' frequent invasions, had taken away the ladder and put the rope in its place, thinking thus to put a stop to their coming on board.   The tide was high, and the great black hull of the ship towered above the wharf like the side of a house.   The boys looked pretty blank at first; but then you know it takes a good deal to stop an enterprising boy when his heart is set on anything; and

presently, after a little talk together, Jack Hardie said he
would see if he couldn't shin up the rope.   So he clasped
the rope tight in his brown fists, twined his
strong legs around it, and up he went, not
very fast, to be sure, but gaining a
bit at every wriggle, until at last he
reached the bulwarks, and the
boys gave him a cheer as he
called out, "Come

RESCUER AND RESCUED.—*See page 185.*

along, fellows; it's not so hard; you can all do it."
Frank Lawson tried next, and he got up all right.   Then
Charley Wright followed.   And now Master Harold thought
he would try his luck.   So, too, did Jim Norton; and
when Harold got the rope first, it made Jim so cross that,
like the rough, heedless chap he was, he gave Hal an angry

push just as the little man had let go from the wharf, and was clinging to the rope.

Of course, Jim did not really mean any harm, but he came pretty near doing dreadful harm all the same; for his push was such a hard one that it loosened unlucky little Hal's hold upon the rope, and with a cry of fright down he dropped between the vessel and the wharf, falling with a great splash into the dark green water.

Poor little Hal! you may well wish you had not disobeyed your mother's orders, for now there is small chance of your ever being able to disobey them again. The tide had begun to run out, and although Harold struggled up to the surface twice, so that his terrified playmates caught a glimpse of his pale, frightened face for a moment, the cruel current dragged him down again, and the horrid salt water rushed into his mouth, as he opened it to cry for help. His father had given him some lessons in swimming that summer, and he tried to put them in practice now, striking out bravely with his plump fists and sturdy legs; but of course such swimming as that could not help him, and he sank deeper and deeper. Then at last he gave up trying to save himself. He lost all sense of suffering, and as he drifted passively away with the current, a strange thing happened to him—something that he will never forget, though he lives a hundred years—and it was this: all his past life appeared before his mind in a series of pictures, in fact, just like the panorama of the American rebellion he had enjoyed the winter before. All his doings, good and bad, but more particularly the bad ones, seemed to come up clearly before him, and as he saw what a naughty, thoughtless boy he had been, he felt sorry enough never to disobey his dear, fond mother again. But wasn't it too late now?

✻   ✻   ✻   ✻   ✻

What! up in the sunshine once more, and sitting on the solid yellow deals, with his companions crowding round him, laughing and crying, and patting him on the back, and acting so comically, while all the time the water is dripping down off his clothes, and making a puddle at his feet, and he does feel so uncomfortable underneath his blouse. And who is the big strong man standing near, just as wet as himself, and looking at him with his handsome bronzed face full of pride and pleasure? And isn't that father coming down the wharf as hard as he can run, with face so white that he looks like a ghost?

Bewildered little Hal couldn't at first understand what it all meant; and when his father, catching him up in his arms, pressed him passionately to his breast, the little man just burst out crying, and hid his wet face on his father's shoulder. In this fashion he went back home, the boys following in a triumphal procession.

An hour afterwards, when Master Harold had got rid of the uncomfortable feeling under his blouse, and put on a warm, dry suit of clothes, Jack Hardie told him how, when he fell plump into the water, the boys had all shouted out for help; and how the mate of the *Roseneath* had sprung out of his cabin at the first cry, and, directed by Jack, without waiting even to take off his coat, had dived right down into the deep, dark water; how he had come up once without finding Hal, and, after taking breath, had gone down a second time in search of him; how he had hunted around in the water until at last, seeing something black below him, he had stretched down his leg, and his toe catching Hal under the chin, the gallant mate drew him up into his arms, and then made for the daylight; and how, when Harold first came out of the water, he seemed to be dead, but in a few minutes came to life again, and sat up, blinking his eyes like a young baby. All this, and more too, did Jack Hardie, proud of having such an audience—for, besides Mr. and Mrs. Owen, a dozen or more of the neighbours had run in to hear all about it--relate with great gusto And as Harold realized how very near he had come to losing his life, and looked into his darling mother's face streaming with tears of joy and gratitude, which but for the brave sailor would have been tears of bitter sorrow, he gathered up his little features into a most determined expression, and said,—

" Mother, I'll never disobey you again."

Thus did his mother get her wish, and Master Harold his lasting impression, which many a time saved him from falling again into disobedience.

HOW WILBERFORCE BRENNAN VISITED
WHITE BEAR CASTLE.

"WILBY! Wilby! come here; I want you," called a woman's shrill voice at the foot of the stairs.

And down from the little attic room came the answer promptly,—

"All right, mother; I'm just coming."

A minute later a stout, hearty lad of fifteen presented himself before his mother, and dutifully awaited her commands.

"Why, Wilby," said she, "I was just thinking I had better send you over to Aunt Matilda's to tell her that your father was going to town to-morrow. She's pretty sure to want him to do something for her, and he goes so seldom nowadays she'll be disappointed if we don't let her know."

"Well, mother," replied the boy, looking rather doubtfully out of the window, from which a vast expanse of desolate, snow-covered fields could be seen, "it's not just the best kind of an afternoon to be going away over to aunty's. There's a heap of snow on the ground, it's awfully cold, and the wind's rising."

"Tut! what does a big strong boy like you care for the cold? Besides, you can put on your snow-shoes, and take the short cut through the wood-lot. You won't feel the wind in the woods. I really must send Aunt Matilda word, and father won't have time to go over himself."

"Very well, mother, if I must I must, I suppose; but, all the same, I wish it could wait till to-morrow."

So saying, Wilby, with a sigh of resignation, went off to get ready for his tramp.

It was no trifling affair, this errand over to Aunt Matilda's, I can tell you. She lived six good miles away by the road, and even taking the short cut through the pasture and wood-lot, it was not less than four miles.

Of course, with fine weather and good going, four miles was not much of a task for Wilby's sturdy legs, and he never failed to get so warm a welcome and such delicious cake at his aunt's that generally he was only too glad to go. But in mid-winter, with four feet of snow on the ground, the thermometer right down to zero, and the wind cutting like a knife, it seemed a very different matter.

However, Wilby, as his mother called him for short (Wilberforce being kept for company or for when she wanted to be very emphatic), was quite as plucky as he was obedient, and a quarter of an hour after his mother first called him he started out on his errand, muffled up to the eyes, with his snow-shoes well strapped to his feet, and his good dog Oscar trotting along beside him. It was well for him that he did have wise old Oscar, as we shall presently see.

Bending his head low, so as to protect his face as much as possible from the keen wind, and swinging his arms to and fro in time with his stride, Wilby went swiftly down the hillside, across the river, and up the other slope, until he reached the shelter of the woods, where the wind bothered him no longer, and he could take things more quietly.

Oscar ran soberly along at his heels, and Wilby was glad of his company, for the short winter day was already drawing to a close, and the lonely wood-lot was not the most cheerful place in the world to be in at that time.

Wilby was a great boy for books, and had just finished reading Colonel Knox's delightful story, "The Voyage of the *Vivian*," of which the most interesting part to him had been that relating to the polar bears; and now, as he trudged steadily along through the silent woods, he fell to thinking about these bears, and wondering what he should do supposing he should meet one.

Of course, he knew well enough that the nearest white bear was at least a thousand miles away, and that even an ordinary black bear had not been seen in that neighbourhood for years; but, all the same, he could not get those cruel white monsters out of his thoughts. In fact, he became quite nervous over them, and would peer eagerly ahead and anxiously around, just as if one of them might rush in upon him at any minute.

At length his nervousness got so much the better of him that walking seemed altogether too slow, and he started off on the hard run. Only two miles of the distance to Aunt Matilda's was left at this time, and one of these soon disappeared as Wilby hurried onward, with Oscar bounding joyfully beside him.

Ten minutes more at the farthest, and they would be safe at their destination. Already Wilby thought he could catch through the trees a gleam of light from the kitchen window, when suddenly something unfortunate happened.

It had been hard work keeping to the wood path, so buried was it under the snow ; and he must have strayed a little from it, for he found his way barred by a huge tree-trunk, which certainly ought not to have been there.

The wisest thing, of course, would have been to retrace his steps a bit ; but instead of that, Wilby rashly tried a running leap over the obstacle, and it was not a success.

Without snow-shoes he might have cleared it easily ; but with these encumbrances on his feet, he not only made a very poor attempt, but in some way or other they got entangled together, and in a violent effort to keep his balance, he sprained his right ankle so badly that, to his great dismay, he found he could no longer bear any weight upon it.

Here was a pretty state of affairs indeed ! A whole mile from Aunt Matilda's, not yet clear of the woods, not a living soul within reach of his voice, his right leg utterly useless and hurting awfully, and the cold growing more intense every minute !

It did not take poor Wilby long to realize that he was in no little danger. As he could do nothing with his snow-shoes, he took them off, and tried to get along without them ; but the snow was so dry and soft that he sank right into it, and could make no advance at all.

His only hope seemed to be to shout at the top of his voice on the small chance of somebody hearing him. So he called for help with all his might.

Oscar was much puzzled by his master's conduct, and circled impatiently around him, as if to urge him onward.

For quite a long time Wilby shouted, until what between cold and weariness there was no more shout left in him. Presently he felt an intense longing to sleep stealing over him. He strove desperately hard to shake it off, for he knew well what it meant; but in spite of all his efforts the deadly drowsiness crept steadily and surely over his senses, and he was just lapsing into unconsciousness when there was a crashing in the underbrush ahead, and before he had time to ask himself what it could be, the small trees in front of him parted violently, and out stepped a great white bear.

" What do you mean by all this shouting ? " he demanded rather crossly.

Curiously enough, Wilby was not quite so terrified as he expected he would be if a white bear happened along, and found courage to say very humbly,—

" Please, Mr. Bear, I hope I didn't disturb you. But, you see, I've sprained my ankle badly, and I was shouting for some one to come and help me."

" Ho, ho ! you are hurt, are you ? " was the reply, in rather a gentler tone. " Well, I'll look after you."

And so saying, the bear picked the big boy up in his arms as though he had been a little baby, and marched off with him through the woods at a rapid rate.

Wilby knew resistance was vain, so he just made up his mind to take things as quietly as possible; which, under the circumstances, was a very wise thing to do.

After about five minutes' walking, his captor came to a large tree which had been torn up by the roots. Under this he quickly dodged, and entered what seemed to be a long, dark passage.

In spite of his good resolution, Wilby could not help a kind of groan at this.

"Shut up!" growled the bear, giving him a by no means gentle cuff on the side of the head.

Wilby did shut up, and for a time nothing was to be heard save the soft thump, thump, thump of the bear's broad feet on the hard floor of the passage.

At last they stopped. The bear gave something a kick, a door flew open inward, and then there burst upon the bewildered Wilby such a sight as he had never even dreamed of in his life before.

He found himself in a large room, flooded with light and warmth from a glorious wood fire that was crackling away in a huge fireplace at one end. At first he thought the whole place had just been newly whitewashed, but soon discovered his mistake.

Everything in and about that room was marble—white marble—pure and glistening as the snow outside. Floor, walls, ceiling, tables—they were all marble alike, and they looked wonderfully fine, with the firelight flashing upon them.

But before Wilby had time to take much more in, he heard a deep bass voice asking,—

"Hallo, Major! what have you got there?"

And turning his head, he saw a splendid white bear, a good deal bigger than his rescuer, coming toward them from the far end of the room.

"Some farmer's son, Max," answered the Major, at the same time gently depositing his load on a couch near the fire. "I found him 'most frozen to death in a snow-drift. I guess we can make him all right again."

"Of course we can," exclaimed another voice, much livelier in tone than the first speaker's, and a third bear, quite as white but not so tall as either of the others, emerged into the firelight from a dark corner, where he had been attending to some household duty.

"Of course we can, if you say so, Minor," growled the one called Max, good-humouredly. "We'll begin by giving him a good dinner, at all events."

By the way, I forgot to mention that the full names of Wilby's new friends were Ursa Minor, Ursa Major, and Ursa Maximus, but for convenience' sake they called one another simply Minor, Major, and Max.

Feeling surprisingly at his ease, in view of his strange surroundings, Wilby stretched himself out on his comfortable couch, and almost forgot the pain from his sprained ankle in his delight at his novel experience.

"What a lot I'll have to tell them at home!" he said

exultingly to himself. "They won't believe one-half of it, I know."

Maximus was evidently head of the household, and superintended in a dignified way, while Major and Minor bustled about getting dinner ready.

In a little while all the preparations were complete, and Major, who seemed to feel especially responsible for Wilby, brought him a steaming bowl of something which the hungry boy was not long in sampling. And it proved to be such delicious rabbit-stew that he could not help exclaiming,—

"My sakes, but this is fine! Mother couldn't make a better stew herself,"—which compliment pleased Minor, who had prepared the stew, so much that he filled Wilby's bowl up again before it was fairly empty.

Besides the stew there were roast partridges and baked potatoes, and also apples and nuts, so that Wilby had just about as much as he could comfortably eat—in fact, perhaps a little more. At all events, his waistband began to remind him it was there.

Dinner over, the dishes were cleared away and the room set in order again, Wilby watching everything with the liveliest interest, determined to have such a story to tell as would make him the hero of the country-side for a whole month at least.

He was particularly struck with the deftness with which the bears went about their work. Although their big paws looked clumsy enough, the dear knows, they did things as handily as Wilby himself could have done them.

When every sign of the dinner had vanished, Max, Major, and Minor drew up their chairs (for they each had a big arm-chair) in front of the fire, and sat down to talk over the events of the day, quite ignoring the addition to their family,—who, indeed, was very well pleased at being left alone, as he much preferred using his eyes to his tongue, when everything around him was so delightfully novel.

The bears' voices were so low and deep that Wilby could not make out one-half they were saying. Besides, what with the warmth of the room and his own weariness, he began to feel very sleepy again, especially as the couch was extremely comfortable. In fact, he had just about dozed off, when he was awakened by Maximus jumping up from his chair, and saying in a loud tone,—

"Come, fellows, let us have a song, and then we'll turn in."

Whereupon the three of them stood up together around the fire, and sang very heartily the following song, the words of which, so far as he heard them, Wilby had no difficulty in remembering, although the tune went completely out of his head. He had not much of an ear for music, any way.

> "Three jolly white bears are we,
> Who can sing right merrily,
> For our hearts are light and free
>   From any care.
> We have always lots to eat,
> And we keep our house so neat
> That it's really quite a treat
>   To be a bear.

> "Yes, indeed, we're happy bears,
> Since nobody knows our lairs,
> Where we mind our own affairs
>   So quietly.
> Of course we have to work,
> But none of us ever shirk;
> For who'd be a lazy lurk,
>   Don't you see?
>
> "When the snow is on the ground,
> We go hunting all around
> For the bunnies which abound
>   Among the trees.
> And when summer-time is here,
> How the berries disappear
> Down our throats—"

But Wilby never heard the end of the third verse, for the simple reason that sleep overcame him just then, and song, singers, and marble palace alike faded away into nothingness.

He had no idea how long he slept, but when he awoke he was both surprised and disappointed to find himself on the sofa in Aunt Matilda's very plain, though cozy, sitting-room, instead of on his couch in White Bear Castle, while now not only his ankle but his whole body gave him pain —every nerve tingling, and face and hands smarting dreadfully.

Minor, Major, and Maximus were all gone too, and in their place dear old Aunt Matilda and kind Uncle Lemuel were bending over him, with faces full of relief at his return to consciousness.

"O Wilby dear, how glad I am to see you open your eyes again!" exclaimed Aunt Matilda joyfully.   "You were so long coming to that I began to fear that it might be all over with you."

"Yes, Wilby, my boy," added Uncle Lemuel, "you've had a close shave. But for Oscar there would not be much life left in you by this time."

Wilby was too dazed for some time to understand it all, but later on his uncle explained the matter.

It seemed that wise old Oscar, as soon as Wilby lost his senses, scampered off to Uncle Lemuel's as hard as he could go, and by barking and scratching at the door soon let them know he was there. Then by signs whose meaning they were not long in guessing, he persuaded them to go back with him, until poor Wilby was found where he had fallen beside the big tree.

Oscar capered about, wild with delight, when his master was carried off to the house, and Uncle Lem could not say enough about his cleverness.

Wilby felt very grateful to Oscar and to his uncle also, and thankful that he had not lost his life. Yet he could not help a twinge of regret at the thought of never seeing his white bear friends again, seeing how kindly they had treated him in spite of their character for cruelty.

However, it was no small consolation to have such a rattling good story to tell, and tell it he did very graphically many a time, much to the enjoyment of his hearers.

Whether they all believed it or not is a question that, if you do not mind, I will leave it to you to settle.

Over-contained
more discipline
- reading

OUTSIDE THE BOOM.

MORT HENSHAW was a boy who had implicit faith
in himself. He cherished the firm conviction
that whatever any other boy could do came within the
range of his capabilities. He had only to find out the
way it should be done in order to accomplish it.

This was a pretty large view to take of things in
general, yet it must be confessed that Mort was not without a fair degree of justification for having what the
Scotch would call so good a conceit of himself.

Blessed with a strong, symmetrical frame, a quick eye,
a sure hand, a perfect constitution, and abundant courage,
he came easily by a mastery of the different sports he
entered into, and had few equals, and fewer superiors, at
cricket, football, lacrosse, baseball, swimming, rowing, and
the other amusements of the day.

There was one pastime, however, of which, although he
had heard much, he knew nothing, and that was sailing.
The pretty little stream which ran by his home afforded
no facilities for this glorious sport, and the pleasures of it
he knew about only from the descriptions of his more
fortunate companions.

Great, then, was his delight when the spring that found him fifteen years of age brought with it an invitation from one of his uncles to spend the whole summer with him at his cottage on Lake Deschenes, a splendid sheet of water not far from the city of Ottawa.

The invitation mentioned, as one of the attractions of the place, that he would be able to have all the sailing that his heart could wish.

"Hurrah! hurrah!" shouted Mort, capering about the room with a face beaming like the sun. "All the sailing I want! Just think of it! Won't that be grand? The very thing I've been looking for."

"It will be grand, Mort dear," said his mother, "provided you take good care not to run any unnecessary risks. You must do exactly what your uncle tells you, just as if he were your father."

"Oh yes, mother, I'll do that," quickly responded Mort, ready to promise anything in the exuberance of his joy. "I'll be his crew, you know, and obey orders just as if I were at sea with him."

Very impatiently did Mort await the coming of the day when he should set forth for Deschenes. His uncle was principal of the Collegiate Institute at Ottawa, and had three months' vacation, which he usually spent at the lake in sailing, rowing, bathing, and fishing, until the return of autumn recalled him to his duties.

It was the last week in June when Mort arrived at Lake Deschenes, and his first question, after exchanging greetings with his uncle and aunt, was,—

"Will you show me your boat, please, uncle?"

Smiling at his eagerness, Mr. Turner took him over to the boathouse, where a number of boats and canoes lay upon the floor, or were suspended upon racks against the wall.

Mort had never seen so many or such fine boats in his life before. They were nearly all built of cedar, and were varnished instead of being painted, the copper fastenings dotting their shining sides with regular lines. The boy gave a great gasp of admiration, and it was some time before he recovered himself sufficiently to ask,—

"And which is your boat, uncle?"

Mr. Turner pointed to one lying just in front of them.

"Oh, what a beauty!" cried Mort. "She's the best of them all."

His uncle smiled a complacent assent, for that was precisely his own opinion. As to beauty of lines, perfection of finish, completeness of outfit, and speed on any tack, he considered the *Gleam* without a superior on Lake Deschenes, and Mort's prompt recognition of the fact pleased him as much as the cordial praise of her baby does a young mother.

"You are not far from right, my boy," said he. "The *Gleam* is both a beauty to look at and a good one to go. as you shall see for yourself very soon."

The *Gleam* belonged to the class of boat known as the "St. Lawrence skiff," the swiftest and safest boats of their size—when not over-canvassed—that carry sails. She was about twenty-two feet long, and had a half-deck all round, with a six-inch combing to keep out the water.

Two tall masts carried big bat-wing sails, which would have soon toppled her over but for the heavy iron centre-board that kept her stiff in an ordinary breeze. Everything about her was of the best, and Mort thought her the most beautiful object his eyes ever beheld.

That afternoon he had his first sail in the *Gleam*, and as, responding perfectly to every puff of the wind and turn of the tiller, she went flying across the lake, his heart thrilled with delight, and became filled with a passionate desire to master the art of handling such a craft.

"O uncle, won't you teach me how to steer and to manage the sails before I go back home?" he pleaded, looking earnestly into Mr. Turner's face.

"Certainly, Mort, certainly," was the kindly reply; "and I think you ought to make a very apt pupil, too."

Mr. Turner was altogether as good as his word. He took much pains in initiating Mort into the mysteries of sailing, teaching him the way to tack, when it was permissible to jibe, how to run before the wind, and so forth, until, by the end of the first month, Mort had become tolerably proficient, and could be trusted to manage the *Gleam* alone in an ordinary breeze.

This special privilege he was then allowed to exercise, provided he did not go outside the "boom"—that is, the long line of shackled logs which enclosed the bay where the boathouse stood, and which was intended to keep the saw-logs from stranding on the beach.

Inside the boom was a stretch of shallow water nearly a mile long by a quarter of a mile wide, on which plenty of sailing might be had without going out through the gap into the body of the lake.

For a time Mort was content with this enclosed space, and, whenever his uncle permitted him, would get the boat out, and go tacking up and down from end to end, feeling almost as proud of his newly-acquired skill as if he had been discoverer of the science of sailing.

But of course it was not many days before he began to cast longing eyes beyond the line of swaying logs, and to feel that the thing he most desired in the world was to be allowed to sail the *Gleam* across the lake and back.

But when he hinted as much to his uncle he met with no encouragement.

"No, no, Mort. You must be content with staying inside the boom; for, besides the chance of a squall, there is the danger of being caught in the current and carried into the rapids, which would soon make an end of both you and the boat."

Now it happened that one morning both Mr. and Mrs. Turner had to go into the city, not to return until by the night train, and Mort was left entirely to his own resources. Of course he turned to the *Gleam* for company, and as soon as the morning breeze came up, taking with him two other lads about his own age, he launched the boat, and went skimming from end to end of the bay.

"This is good fun," said Ted Day, "but it would be better still outside the boom."

"Oh yes!" cried Charlie Lister "Do go outside; just a little bit. Mort '

Mort shook his head, and tried to look very decided. His own heart was beating a lively response to the suggestions of his companions, but his answer was,—

"No, Charlie; uncle does not allow me to go outside, you know."

Once the idea had been mooted, however, it refused to go to rest again. The morning seemed a perfect one. There was a steady breeze from the north-west, just the

direction best suited for a slant across the lake and back without having to tack at all.

Ted and Charlie begged and coaxed Mort to make one trip out, any way. Mr. Turner would never know anything about it, and they could easily be back before midday.

Mort's resolution, which had been rapidly weakening, finally gave way altogether.

"All right," said he, allowing a sudden spirit of reckless

ambition to submerge his compunctions at doing what he knew well enough was a mean betrayal of his uncle's confidence in him. "We'll just make one trip across. It does seem a pity to lose the chance this glorious morning."

So out through the gap the *Gleam* darted, as if glad of her freedom, and went flying over the blue water toward Blueberry Point.

"My, but this is grand!" exclaimed Charlie rapturously, as the boat careened before the freshening breeze, so that the water lapped the lee-combing.

"You are right; it is—eh, Mort?" echoed Ted, turning to Mort, who, holding the tiller in one hand and the end of the main sheet in the other, watched every move of the boat with feelings strangely divided between anxiety and proud delight.

The passage across was quickly made, and then, being thirsty, Charlie proposed that they land for a few minutes to get a drink at a spring near the shore. After the drink Ted suggested a bathe; and thus an hour slipped by, during which an ominous change took place in the weather. The sky clouded over, the wind, which had been steady, began to come in fitful gusts.

"I don't like the look of things," said Mort, in a tone of concern. "I wish we were inside the boom."

"Well, let's hurry and get there as quickly as we can." responded Ted.

It was all well enough to say this, but with the change of weather had come a change of wind, which was now against them, so that they would have to tack all the way home.

By dint of careful sailing they had got about a third of the distance, when suddenly the sky darkened, some large drops of rain pattered upon them, and the next moment a sharp squall struck the *Gleam* full upon her quarter.

In order to give his whole attention to the steering, Mort had asked Charlie to hold the main-sheet, impressing upon him to take only one turn around the cleat. But Charlie, who was of the lazy sort, finding the sheet hard to hold, had taken two turns, and done it in such a way that the rope had jammed. Consequently, when Mort shouted to him, as he put the tiller hard a-port, " Let go the main-sheet instantly, Charlie ! " and he attempted to obey the order, he could not do so in time to meet the emergency, and the next instant, amid simultaneous shrieks from all three boys, the *Gleam* went over on her beam ends.

Fortunately they were all good swimmers, and did not get entangled in any of the ropes, so that, without much difficulty, they succeeded in climbing up on the side of the boat, where it was easy enough to hold on for a while.

There was no fear of the *Gleam* sinking, as she bore no ballast to carry her down, and had air-tight compartments in both bow and stern. Nevertheless, the position of the boys was one of great peril, for the boat was right in the channel leading to the rapids at the lower end of the lake, in the direction of which the wind was now blowing. To get into these rapids meant utter destruction for both boys and boat, yet to keep out of them was impossible without help, while to swim ashore was far beyond their powers.

They shouted and shrieked for aid, but there was no one in sight to hear them, and soon the storm burst upon them in full fury, blotting out the shore on both sides, and threatening to beat them off the boat as it tossed up and down in the white-caps.

How bitterly Mort regretted having ventured beyond the boom, and how fervently he vowed never to do so again if he could only be saved this time!

When the squall passed and the air cleared, he saw that they were fast drawing near the rapids.

" O Charlie," he groaned, " why did you make me go outside the boom ? "

Charlie made no reply. He could think of nothing else but his imminent danger.

Steadily and surely the *Gleam* drifted downward. In another fifteen minutes she would be in the remorseless grasp of the rapids. The wind went down almost to a calm, but the current grew stronger, so that there was no slacking of her speeding toward destruction.

The boys held desperately on to the keel, saying nothing to each other, but praying as best each could.

On, on the boat moved. Oh, was there no chance of help ? Must they go down to death in sight of so many homes ?

A couple of hundred yards above the rapids was a floating stage, strongly moored, which was used by the men looking after the saw-logs that came down the river in great droves from time to time. As they neared this a bright thought flashed into Mort's mind.

"Say, boys," he cried, "I've got it! Do you see that float? Let's push the *Gleam* over to it."

The others caught the idea at once. All getting on the same side of the boat, they proceeded to push her toward the stage by swimming with their legs.

It was exhausting work, but they were encouraged by seeing that they were making headway, and they persevered until at last success crowned their efforts, and with a glad cry of relief Mort crawled upon the stage and fastened to it the boat's painter.

All actual danger was now over, and at once Mort regained his self-possession. Under his directions the masts were taken out, the boat righted and bailed dry, and everything stowed snugly aboard. Then with the oars she was rowed back to Deschenes, not a whit the worse for her wetting.

As soon as his uncle returned, Mort told him the whole story.

Mr. Turner was very sorry to learn of his nephew's breach of trust, and, as a penalty therefor, withdrew from him for the rest of the summer the privilege of taking the boat out alone, which was a sore deprivation; but Mort felt that it was richly deserved, and it only strengthened his resolution to be more obedient to orders in the future.

FOUND AFTER MANY DAYS.

"EDIE! Edie!" rang out in a clear, strong voice from the door of a farmhouse, where stood a comely, brown-faced woman, shading her eyes with her right hand, as she swept the sunny space around in search of her daughter.

"I'm coming, mother," was the prompt response.

And the next instant there appeared from behind the barn a little girl not more than eight years old, who looked the very picture of health and happiness.

"You know where your father's chopping to-day, don't you, Edie?" asked Mrs. Hazen, with a glance of affectionate pride at the sturdy little figure before her.

"Oh yes, mother," replied Edie, swinging around and pointing with her plump forefinger, stained by the juice of the raspberries she had just been picking, to the top of the hill that sloped upwards from the other side of the road. "Father's over there in the back pasture, near the blackberry patch."

"That's right, pet," said Mrs. Hazen, lifting up the bright face for a hearty kiss. "And now wouldn't you like to take him his dinner?"

" Indeed I would," cried Edie, dancing around and clapping her hands. "And may I stay with him until he comes home ?"

" I suppose so—if he wants you," assented Mrs. Hazen. " But in that case you must come in and have your own dinner first."

A half-hour later, with a well-filled basket on her arm, and her mother's parting injunction not to loiter on the way in her ears, Edie set forth full of joy on her mission.

" She's a little thing to send so far," mused the mother, following the retreating figure with eyes full of tender concern. " But she does so love the woods, and seems to make her way through them like an Indian."

With heart as light as any bird chirping by the wayside, Edie hastened through the gate, across the road, between the lower bars of the pasture gate, and then, climbing the hill behind which lay the back pasture, entered the bush, in which her pink calico sun-bonnet soon vanished from view.

Mr. Hazen's farm stood on the very edge of civilization, in the northern part of New Brunswick. The most of his acres he had cleared himself, and he never lost an opportunity of hewing his way further and further into the mighty forest, whose billows of birch, pine, and hemlock rolled away northward, eastward, and westward for uncounted leagues.

This day he was working at a bunch of timber a little beyond the eastern edge of the clearing, called the " back pasture.'

As mid-day drew near he began to feel hungry, and more than once paused in his work to go to the edge of the clearing, to see if there were any signs of an approaching dinner.

"I hope Esther hasn't forgotten me to-day," he thought, after doing this for the third time to no result. "It's not like her to do it."

The great golden sun moved steadily on to the zenith. and then inclined westward, but still no messenger appeared bearing the needed refreshment.

Mr. Hazen felt strongly tempted to shoulder his axe and go home. But the day was so favourable to his work that, after a good deal of grumbling at what he supposed to be his wife's neglect, he decided not to quit it. So, tightening his belt, he grasped his axe anew and strove to forget his hunger in the ardour of his toil.

He did not, however, work as late as common that day, for in addition to his hunger, there grew upon him a feeling of uneasiness, which at length became so disturbing that he could not endure it. Accordingly, fully an hour before his usual time, he shouldered his axe and strode off homeward, saying to himself,—

"I hope nothing's gone wrong; but I don't know what gives me such an apprehensive feeling."

When he approached the farmhouse, he caught sight of his wife coming up the road that led to the nearest neighbour, about half-a-mile away.

Hurrying on to meet her, he asked in a tone not altogether free from irritation at his needless fears,—

"Why, Esther, where have you been? And where is Edie?"

"I ran over to neighbour Hewett's for the paper," Mrs. Hazen responded. "But"—and her face filled with sudden alarm—"Edie? Wasn't Edie with you?"

"Why, no!" replied Mr. Hazen, while in his face was reflected the expression of his wife's; "I haven't seen her since breakfast."

"Not seen her!" repeated Mrs. Hazen. "O Henry, what has happened? I sent her with your dinner just before mid-day, and she asked me if she might stay with you until you came home."

Mr. Hazen was a man prompt to action. Taking his wife's arm and fairly pushing her along the road, he said,—

"There's not a moment to lose, Esther. Edie's lost her way, and we must go after her."

Without returning to the farmhouse, they pressed up the hill and through the back pasture into the forest.

Hither and thither they hunted, now one and now the other raising the echoes of the leafy fastness by calls of "Edie! Edie!" but getting no response save the cries of startled birds or the mocking chatter of a squirrel.

As night drew on Mr. Hazen realized that a more organized effort was necessary; and hastening home with harrowed hearts, his wife got ready some food, while he rode over to Hewett's to obtain assistance.

Both Mr. Hewett and his eldest son returned with him. They hurriedly snatched a meal, and then, provided with guns and lanterns, set off to renew the search.

All that night they tramped through the gloom of the forest, meeting from time to time to take counsel together, and then separating, to cover as much ground as possible.

But the day dawned without bringing any comforting news for the haggard woman who anxiously waited their return at the gate, and, when they came without her daughter, sank down on the ground, half fainting with uncontrollable grief.

As soon as possible the eager search was renewed, and continued from day to day, until at last even the heart-broken parents had to give up all hope, and strove to resign themselves to the awful conviction that their darling Edith—their only one—had met her death all alone in the depths of the great forest, having either died of hunger and exposure or fallen a victim to the bears and wolves with which its solitudes abounded.

In the meantime, how had it fared with Edie, who had gone forth so joyously to carry her father's dinner to him ?

Her intention at the start was certainly to make a straight course to her destination. But the attention of little folks is easily attracted, and in this instance, just as she entered the edge of the forest, and should have turned off to the left, a saucy little squirrel challenged her on the right, and in trying to get near him Edie pushed further and further into the forest, until presently she began to wonder if she had not lost her way.

At once losing interest in the squirrel, she put down her basket to look about her. With a pang of sharp dismay, the child realized that she had lost her bearings, and did not know which way to turn.

Just at that moment her keen ear caught a sound that she immediately recognized. It was the regular blows of an axe falling upon a tree-trunk.

Her face lit up, and she clapped her hands for joy.

"That's father chopping!" she exclaimed. "Now I know which way to go!"

And picking up her basket, Edie trotted off in what she took to be the direction from which the sound came.

On she trudged bravely for some distance, hoping each minute to come upon her father, until, growing weary of her burden, she put it down to rest a moment.

As she rested it seemed to her that the sound of chopping had grown fainter—so much so, indeed, she could hardly make out which way it came to her ears.

"Oh dear!" she sighed; "where can father be? I'll call for him." And she made the place ring with shrill cries of "Father! father! Where are you?"

But they evoked no response, and then, more alarmed than ever, Edie picked up her basket again, and pushed on with all her little strength.

Unhappily every step increased the distance between Mr. Hazen and herself; for it was not the real sound of the chopping Edie had followed but the echo, and instead of making toward him, she had been going in directly the opposite direction.

At the end of an hour she felt very tired, and throwing herself down on a bank of moss at the foot of a forest monarch, gave way to the tears that hitherto she had resolutely restrained.

"Oh dear!" she said, "I'm lost, I'm lost! and how ever will father find me?"

After the first passion of tears had passed, Edie began to be conscious of the pangs of hunger, and the thought came that she might as well eat something out of the basket, as she could not find her father to give it to him.

So she ate a little of the bread and meat, and took a sup out of the bottle of milk, and then, feeling refreshed, renewed her tramp, first listening eagerly, but in vain, for the sound of her father's axe.

All that afternoon the lost child alternately walked and rested, often crying softly to herself, then drying her tears and seeking to take heart from the hope of yet finding her father before darkness came on.

She was a brave little thing, accustomed to a good deal of outdoor life, and to running through the woods; but when night closed around her and the forest shade deepened into impenetrable gloom, poor Edie gave up the struggle, and sank down in a mossy hollow, shivering with terror.

Yet so weary was she that presently she fell asleep, and did not awake until dawn, when, though feeling very stiff and sore from the unwonted exertions of the day before, she ate her breakfast out of the basket and renewed her progress.

The following day she wandered about, only getting deeper and deeper into the forest. Her basket was empty before evening, and she was fain to make her supper of

the berries, which fortunately were very plentiful. They
were not altogether satisfying, but they were better than
nothing.

Another day passed, the weather providentially continu-
ing bright, clear, and warm,
and the little wanderer still
kept on, not knowing
whither she was going
That night strange things

began to happen. She was
more wakeful than usual, and
as she lay at the foot of a tree, she saw some large animals
moving about in the dim light, and her bosom thrilled
with joy, for she thought they must be her father's oxen.
So she called out,—

"Buck! Bright! Come here!"

But at the sound of her voice they started as if
greatly frightened, and at once dashed off through the
woods at the top of their speed; which showed her that

they must have been moose, such as her father sometimes shot.

The following night two great, black, shaggy dogs, which she supposed must be neighbour Hewett's, came near her; but when she called them by their names they seemed more surprised than the moose, for they stood up on their hind legs, looked very hard at her for a few moments, and then, dropping down on all fours, hastened away into the darkness again, where, as Edie thought, she heard them howling. In this, however, she must have been doubly mistaken.

What she took to be dogs were no doubt black bears, then quite numerous in that district, being attracted by the berries; and the howling, of course, was done by wolves, which, luckily, seemed afraid to attack her.

On the fourth afternoon, Edie, by happy chance, came across the deserted shanty of an early pioneer, standing in the middle of a clearing that was thickly overgrown with raspberry bushes.

Here she remained for three days, feeding upon the berries during the daytime, and sleeping in the shanty at night. The nights were so warm that she needed no fire, and inside the shanty she was safe from the attacks of bears or wolves. It was dreadfully lonely, yet still she hoped that her father would come and find her.

A whole week thus passed away. Edie had been given up for lost by her heart-broken parents, and the neighbours who were assisting in the search had returned to their homes, when a gentleman—Mr. Barker by name—

had an experience such as no sportsman surely ever had before.

He had been out on a hunting expedition for a fortnight, and that day came to the banks of Bear Creek.

He was preparing to cross on a fallen log almost spanning the stream, when his keen ear caught the sound of soft footsteps, accompanied by a continuous rustling movement in the thicket of wild raspberries that covered the opposite bank.

At once with a tremor of delight he suspected the approach of a deer, or possibly a bear, and dropping behind a bush, he levelled his rifle in readiness to fire.

The next moment, as his eager eyes intently scanned the raspberry bushes, his sportsman's feeling of delight suddenly changed to a thrill of horror when a tiny brown, berry-stained hand was quietly raised to pull down a loaded branch of fruit.

"Well, of all things!" cried the hunter, as his finger fell from the trigger that had so nearly sent the bullet upon its fatal mission. "What an awful mistake I almost made!"

Throwing down his rifle he sprang across the log, to catch in his arms a little girl not more than eight years old, whose torn garments, tangled locks, soiled hands, and thin, pale face, told in a glance the story of many days' hapless wanderings.

Oh, how glad poor Edie was to see him, and how artlessly she told the story of her wonderful adventures! And how thankful to Providence the hunter was that he had chanced to find her ere it was too late!

Forgetting all about his hunting, her rescuer now applied

himself to the task of getting her home. They were far from the nearest house, and the poor child was so weak from lack of proper food that he had to lift her up on his broad shoulders.

But Mr. Barker was as strong as he was kind-hearted, and he pushed resolutely on, guiding himself by his compass, until at last, just as dusk was closing around them, and he began to fear they would have to pass another night in the forest, they came upon a clearing, at the far side of which stood a neat log house.

Edie shouted her joy at the sight. It meant that all her perils were over; and the hunter, putting on a big spurt, dashed across the clearing at a run and deposited her on the doorstep, exclaiming in a tone of vast relief,—

" There now, my child, that's the end of your wanderings!"

The good people of the house gave them both a warm welcome. Edie received every attention ; and the following morning, looking altogether a different girl, with dress mended, hair neatly brushed, hands free from berry-stains, and face radiant at the prospect of returning to her parents, she took her seat in the farmer's waggon to be driven home.

How shall the joy of the Hazens be described when the little daughter they had mourned for as dead came back to them, looking thin and worn, it is true, but otherwise not a whit the worse for her thrilling experience !

Mr. Barker watched them with brimming eyes, murmuring, as he fondly patted the stock of his Remington,—

" The best day's work you ever did was when you didn't go off at all   A lucky chance, indeed ! "

MRS. GRUNDY'S GOBBLERS.

MRS. GRUNDY (or, as the boys disrespectfully called her, Mrs. Grumpy) was certainly not a favourite with the young people of Westville. In the first place, she did not like children. The fact that she had never been blessed with any of her own no doubt had a great deal to do with this dislike for other people's, which she manifested by vigorous use of hand and tongue at the slightest provocation.

Many a sharp speech and stinging slap did Mrs. Grundy inflict—and not always upon those who deserved it most, either; for so hot was her temper, so hasty her action when irritated, that she would visit her wrath upon the first youngster she could reach, without waiting to investigate the extent of her luckless captive's guilt.

Another reason why Mrs. Grundy was not popular was that, although she owned the finest orchard and garden in all Westville, not one crimson strawberry, purple plum, or golden apple was she ever known to bestow upon boy or girl; and woe betide the adventurous urchin that dared to take one unbidden, even though it be a half-spoiled windfall, if he fell into her strong hands! Forthwith he was marched off, amid a storm of slaps and scolding, despite his sobs and vows of penitence, into the awful presence of Squire Hardgrit, and, his alarmed parents having been duly summoned, was in their presence condemned to that most appalling of punishments—a whole day in the house of detention !

This method of dealing with the would-be or actual fruit-filchers had one advantage, so far as Mrs. Grundy was concerned—it gave her a sharer in the burden of her unpopularity, which perhaps might otherwise have proved insupportable ; for so hard, cold, and unsympathetic was Squire Hardgrit, and such evident pleasure did he take in imposing his penalties, that if the Westville boys hated anybody as cordially as they did Mrs. Grundy, it was certainly the stern, severe squire

For some time past the relations between these two worthies and the boys had, as the newspapers say about the great Powers, been more than usually strained. Not content with fiercely defending her garden and orchard from juvenile depredation, Mrs. Grundy had asserted her right to keep everybody off the broad, smooth plot of grass that lay between her cottage and the road, and had been upheld in her claim by the squire, to the profound disgust of the boys, who had long made it their gathering-place in the summer evenings ; for although too small to play a game of baseball upon, it was big enough for pitching and catching, chase, leap-frog, and that sort of thing.

This appropriation of the grass plot, which had hitherto been regarded as public property, was quite too much for the boys. It was the last drop in the cup of bitterness, and in desperation they called a meeting to be held in Thompson's barn on Saturday night to consider the situation.

Saturday night came, and a dozen of the brightest boys of Westville gathered in solemn conclave around a lantern to see if some way could not be devised of getting even with Mrs. Grumpy and the squire.

As the barn belonged to his father, Charlie Thompson was chosen chairman, and he promptly opened the meeting as follows:—

"Now, fellows, we can't stand this sort of thing any longer. Something must be done, if we perish in the attempt. The honour of the country demands" (Charlie, whose memory was particularly good, had not yet forgotten the last 4th of July oration) "that measures should be taken to show to our oppressors that we are not slaves and cowards. The meeting is now open, and the chair will be pleased to receive suggestions."

And amid a vigorous round of boot-heel applause Charlie sat down, feeling that he had proved himself quite equal to the occasion.

For a few moments there was a dead pause, all having some sort of a scheme, more or less hazy, in their heads, but none wishing to speak first.

At last little Tommy Short, the youngest in the group, piped out,—

"Let's tar and feather 'em. Father has lots of tar in his back shop, and I know where there's a big pot."

A roar of laughter greeted this suggestion, the impracticability of which was exceeded only by its absurdity, could it have been carried out.

Dame Grundy and Squire Hardgrit would certainly have made a most mirth-provoking sight, done up in suits of tar and feathers.

The speech served its purpose, however, in loosening the other tongues, and plans and projects now poured in thick and fast.

"S'pose we burn their barns down," said Dick Wilding, who was a great reader of cheap-novel literature.

But all the rest shouted "No!" at once.

"What do you say to ham-stringing their horses?" asked Bob Henderson, in rather a dubious tone, as if he had not much confidence in the wisdom of his scheme, which, in fact, just occurred to him because he had read that that was the way the Arabs treat their enemies' horses when they get the chance.

"Stuff and nonsense!" cried the chairman. "That's not the sort of thing we mean at all. We're not hankering after the penitentiary."

"Give us your plan, then, Mr. Chairman," said Dick Wilding.

"Well, fellows, I'll tell you what I was thinking of. Let us hook the old lady's gobblers, and hide them until she thinks they're gone for good. You know what a heap she thinks of them, and it will worry her awfully to lose them."

"Capital! capital!" shouted the rest of the boys. "The very thing!"

"But where shall we hide them?" asked Sam Lawson. "It'll have to be a pretty safe place, for Mrs. Grumpy will turn the town upside down hunting for her precious turkeys, you may be sure."

While all this talk was going on, Harold Kent had been sitting on an upturned box which served him as a chair, without opening his mouth. Now, however, taking advantage of the pause which followed Sam's question, he said quietly,—

"Why not hide the gobblers in one of the empty rooms in Squire Hardgrit's building? You know, the squire's been trying to get these Bronze Gobblers from Mrs. Grumpy for ever so long, and she won't let him have them; and if they're found on his premises, she'll be sure to think that he had something to do with hooking them."

It was just like Harold to propose something so original and daring in its conception as to fairly take his companions' breath away, and they now looked at him with feelings divided between admiration and amazement.

The chairman was the first to speak. Bringing his hand down upon his knee with a crack that made the others jump, he cried,—

"Magnificent! Boys, we'll do it, or perish in the attempt."

Whereat the others shouted in chorus,—

"Hoorah! We'll do it!"

"Since we're all agreed, then," said Charlie, "the next business before the meeting is to plan how to do it."

As before, all sorts of wild suggestions were put forward, and again it was left for Harold Kent to advance the most practicable scheme.

This was it: the shed in which Mrs. Grundy's famous flock of turkeys was carefully secured at night stood at some distance to the back of her house, and as she slept in one of the front rooms, there was slight risk of her seeing or hearing anything. What Harold proposed was, that, slipping out of their rooms after everybody was asleep, they should meet behind the turkey-shed, bringing with them three gunny sacks and a dark lantern. Having got the gobblers safely into the sacks, they would then creep round the back way to the building in which the squire's office was situated, climb in through a lower window, and so upstairs to the room in which the turkeys were to be left.

"You've a great head, Hal," said Jack Wilding admiringly, when all this had been detailed, "and you can count on us every time—can't he, boys?"

"You bet he can," chorused the crowd.

A satisfactory plan of campaign having thus been settled upon, the meeting was adjourned until Monday midnight, then to assemble behind Mrs. Grundy's turkey-shed.

The eventful night came; and as midnight drew near, one by one the boys gathered with throbbing hearts at the rendezvous.

At length all but Tommy Short, whose courage had failed him, and Bob Henderson, whose father had nabbed him in the act of slipping out, and sent him back to bed with a spank, turned up.

"THEY WERE TOO BEWILDERED BY THE BLAZE TO MAKE ANY NOISE."

Page 227

It was an intensely dark night and blowing half a gale, all of which was in favour of the enterprise. The shed door was found to be simply secured with a wooden latch, and lifting this the conspirators tip-toed inside; and then Charlie Thompson, who carried the dark lantern, suddenly turned its glare full upon the startled gobblers as they nodded solemnly side by side upon their roost.

They were too bewildered by the blaze to make any noise, and before they could recover their self-possession sufficiently to exclaim at so extraordinary an apparition, the other boys had stepped behind them, and with quick, deft movements slipped the big sacks over their heads, thus reducing them at one bold stroke to helpless captives.

The poor turkeys struggled and "gobbled" a good deal in their narrow quarters, but all to no purpose; and full of terror, no doubt, at their strange treatment, were hurried out of the shed into the lane, and thence through dark and silent ways to the rear of the squire's building. Here the conspirators paused for breath and consultation.

"Now, fellows," whispered Harold Kent, "we needn't all go inside, you know. I'll take the lantern, while the three biggest of you carry the gobblers, and the rest will stay here until we come back."

Somewhat reluctantly this was assented to, for all wanted to share the danger as well as the fun; and then Harold, lantern in hand, followed by Dick Wilding, Sam Shaw, and Frank Cushing, each bending beneath a bag of struggling, "gobbling" turkey, climbed in through the low window, crept softly in stocking feet along the narrow hall and up the creaking stairs; while their companions, with hearts beating like trip-hammers, shrank close together in the darkest corner outside and anxiously awaited their return.

It was no easy task that the four boys had in hand. True enough that the building was uninhabited at night, but there were people living next door, and any unusual noise could hardly fail to be heard through those thin wooden walls; while, late as the hour was, the sound of footsteps on the plank side-walks would ever and anon send a chill of terror through the anxious watchers below.

Moreover, to carry three big turkeys up a flight of stairs and deposit them in an empty room without filling the whole place with their noise was the hardest part of all. Nevertheless they succeeded admirably.

Five minutes after they disappeared they rejoined their companions, trembling but triumphant, having left their captives in good order and condition in the front room, just across the room from Squire Hardgrit's office, where they would be certain to make themselves seen and heard in the morning.

This done, the boys scattered to their homes, creeping back noiselessly to their beds, in which, being thoroughly tired out, they slept as soundly until morning as if they had not been up to any mischief whatever.

The great gathering-place of the Westville boys was the blacksmith's forge, which stood across the road from Mrs. Grundy's, and thither the conspirators came one by one the following morning in expectation of seeing the fun.

Nor were they disappointed. Their enemy thought too much of her precious turkeys to intrust any person else with the duty of feeding them, and so every morning carried them a big dish of corn-meal mush after she had finished her own breakfast.

"There she goes!" exclaimed Dick Wilding presently, as the boys were laughing and talking somewhat nervously together.

And, sure enough, Mrs. Grundy's portly figure emerged from the house and went slowly toward the shed.

Soon after a sharp cry of "Susan! Susan!" cut the still morning air, and the prim maid-servant was observed to hurry to her mistress.

A moment later the two women could be observed running hither and thither through the garden and orchard, calling, "Turkey! turkey! turkey!" at the top of their voices.

Great indeed was Mrs. Grundy's concern, and soon the whole neighbourhood was made aware of her loss.

"It's those rascally gipsies, sure's I'm alive," she cried. "Who else would steal my beautiful gobblers, that I wouldn't sell even to the squire? I'll have every one of them sent to jail, see if I don't. Just wait till the squire comes!"

And so she stormed while awaiting the arrival of the squire at his office.

The moment he appeared she poured her woful tale

into his ears, while a curious crowd gathered outside, eager to see what the majesty of the law could effect.

Most prominent in the crowd were, of course, the boys, who alone held the clue to the mystery, and were now eagerly expecting the grand *denouement.*

It was not long in coming. Mrs. Grundy had only about half finished her confused recital of facts, suspicions, and theories to the gravely listening squire, when a vigorous "Gobble-gobble-gobble!" was distinctly heard coming from somewhere near at hand, just as a shout broke in from the street of,—

"There they are—up in Squire Hardgrit's room! Look at them!"

Before the squire could take in the situation, his excited client sprang to her feet, rushed out of the office, across the hall, threw open the door into the opposite room, and there, behold! as large as life, and as cross as three gobblers could be, were her missing turkeys, who, the instant the door was opened, charged straight through it, almost upsetting their mistress, and went flapping violently downstairs and out into the street, where they were greeted with a shout of laughter from the surprised spectators.

It would be impossible with either pen or pencil to give an adequate conception of the old lady's countenance as she returned to the squire's office, and met that worthy magistrate just rising from his chair.

Surprise, suspicion, indignation, and wrath chased one another swiftly across her features, and, once her feelings found utterance, there was poured upon the amazed squire such a torrent of reproach and contumely that he was fairly stunned into silence; and before he could recover himself sufficiently to make his defence, his accuser, with a scornful swing of her ample skirts that was simply magnificent, flounced out of the office, while he sank back into his chair, the very picture of helpless bewilderment.

That he, Squire Hardgrit, the incorruptible guardian of the people's rights, should be suspected of having stolen, or causing to have stolen for him, the turkeys of a neighbour, whose situation as a lone widow was such as to make the crime seem particularly heinous—that any person should for one moment suspect anything so abominable; and not only suspect it, but charge him to his face with his supposed guilt before the whole village (for the squire was well aware that Mrs. Grundy's shrill utterances had been audible clear across the street), it was awful, perfectly awful, and not to be borne for a moment! He must see Mrs. Grundy immediately, and compel her to listen to him.

Accordingly, away he posted to the widow's cottage, where he arrived just in time to check the poor dame from going off into a fit of hysterics.

Her turkeys being once more safely in her yard, and her anger pretty well abated, Mrs. Grundy was quite willing to listen believingly to the squire's indignant denials, and graciously accept his assurance that no pains would be spared to ferret out the real delinquents.

The former harmony was restored, and an alliance,

offensive and defensive, sealed with a glass of gooseberry wine, for both were strongly of the opinion that "those wicked wretches of boys" were at the bottom of the whole mischief.

Thanks to those same boys holding their tongues, however, neither Mrs. Grundy nor the squire could ever get hold on any evidence more solid than their own suspicions, and they both had too much sense to take any action upon them.

But the nocturnal travels of the turkeys were not in vain; for their mistress, realizing that the boys, if pressed too far, might do something worse next time, thought it wise to mitigate her severity toward them, and even softened to the extent of calling a lot of them into her orchard that very autumn to fill their pockets with the windfalls.

This stroke of diplomacy was not lost upon the boys, who reciprocated after their own fashion; and thus matters went smoothly on, until at length most harmonious relations were established, and in all the countryside no creatures were safer from the youngsters' mischief than Mrs. Grundy's gobblers.

ONE of the Fur Commissioners of the Hudson Bay Company at Winnipeg was entertaining a number of the factors and other officials at Christmas dinner, and after the successive courses had received appreciative attention, the guests settled themselves at ease about the table to enjoy the excellent cigars and one another's conversation.

Made up as the gathering was of men who had for ten, twenty, thirty years or longer, in the pursuance of their vocation, experienced most moving adventures by flood and field, good stories followed fast. One told of a thrilling trip through the dangerous rapids of the Portage of the Drowned; another, of the narrow escape from meeting death at the hands of a grizzly among the foot-hills of the Rockies; while a third held the attention of all as he graphically described the fearful struggle that he had with a wounded bull bison in the valley of the Bow River.

Thus the story-telling went around until it reached Hugh M'Kenzie, one of the oldest officials in the active service, who, in response to a unanimous demand, spun the following interesting yarn of mountain-sheep hunting.

"It was in the third year of my clerkship, and they had sent me away out to Fort George, right in the heart of the Rockies. I would rather have stayed on the plains, where the buffalo were in plenty; but you're not asked as to what you'd like best in the company. You're just told to go, and there's an end of it. I found it very dull at Fort George, and to while away the time I did all the hunting I could. To help me in this I had two fine dogs, of whom I was extremely proud. They were half-bred collies, not particularly handsome creatures, but full of pluck, and as knowing animals as ever wagged tails.

"Having had pretty good luck with bear and other game to be found in the neighbourhood of the fort, I became possessed of a strong desire to secure the head of one of those Rocky Mountain sheep which have their home high up among the peaks, and are as difficult animals to hunt as there are in the world.

"Again and again I went out without success, although my dogs, Bruce and Oscar, seemed as eager to get sheep as I was myself; but instead of becoming disheartened, I grew all the more determined, and longed for the winter to come, when the snow, by covering their higher pasturing grounds, would drive the sheep lower down the mountain, and thus make them more getatable.

"The winter began with a series of heavy snowfalls which shut us all up in the fort for several weeks, and it was early in December before I thought it safe to have another try after the sheep.

"Then one fine, bright morning I started off, feeling very

hopeful that I would return with my much-coveted prize. The dogs, of course, went with me, but I had no other companion, nobody else having sufficient sporting ardour to share in the risks of my expedition; for it certainly was full of risks, and had I been older and wiser I would never have undertaken it. But I was young and strong and full of spirit, and my eagerness to obtain a set of horns had become a bit of a joke against me with the fellows; so that I was not in the mood to soberly weigh the pros and cons of the matter.

"Thinking it possible I might be out all night, I rolled up some provisions and matches in my thick plaid, and strapped it on my shoulders. With hatchet and hunting-knife in my belt, a full powder-horn at my side, snow-shoes on feet and rifle in hand, I set out amid the good-humoured chaffing of my fellow-clerks.

"Up into the mountains I climbed, keeping a keen look-out for signs of the game I was seeking, while Bruce and Oscar ranged right and left, so that we covered a good deal of ground between us. By mid-day the climbing became so steep and difficult that I had to take off my snow-shoes, and strapped them on my back. They were no longer necessary, at any rate, for the snow was covered with a crust which bore me up admirably, and made easy going for my moccasined feet.

"It was not until afternoon that the first sheep were sighted, and, much to my delight, they seemed not far away, and easy to get at. There were five in the flock: a huge ram with superb horns—just the thing I hankered after--and four fine ewes, which, however, had nothing to fear from me.

"Calling the dogs to heel, I proceeded to stalk the unsuspecting creatures with all the skill I possessed. It proved a harder job than I thought. They were on a kind of ledge several hundred feet above me, and in order to get a proper shot without giving them warning, it was necessary to make a wide circuit, so as to reach a point opposite their ledge from which a capital chance might be had.

"By dint of great exertion, however, I reached the point all right, and was just waiting a moment to catch my breath before taking aim at the ram, when Oscar's impatience overcame him, and he gave a sharp bark. Instantly the whole five animals started to flee. I threw the rifle to my shoulder and pulled the trigger. It was nothing better than a snap-shot, yet it did not miss; for with the report the ram sprang into the air, stumbled as he came down, and then dashed off again, leaving behind him a plain trail of blood-drops on the white snow.

"With an exultant shout I sent the dogs forward, and followed as fast as I could. I had to go down into a ravine and get up the other side before reaching the bloody trail. Forgetting everything else in my wild excitement, I pressed on, guided by my dogs' sharp barking. It was terribly hard work, and I had many a slip and stumble; but the red splashes in the snow grew larger the further I went. Bleeding at the rate he was, the ram surely could not keep up his flight for any great distance.

"Presently I came to a place that at any other time would have brought me to a full stop. A ridge of hard frozen snow stretched between two rocky ledges. On the one side it reached down to the edge of a precipice, which then fell away abruptly into an unknown depth. On the other side, in one unbroken sheet, it sloped down full five hundred feet to a level upon which the snow lay in great drifts. The ram was already half-way across the ridge, although evidently in distress, and the dogs were hard at his heel, barking fiercely, for they knew that victory was not far off.

"Throwing all considerations of prudence to the winds, I set out to follow them. So narrow was the ridge that I could not stand erect, but had to sit astride it, and push myself forward by using both hands and feet. I never glanced below me, lest I should lose my head; and at length, almost completely exhausted, I succeeded in making the other side.

"Here awaiting me was my quarry, standing at bay against the cliff, and butting off the dogs that were springing for his throat. It was some minutes before my nerves were sufficiently steadied for me to use my rifle; then one shot was sufficient. With a convulsive spring the noble animal scattered the dogs and fell dead at my feet.

"Oh, but what a proud moment for me! The horns were splendid. A man might not get a finer pair in a lifetime. With the utmost care I detached the head, and then, for the first time since the chase began, sat down to rest.

"I was so tired that I would have been glad to camp here for the night. But there was absolutely nothing in the way of shelter, and it promised to be bitterly cold and windy. I must get back to the lower level before darkness came on.

"Securing the ram's head on my shoulders, where I must say it felt abominably heavy, I returned to the ridge. Not until then did I realize into what a critical position my reckless ardour had brought me. One look at that perilous passage-way was sufficient to assure me that in my wearied and unnerved condition to recross it was a feat utterly impracticable. My dogs—two clever, sure-footed creatures as they were—shrank back in evident dismay, although I sought to urge them forward; yet for me to remain on that exposed ledge meant death by freezing before morning.

"I was in a terrible predicament. Little more than an hour of daylight remained. Whatever was to be done needed to be done right away. While I stood there bewildered and irresolute, Oscar again ventured out a little distance on the ridge, but, becoming frightened, tried to turn back. In so doing he lost his footing, and, despite desperate efforts to regain it, shot swiftly down the slope that ended in a level five hundred feet below.

"With keen concern I watched him through the waning light rolling helplessly over and over until after a final tumble he landed in a great drift, out of which, to my great joy, he emerged the next moment, shook himself vigorously, and sent back a brisk bark as though to say, 'Come along; it's not so bad as it looks.'

"Instantly I caught the idea. If my dog made the descent uninjured, why could not I? Great as the risk might be, it was, after all, no worse than staying on the ledge all night. To think was to act. Loosening the ram's head from my back, I sent it down after Oscar. It sped to the bottom and buried itself in a snow-bank. Next I tied my rifle, hatchet, and hunting-knife on one of the snow-shoes, and despatched them. They, too, made the trip all right, and vanished in the snow. Then came my turn. Rolling up the plaid I lashed it on the remaining snow-shoe, and committed myself to this extemporized toboggan.

"What followed is more than I can tell. So steep was the slope that I seemed to drop into space. I was not conscious of touching anything, but simply of being shot through the icy air, blinded by particles of snow, and choking for lack of breath, until I was hurled like a stone from a catapult into a mass of loosely-packed snow, and lost consciousness.

"When I came to myself, Bruce and Oscar were both beside me, licking my face with affectionate anxiety. At first I could not move, and my whole body was so full of pain that I feared I had been seriously injured. But, after lying still awhile, I made shift to get upon my feet, and to my vast relief found myself none the worse of my wild descent, save for a scratched face and a severe shaking.

"My next thought was for the horns. I had no diffi-culty in extricating them or the rifle from their snowy bed, and found both were uninjured. Strapping them once more on my shoulders, and adjusting my snow-shoes, I set off down the ravine.

"To get back to the fort that evening was, of course, out of the question, but I hoped to find some cavity in the cliff where I could spend the night safely. Just before dark I discovered a snug little place, perfectly protected from the wind; and there, with my plaid wrapped tight around me, and my dogs curled up close against me, I put in quite a comfortable night. As soon as the day broke I started for the fort, and reached it by noon, half starved and very tired, but as proud of my trophy as David was of Goliath's head."

A hearty round of applause followed the conclusion of the old Scotchman's story, and by general consent it was voted the best told during the evening.

THROUGH THE TRACKLESS FOREST.

THE two features of nature in which her might, her majesty, her mystery, find fullest expression, are the ocean and the forest. Regarding their vastness and their unchanging character, in our weak endeavour to find terms for the infinite we have made them symbols of eternity. Irresistible, perennial is the fascination they possess for man, and all-satisfying the measure with which they respond to his demands. On ocean's bosom or in the forest's heart he finds free play for his noblest qualities. In making them subservient to his will he has achieved his grandest development.

Nowhere round the globe are the forests finer than on this continent of ours. Boundless in extent and endless in diversity, the eye never wearies of resting upon them or seeking to penetrate their depths. Happily free as they are from the dense matted undergrowth that makes progress through the forests of the tropics a continuous penitential pilgrimage, they present glorious vistas of silvan shade, shot through with golden shafts of sunlight, down which you may wander at your ease in unchecked communion with nature.

By way of comparison just place these two pictures side by side.

Seeking to give some conception of the interminable Congo forest, in which he spent so many months of misery, Stanley exclaims: "Take a thick Scottish copse dripping with rain; imagine this copse to be a mere undergrowth, nourished under the impenetrable shade of ancient trees, ranging from one hundred feet to one hundred and eighty feet high; briers and thorns abundant; lazy creeks meandering through the depths of the jungle, and sometimes a deep affluent of a great river. Imagine this forest and jungle in all stages of decay and growth—old trees falling, leaning perilously over, fallen prostrate; ants and insects of all kinds, sizes, and colours murmuring around; monkeys and chimpanzees above, queer noises of birds and animals, crashes in the jungle as troops of elephants rush away; rain pattering down on you every other day in the year; an impure atmosphere, with its dread consequences, fever and dysentery, gloom throughout the day and darkness almost palpable throughout the night."

Turn now to Parkman, who knows and loves his forests as Miss Murfree her mountains, and who has once and for all time painted the picture of the great American forest: " Deep recesses, where, veiled in foliage, some wild, shy rivulet steals with timid music through breathless caves of verdure; gulfs where feathered crags rise like castle walls, where the noonday sun pierces with keen rays athwart the torrent, and the mossed arms of fallen pines cast wandering shadows on the illumined foam; pools of liquid crystal turned emerald in the reflected green of impending woods; rocks on whose rugged front the gleam of sunlit waters dances in quivering light; ancient trees hurled headlong by the storm to dam the raging stream with their forlorn and savage ruin; or the stern depths of immemorial forests, dim and silent as a cavern, columned with innumerable trunks, each like an Atlas upholding its world of leaves, and sweating perpetual moisture down its dark and channelled rind—some strong in youth, some gouty with decrepit age, nightmares of strange distortion, gnarled and knotted with wens and goitres, roots intertwined beneath like serpents petrified in an agony of contorted strife; green and glistening mosses carpeting the rough ground, mantling the rocks, turning pulpy stumps to mounds of verdure, and swathing fallen trunks, as, bent in the impotence of rottenness, they lie outstretched over knoll and hollow like mouldering reptiles of the primeval world, while around, and on, and through them springs the young growth that fattens on their decay—the forest devouring its own dead. Or, to turn from its funereal shade to the light and life, to the open woodland, the sheen of sparkling lakes, and mountains basking in the glory of the summer noon, flecked by the shadows of passing clouds that sail on snowy wings across the transparent azure."

No pestilent fever or insidious deadly miasma lurks in our forests. On the contrary, their pure, piny breath brings back health to many an ailing mortal, and beneath their feathery hemlocks and aromatic spruces one may lie down at night in sweet security from snakes, or centipedes, or other crawling horrors that make each night in a tropical forest a period of peril.

Is there one of us recalling the life of the *coureurs de bois*, the men who above all others made the trackless forest their own, does not feel a stirring of the pulses of admiration and envy, and a pathetic regret that those romantic days in which they flourished are over for ever? They were the natural outcome of the beaver trade, which in the earliest stage of Canadian history formed the struggling French colony's chief source of support. All that was most active and vigorous in the colony took to the woods, thereby escaping from the oppressive control of intendants, councils, and priests, to the savage freedom of the wilderness. Not only were the possible profits great, but in the pursuit of them there was a fascinating element of adventure and danger, which irresistibly appeals to the spirit of enterprise and daring that civilization has not yet quite extinguished within our breasts.

Though not a very valuable member of society, and a thorn in the side of princes and rulers, the *coureur de bois* had his uses, at least from an artistic point of view; and his strange figure, sometimes brutally savage, but oftener marked with the lines of a dare-devil courage, and a reckless, thoughtless gaiety, will always be joined to the memories of that grand world of woods which the nineteenth century is fast civilizing out of existence.

Lost in the forest! What a thrill runs swift to the heart as we repeat the words! Ever since our young eyes overflowed at the immortal legend of the babes in the

COUREUR DE BOIS.

Page 244.

wood, sleeping the sleep that knew no awakening beneath the leafy winding-sheet brought them by their bird mourners, we seem to have had a clear conception of all the terrors the phrase implies, and we follow with throbbing pulses and bated breath the recital of such an experience as the foremost and noblest of all the pioneers of these North American forests had.

One eventful autumn, nearly three centuries ago, Champlain had caught sight of a strange-looking bird, and left his party to go in pursuit. Flitting from tree to tree, the bird lured him deeper and deeper into the forest, then took wing and vanished. On essaying to retrace his steps Champlain found himself at a loss. Whither should he turn? The day was clouded, and he had left his compass in camp. The forest closed around him, trees mingled with trees in limitless confusion. Bewildered and lost he wandered all day, and at night slept fasting at the foot of a great tree. Awaking chilled and faint, he walked until afternoon, then happily found a pond upon whose bosom were water-fowl, some of which he shot, and for the first time broke his fast. Kindling a fire he prepared his supper, and lay down to sleep in a drenching rain. Another day of blind and weary wandering succeeded, and another night of exhaustion. He found paths in the wilderness, but they had not been made by human feet. After a time the tinkling of a brook touched his ear, and he determined to follow its course, in the hope that it would lead him to the river where his party was encamped. "With toilsome steps he traced the infant stream, now lost beneath the decaying masses of fallen trunks or the impervious intricacies of matted windfalls, now stealing through swampy thickets or gurgling in the shade of rocks, till it entered at length, not into the river, but into a small lake. Circling around the brink, he found the point where, gliding among clammy roots of alders, the brook ran out and resumed its course." Pressing persistently forward, he at length forced his way out of the entanglement of underbrush into an open meadow, and there before him rolled the river, broad and turbulent, its bank marked with the portage-path by which the Indians passed the neighbouring rapids. The good God be praised! he had found the clue he sought. Inexpressibly relieved, he hastened along the river-side, and in a few hours more was being joyfully welcomed by his companions, who had been anxiously searching for him. "From that day forth," we are told, "his host, Durantal, would never suffer him to go into the forest alone."

Although the *coureur de bois* has long since made his exit, there still remains in Canada a class of men who have somewhat in common with him. These are lumber-scouts or bush-rangers, whose business it is to seek for "limits" that will pay handsome profits. It is boards, not beavers, they have upon their minds. They are often Indians or half-breeds, and the skill of these self-taught surveyors is sometimes very remarkable. They will explore the length and breadth of the *terra incognita*, and report upon the kind and value of its timber, the situation, and capability of its streams for floating out the logs, and the facilities for hauling and transportation. They will even map out the surface of the country, showing the position of its streams and lakes, its groves of timber, and its mountainous or level appearance, with a skill and accuracy bewildering to ordinary mortals, in whose eyes the whole district would be one great confused wilderness.

No more interesting experience in woodcraft could be had than a scouting excursion in such company. The trackless forest has no terrors, no mysteries for them. To them Nature opens her heart, and tells all her secrets. In lightest marching order, each man's entire equipment being carried in a shoulder-pack upheld by a " tump-line " around the forehead, they plunge into the wilderness. With un-erring instinct they pursue their way, now following the course of some winding stream, now circling a tiny lake lying gem-like in a verdurous setting, now scrambling amongst cliffs, where, to paraphrase Parkman, seeing but unseen, the crouched wild-cat eyes them from the thicket; now threading a maze of water-girded rocks, which the white cedar and the spruce clasp with serpent-like roots; then diving into leafy depths where the rock-maple rears its green masses, the beech its glistening leaves and clear smooth stem, while behind, stiff and sombre, stands the balsam fir, and the white pine towers proudly over all.

When night falls they make their simple bivouac, and their roaring camp-fire like a magician's wand strangely transforms the scene. As the flame casts its keen red light around, wild forms stand forth against the outer gloom— the oak, a giant in rusty mail; the mighty pyramid of the pine; the wan and ghastly birch, looking like a spectre in the darkness. The campers gather close around the ruddy flame made welcome by the cool breath of approaching autumn, and after the broiled trout or roast duck have disappeared, and an incense offering of fragrant smoke ascended from their pipes, they curl up in their blankets, and sleep as only those who live such a life can sleep, serenely oblivious of the harsh shriek of the owl, the mournful howl of the wolf, or the soft footfall of some prowling beast that breaks in upon the breathless stillness.

Splendid as our forests are at midsummer when the delighted eye roams unweariedly over their billowy expanses of sumptuous verdure, it is in the autumn time that they reach their rarest beauty. Then for a brief space before they strip themselves of their foliage to stand bare and shivering through the long, cold winter, they change their garb of green into a myriad of hues of gold and flame.

A keen frosty night following upon the decline of summer heat, and lo, as though some mighty magician had been at work, a marvellous transformation awaits our admiration! Where yesterday a single colour in various tints prevailed, to-day we behold every possible shade of brilliant scarlet, tender violet, sombre brown, vivid crimson, and glittering yellow. The beech, the birch, the oak, and above all, the maple, have burst forth into one harmonious and entrancing chorus of colour—the swan song of the dying foliage—the stern, straight fir alone maintaining its eternal green, as if it said: "Behold in me the symbol of steadfastness." Verily, the wide world round, a more splendid and enchanting silvan panorama cannot be found.

WRECKS AND WRECKERS OF ANTICOSTI.

RIGHT in the mouth of the great St. Lawrence, which without exaggeration has been called "the noblest, the purest, the most enchanting river on all God's beautiful earth," lies a long, narrow island that might with equal propriety be called the dreariest, most inhospitable, and most destructive island on the earth; for it is doubtful if any other spot of corresponding size has caused so many shipwrecks and so much human suffering.

In ten years, according to official records, there have been as many as one hundred and six wrecks, including seven steamships and sixty-seven sailing-ships or barques, having on board no less than three thousand precious souls, and cargoes worth millions of pounds.

Years ago, before the Canadian Government erected lighthouses and established relief stations, the wrecks were more numerous still, and were rarely unattended with loss of life. But times are better now, and when a wreck occurs, unless it be in one of those terrible winter storms that seem to make this ill-omened isle their centre, the crew generally manage to make the land in safety, where they are well cared for by the government officials.

Far different was it in 1737, when the French sloop-of-war *La Renommée* stranded upon a cruel ledge of rocks, hardly a mile off shore, about eight leagues from the southern point of Anticosti.

It was in the month of November, just as winter, which could nowhere have been more dreadful than on that bleak, barren, shelterless island, was fast closing in. In their mad haste to reach the land—for the waves were breaking high over the vessel—the crew took little food with them, although gallant Captain de Freneuse did not forget to take the ship's colours.

When in the gray, grim morning they came to reckon up, they found, to their dismay, that with six months of hopeless captivity before them, they had barely enough food for forty days, allowing the scantiest of daily rations to each of the sixty-five men who had survived the ship-wreck.

The sequel, as related with simple, graphic pathos by Father Crespel, one of the few who ultimately emerged from the terrible ordeal, constitutes as grand a record of human courage and endurance and as harrowing a history of human suffering as ever has been told.

The poor castaways had nothing but a little canvas to shelter them from the keen, biting blasts. Fever presently broke out amongst them. Then half of them set forth in two small boats to coast around that merciless shore for forty leagues, after which they made a hazardous dash across twelve leagues of open sea to Mingan, where French fishermen were known to winter.

The "jolly-boat" was swamped after they had been five days out, and its thirteen occupants were thus spared further misery. At last the ice setting in made the progress of the other boat impossible, and they had no alternative but to go into winter quarters and wait for the tardy spring.

With two pounds of damp, mouldy flour and two pounds of unsavoury fox-meat per day, these seventeen men, housed in rude huts of spruce boughs, prepared to endure the long agony of winter. Once a week a spoonful of peas was served out to each man; which constituted such a treat that, as Father Crespel naively puts it, "On those days we had our best meal."

Hunger, cold, and disease carried off one by one as the months dragged themselves along, until at length only three still lived, when a band of Indians came just in time to save this remnant from perishing.

All this and more is told by heroic Father Crespel with a quaint simplicity, a minuteness of detail, and a perfect submission to the Divine will, that renders his recital extremely touching.

Not less saddening is the story of the stout brig *Granicus*, which in 1828 went to pieces off the east end of the island, also in the month of November. Many of the crew escaped to land, but with little more than the clothing they wore.

Winter soon closed in upon them. No succour came. Their provisions gave out, and what followed may be judged from the awful sight that met the eyes of some

"HUNGER, COLD, AND DISEASE CARRIED OFF ONE BY ONE, UNTIL ONLY THREE STILL LIVED."

government officials when the following spring they stumbled across a rude hut strewn with human skeletons, and, in the pot that hung over the long-dead ashes, some bones that were not those of an animal.

Those dreadful days are happily past and gone. Few lives are lost on Anticosti now   Four fine lighthouses send their cheering rays across the anxious mariner's path, signal-guns and steam-whistles sound friendly notes of warning when the frequent fogs dim the lights, and half-a-dozen telegraph-stations at different points are ready to speed at once the news of disaster to the mainland by means of the submarine cable.

Where wrecks are plentiful, and the controlling hand of the law is absent, wreckers are sure to be plentiful also. Anticosti has been no exception to this rule.   The island has had its share of those who did not hesitate to pursue this nefarious business.

From the earliest times the place has held out attractions to the fisherman and the hunter.   The cod, halibut, herring, and other fish that it pays to catch, abound along the coast ; huge lobsters play hide-and-seek among the sea-weeds, and very good salmon and trout may be caught in some of the streams, while round-headed, mild-eyed seals spend the greater part of the year sporting in the waves or basking on the shore.

Then away inland there are, or used to be, bears, otters, martens, and foxes, to be had for the shooting or trapping.

Coming first to fish and hunt, the fishermen and hunters in many cases stayed to play the part of wreckers.   There was a good deal more money to be made out of the flotsam and jetsam that the storms sent their way than out of fish or fur, and they made the most of their opportunities.

One thing, however, must be said in their behalf. They have never been accused of luring vessels to destruction by false lights, or of confirming their title to the goods cast up by the sea by acting upon the principle that dead men are not competent witnesses in court, and by despatching any of the shipwrecked who might have survived the disaster. On the contrary, more than one unfortunate crew have owed the preservation of their lives to these very wreckers.

The most renowned of them all—a man of whom it might in truth be said that there was not a St. Lawrence pilot or a Canadian sailor who knew him not by reputation, or a parish between Quebec and Gaspé where marvellous tales were not told about him around the evening fire—was Louis Olivier Gamache. In these stories he figured as the beau-ideal of a pirate, half ogre, half sea-wolf, who enjoyed the friendship and special protection of a familiar demon.

The learned and loquacious Abbé Ferland, in his dainty little volume of "Opuscules," which I hold in my hand, tells us about this wonderful Gamache, that, according to popular rumour, he had been seen to stand upright upon the thwarts of his sloop, and command the demon to bring him a capful of wind. Instantly his sails were filled, though the sea around him was in a glassy calm, and away he went, while all about him were vessels powerless to move.

During a trip to Rimouski he gave a grand supper to

the devil, not to a devil of the second class, but to the veritable old gentleman himself. Aided by invisible assistants, he had massacred whole crews, and appropriated to himself the rich cargoes of their vessels. When hotly pursued by a government boat sent to capture him, and just about being overtaken, both sloop and Gamache suddenly disappeared, leaving nothing behind but a blue flame that went dancing over the waves in mocking defiance of the disappointed minions of the law.

Upon such thrilling legends as these was founded the reputation of the "Wizard of Anticosti," and so generally were they believed that the genial abbé assures us that the majority of the mariners in the gulf would rather have attempted to scale the citadel of Quebec than to approach by night the bay where Gamache was known to have his stronghold.

We can put plenty of confidence in the abbé, for in the year 1852 he had the courage to pay the wizard a visit, and I am sorry that I have not room to give the full particulars of that visit as they are brightly presented by this ever-entertaining writer.

He found the terror-inspiring Gamache to be a tall, erect, and vigorous old man, with snow-white hair but piercing eyes, who came forward to meet his visitors with an easy, dignified bearing that betrayed no concern or troubled conscience.

His house appeared to be a perfect arsenal of deadly weapons. No fewer than a dozen guns, many of them double-barrelled, grimly adorned the walls of the first room they entered, and every other room up to the very garret had at least two or three more, loaded and capped; they hung upon racks, surrounded by powder-flasks, shot-bags, swords, sabres, daggers, bayonets, and pistols, in most imposing profusion.

The house itself was something of a fortress. Every possible precaution had been taken to prevent persons entering it without the permission of its master. All the doors and windows were strongly barred and shuttered, and so complete were the defences that one man inside might have defied twenty outside. In the sheds, arranged in the most orderly manner, were long rows of barrels, bales, casks, and other gifts of the sea.

Such was the den of the dreaded wrecker, a man not one tithe so bad as wild rumour made him, but who, nevertheless, took pains to intensify the public feeling about himself, in order that he might be the more undisturbed in the solitude he had chosen for himself in that strange, wild place.

He had not always been alone, either. Twice had a woman been found willing to brave the rigours of his life for love of him, and in both cases they had succumbed to the terrible loneliness and desolation. His second wife died suddenly, while he was off on a hunting-trip in midwinter; and he returned, after a fortnight's absence, to find her frozen form clasping to its icy breast the bodies of their two little children, the one five and the other six years old.

"That is how they will find me some day. Each one

in their turn. Ah! well—since she is dead we can only bury her."

That was all the strange, taciturn man said to his companion, a hunter who had been with him, and yet he had always shown his wife the greatest kindness and affection. It was not that he was heartless, but that he would rather have died than reveal the depth of his feeling.

He amused the abbé very much by relating the various devices to which he had resorted in order to heighten his reputation for diabolic associations. He would go to a country inn, for instance, order a supper for two to be served in a private room, stating that he expected a gentleman in sable garments to share it with him.

When the supper was ready he would then lock himself up in the room, polish the supper off unaided, and summon the astonished landlady to clear the remains away, as he and his friend had supped and were satisfied. He would further increase their mystification by sundry rappings, and inexplicable openings and shuttings of doors.

He could also employ more sinister means of protecting himself when necessary. One day, when he was quite alone, a canoe glided into the bay, and presently a gigantic Montagnais Indian stepped ashore, armed to the teeth, and advanced with a firm step towards the house.

He was evidently crazed with fire-water, and Gamache felt in no mood to try a tussle with so brawny an opponent. Standing in the doorway, with a rifle in his hands, he called out in his sternest tones,—

"Stop! I forbid you to advance."

The intruder took not the slightest notice of him.

"Take another step and I fire," shouted Gamache. The step was taken, but before it could be repeated, the rifle spoke and the Indian fell, his thigh-bone smashed with the bullet. In an instant Gamache was beside the wounded man. Removing his weapons, he lifted him to his shoulder, and bore him tenderly to the house, and there nursed him until he was completely recovered.

Then filling his canoe with provisions, he sent him back to his tribe, with a warning never to intrude upon Gamache again unless he wanted a bullet through his head instead of his thigh.

In 1854, Louis Olivier Gamache died, like his poor wife, alone and unattended. For weeks no one had visited his abode, and when at last some seafarers chanced that way they found only the corpse of the once dreaded wizard, whose supposed league with evil spirits did not avail to save him from fulfilling his own prophecy.

The wrecks continue at Anticosti. Not long ago the shattered skeletons of four fine ocean steamers might have been seen upon its fatal shores, but with Gamache the reign of the wreckers ended, never to return.

A LUMBER CAMP.

THERE is no summer in a Canadian lumber camp; that is to say, there is nobody in the camp in summer, which amounts to the same thing. The season of activity in the camps, or the "shanties" as they are generally called, extends from late September to early April, and all summer long they are left to the care of birds that chirp and squirrels that chatter on the roof.

In the month of September the Canadian lumberman joins the gang of sturdy, active men who are bound for the "shanties," where a winter of hard work awaits them. For him the forests exist only to be remorselessly cut down; but though he may never stop to think about it, his is a very romantic and fascinating occupation.

September is one of the loveliest months in the Canadian calendar. The days are still long and sunny. The heat of summer has passed away, and the chill of autumn not yet come. One cloudless day follows another, and nature seems to be doing her best to make existence a delight. This is the time when the shantymen gather into gangs, and by rail or steamer journey northward until they pass

the limits of settlement. Then taking to " shanks' mare "
they make their way into the depths of the forest.

Let us follow a gang that is going upon a "limit" still
untouched by the axe, far up the Black River, a tributary
of the Ottawa, a hundred miles or more from the nearest
village. This gang consists of about forty men, including
the foremen, clerk, carpenter, cook, and chore-boy, all active,
sturdy, and good-natured fellows. Most of them are French-
Canadians—*habitans*, as the local term is—but English,
Scotch, and Irish are found among them too, and quite
often swarthy, wild-eyed men whose features tell plainly
of Indian blood.

Scouts have previously selected the best site for the
camp. It is usually in the midst of the " bunch " of timber
to be cut, so that little time may be lost in going and
coming. On arriving, the first thing done by the gang is
to build the shanty, which is to be its home during the
long, cold winter.

This edifice makes no pretence to architectural beauty,
but nothing could be better adapted to its purpose. It is
an illustration of simplicity and strength combined. With
all hands helping heartily, a shanty forty feet long by
twenty-eight feet wide can be put up in five days. Meantime the builders live in tents.

This is the way they go about it :—First of all, a number
of trees are cut down. The trunks, cleared of all their
branches, are sawed into proper lengths, and then laid one
upon another until an enclosure with walls eight feet high
is obtained. Upon the top of these walls strong girders

are stretched, which are supported in the centre by four great pillars called "scoop-bearers."

Then comes the roof. A Canadian shanty roof is neither tiled nor shingled, but "scooped." What is a "scoop"? It is a piece of timber something like a very long railway tie, one side of which is hollowed out, trough-wise, clear to the ends. Place two of these side by side, with the concave sides upward, and then lay another on top of them, concave side down, so that the edges overlap and fall into the troughs, and you have a roof that will defy the heaviest rains or wildest snow-storms that Canada can produce.

A floor of roughly-flattened timbers having been laid and a door cut, it only remains to construct the "camboose," or fireplace, and the bunks, and the shanty is complete; provided, of course, every cranny in the walls has been chinked with moss and mud, and a bank of earth thrown up all around the outside to make sure that no draughts can sneak in when the mercury is far below zero.

The "camboose" is quite an important affair, and occupies the place of honour in the centre of the room between the four massive scoop-bearers. Its construction is as rude and simple as that of the rest of the shanty. A bank of sand about two feet deep and six feet square makes the hearth. Over it hang two wooden cranes that hold the capacious kettles, which are always full of the pea-soup or fat salt pork that constitute the chief items in the shantymen's bill of fare.

A mighty fire roars and crackles unceasingly upon the hearth, its smoke escaping through a square hole in the roof—a hole so big that one may lie in the bunks and study the stars. This rude chimney secures the best of ventilation to the shantymen. The bunks, which are simply sloping platforms about seven feet in length, running around three sides of the room, offer the sweet allurement of the soft side of a plank to the tired toilers at the close of the day.

Such is a shanty of the good old-fashioned sort. In later days such refinements of civilization as windows, stoves, and tables have been added by progressive lumbermen, but there are still scores of shanties to which the above description applies.

The shantymen are now ready to begin operations against the great trees that have been standing all about, silent, unconscious spectators of the undertaking. The forty men are divided according to the nature of their work. The clerk, cook, and chore-boy are the "home-guard." The others, according to their various abilities, are choppers, road-cutters, teamsters, sawyers, and chainers.

The only duty requiring explanation is that of chore-boy. It is usually performed by the youngest member of the gang, although sometimes it falls to the lot of a man well up in years. The chore-boy is the cook's assistant and general utility worker of the shanty. He has to chop the firewood, draw the water, wash the dishes, and perform a multitude of such odd jobs, in return for which he is apt to get little thanks and much abuse.

The choppers have the most important and interesting part of the work. They always work in pairs, and go out against the trees armed with a keen axe apiece and a cross-cut-saw between them. Having selected their victim—say a splendid pine, towering more than a hundred feet in the air—they take up their position at each side. Soon the strokes of the axes ring out in quick succession. For some time the yellow chips fly fast, and presently a shiver runs through the tree's mighty frame. One of the choppers cries warningly to the other, who hastens to get out of the way. A few more strokes are given with nice skill. Then comes a rending crack, whose meaning cannot be mistaken; and the stately tree, after quivering a moment as though uncertain which way to fall, crashes headlong to the ground, making a wide swath through the smaller trees standing near.

A good chopper can lay his tree almost exactly where he likes, and yet somehow accidents are of frequent occurrence. Every winter additions are made to the long list of men whom the trees have succeeded in involving in their own ruin. A gust of wind, the proximity of another tree, or some such influence may cause the falling trunk to swerve, and fall with fatal force upon the unwary chopper.

The tree felled, the next proceeding is to strip it of its branches, and saw it up into as many logs as can be got from it. Two, three, four, or even as many as five logs may be obtained from a single tree—the length of each being thirteen and a half feet or sixteen and a half according to the quality. The odd half-foot is allowed for the "brooming" of the ends as the logs make their rough journey down the streams to the mills.

LUMBERING.

Page 266.

Eighty logs felled, trimmed, and sawed is quite an ordinary day's work for one pair of choppers; and when the choppers have been "striving"—that is, each pair trying its best to outdo the others—six hundred logs have been turned in by a single pair as the splendid result of a week's work.

The logs are at first piled up on "roll-ways," which are simply two tree-trunks placed a little distance apart. Later on, when the road-makers have done their part, the teamsters bear them off to the bank of the stream or out upon the ice of the lake, where they wait the coming of spring to begin their journey by water to the mills.

The shantyman leads a free, hearty, healthy life. From dawn until dark he works in the open air, exercising lungs and muscles. When the autumn rains are over, and the snow has come to stay, he breathes for four months the clear, cold, bracing air of the Canadian winter, fragrant with the scent of pine and cedar. No matter how fond of drink he may be, not one drop of liquor can he have, although he may and does drink long and deep from the "cup that cheers."

His fare possesses at least two sterling merits. It is substantial in quality and unlimited in quantity. He enjoys it most when the day's work is over, and, no less weary than hungry, he trudges home to the shanty. There he finds the warm welcome of a steaming supper awaiting him.

Drawn up about the blazing fire he sees a pot of excellent pea-soup, a boiler of strong tea, a big pan full of fat pork fried and floating in gravy, another pan containing slices of cold boiled pork, huge loaves of bread baked in great iron pots buried deep in the ashes of the "camboose"—and better than city baker ever made—and a pile of bright tin basins.

Picking up two of the basins, he fills one with soup and the other with tea. Helping himself to a generous slice of the hot bread, he makes use of it as a plate for a slice of the pork. Then he retires to the edge of his bunk, and with the aid of his clasp-knife discusses this solid if not varied repast.

There is not much change in the bill of fare all winter. Occasionally, perhaps, if the roads permit, fresh beef "on foot" will be sent up from the depot, and the lumbermen may enjoy the luxury of steaks and roasts. Quite often, too, a bit of game will fall in their way while they are working in the woods. Great is the rejoicing when François or Alec succeeds in bringing down a fat deer. Bear-steak, too, is not unknown. The bear is trapped in a "dead fall," or small hut above the door of which a heavy log is hung in such a way that it drops with crushing force upon the bear pushing in to get at the bait.

Sometimes the shantymen do a little trapping on their own account. One of them, who wished to obtain a fine bear-skin, paid dearly for his prize. He had set his steel spring trap, and returning after an interval, found that it had disappeared. The marks in the snow made tracking easy; and hurrying along, he presently reached a great log over which the trap had evidently been dragged. His haste made him careless, and springing across the broad trunk without stopping to reconnoitre, he threw himself right into the arms of the bear. The animal, weary of dragging the heavy trap, was resting on the other side.

The hunted creature was furious with pain. The shantyman's only weapon was his sheath-knife, which he drew and stabbed the bear again and again in the breast. But stab as he might he could not loose the brute's fatal grasp. Next day his comrades, anxiously following up his trail, found him dead, with the dead bear's paws still holding him fast.

The shantyman's recess comes when the evening meal has been despatched. He has an hour or more before bedtime. It is pipes all round, and song and joke and story win generous applause from the not over-critical audience. The French-Canadians are especially fond of singing. They have many songs, some of which, like "À la claire fontaine" and "En roulant ma boule," are full of spirit and beauty. If François or Alec has remembered to bring his fiddle with him—and he seldom forgets it—the singing is sure to be followed by dancing as the evening goes on.

Bedtime comes early in the shanty. By nine o'clock, at the latest, all have "turned in." The process of going to bed consists simply in taking off one's coat and boots, and rolling up snugly in a couple of thick blankets. Many a millionaire would gladly give one of his millions for the ability to sleep as soundly and restfully in his soft bed as does the shantyman upon his pine boards.

In the dusk of early morning the foreman's loud voice is heard calling to the men,—

"Turn out now, and get your breakfast!"

The lumberman has been asleep ten good hours, but he feels as if he had just lain down!

Sunday is the day the shantyman likes best. No work is done upon that day. He can spend the time as he pleases. Generally he is content to lounge about smoking, and enjoying the luxury of doing nothing. A religious service is so rare a treat that when there is one all attend it without reference to their creed.

Thus the long winter slips by. The logs accumulate upon the river bank or out upon the icy lake. When the warm days of spring come the lumberman's labours are at an end, so far as the shanty is concerned. The great spring drive begins. The logs start upon their journey southward, and the shantyman becomes a river-driver. Armed with pike-pole or camp-hook, he hurries his awkward squads of logs down stream as a shepherd drives his flock to market.

This is often a very exciting and dangerous occupation. The Canadian rivers abound in falls and rapids, past which the flocks of tree-trunks have to be guided skilfully. Many a time the river-driver's life is in peril as he wades through the turbulent, ice-cold water, or leaps from rock to rock, or from log to log, in his efforts to prevent his charges from stranding.

When the drive is finished the shantyman's labours are over, until the return of autumn recalls him to the forest.

LACROSSE.

WHAT the game of cricket is to England, and the game of base-ball to the United States, is the game of lacrosse to Canada; and yet it is worth noting that both cricket and base-ball flourish in Canada, which goes to show that the young Canadian seeks for quantity as well as quality in his sport.

The Indians invented lacrosse, just as they invented the canoe, the snow-shoe, and the toboggan, and it is not likely that their pale-face brother will be able to invent something surpassing any of them. How long ago they invented lacrosse is a question not even Parkman nor Catlin can tell us. The redskins have never had newspapers, and seem to have been poor hands at keeping diaries; consequently we can never hope to know when first the Iroquois champion team, led by the famous chief "Throw-the-ball-half-a-mile," defeated the Cree champions under the no less renowned "Stop-it-with-his-stomach-every-time."

Catlin, who saw it played by six hundred, eight hundred, or even one thousand Choctaws at a time, tells us that the players would trip and throw each other, and sometimes take flying leaps over the heads of their stooping opponents, or dart between their extended legs. "There are times," he adds, "when the ball gets to the ground, when there is a confused mass of sticks, shins, and bloody noses." I may add on my own account that those times are not altogether past and gone. Scratched shins and crimsoned noses are still to be found on the lacrosse-field.

There is, of course, a good deal of difference between lacrosse as played by the whites to-day and as it was played by the redskins half a century ago. In the first place, the ground was not a level, smooth-shaven lawn, with a cinder path around it, and beyond that rows of seats for spectators, but a glade in the forest, interspersed with stumps of trees, fallen trunks, and clumps of young spruce. The goals were single poles or stakes, about eight feet high, and the distance between them varied, in proportion to the number of players, from five hundred yards to half-a-mile, or even more. Then the crosse was much shorter, and smaller as to its netting, while among some tribes no netting at all was used, but instead thereof two sticks having spoon-shaped ends, between which the ball was caught and carried. As to the dress of the players—well, the difference is not so very great. The white men wear a little more on their backs, and canvas shoes instead of moccasins on their feet, and that is about the sum of the matter.

I will now try to describe the game as it is played by the Canadian clubs to-day The ground should be a smooth, level field one hundred and fifty yards in length by one hundred in breadth at the very least, and for championship matches another fifty yards each way is most desirable. The goals should be one hundred and twenty-five yards apart, but a lesser distance may be agreed upon between the two captains if the nature of the ground requires it. The side boundaries are formed by the fence or ring of spectators, as the case may be. If the ball goes over the one, or gets tangled up with the other, it has to be brought out and " faced." The nature of " facing " will be explained further on. The goals are simply two poles six feet high and six feet apart, and in front of them, at a lacrosse stick's length from their base, a line is marked with whitewash, inside of which no attacking player must enter unless the ball has preceded him. If he enters in advance of the ball, the goal-keeper may drive him out at the point of his stick, and use any violence necessary for that purpose.

The side consists of twelve players and a captain. The captain does not play ; he simply runs round and shouts at the other fellows. It looks like an easy job, but it is far from being so. Upon the captain very often depends the fate of his team, and he should always be a cool, clear-headed, experienced player, thoroughly up to all the tricks and subtleties of the game. The lacrosse-sticks, or crosses as they are called, are light, strong sticks, made of either hickory, ash, or rock elm; the Indian preferring the first because of its strength, and the white man the other two because of their lightness. There is no rule as to the length of a stick, but practical experience has shown that the most convenient length is equal to the distance from the toe to the hollow under the arm. Each player can therefore suit himself in the matter. The netting is of gut, and should be about twenty-nine inches long, and *must* not be more than twelve inches wide at its widest part. Nine inches is a good average width. There must be no "bag" to the netting, and to guard against this the referee is required to inspect the crosses carefully before allowing the match to begin. The ball is of sponge india-rubber, about half-an-inch less in circumference than a base-ball, and weighing about four ounces. It should bounce freely, as this adds greatly to the uncertainty and interest of the game.

All the preliminaries having been satisfactorily arranged, a fine day, a good ground, and a large gathering of spectators secured, we will suppose that a championship match between the representative teams of Montreal and Toronto is about to take place. At the appointed hour the teams issue from their dressing-rooms amid the cheers of their adherents and line up before the referee and umpires. That is, they face one another in two parallel lines, and then the referee proceeds to examine their crosses lest they should be "bagged," and their shoes lest they may be spiked. He also addresses a word of warning to them upon the subject of rough play, which, unhappily, has become far too common of late. He then dismisses them, and they take up their places on the field. When this is done they take their positions in pairs, each man having an opponent opposite him. Thus the Montreal goal-keeper has the Toronto "inside home" just in front of him; each of the fielders has a man to "cover" him, as the term is, and there is a Toronto "centre" as well as a Montreal centre.

The game is begun by the two centre fielders. They half kneel opposite each other, and lay their crosses on the ground, face to face, every nerve and muscle tingling with excitement, for much may depend upon which gets the advantage at the start. This is called "facing the ball," and when the referee is satisfied that everything is in readiness, he places the ball between the two crosses, taking care that it is exactly in the middle. At his shout of "Play," the two centres strive, by a sharp, sudden twist of the crosse, each to draw the ball in his own direction. The successful one immediately passes it to the nearest fielder on his own side, who is instantly pounced upon by his "cover," and then the fun begins in fierce earnest.

It is quite out of the question to convey through the medium of print any adequate conception of the interest and excitement that a game of lacrosse between two well-matched teams affords. For brilliancy of individual effort as well as of combined team play, for incessant movement and thrilling situations, for cheer-inspiring displays of undaunted pluck or untiring fleetness, there is no game that can compare with it. The ball flies all over the field, now soaring like a bird through the air, now skimming along the ground like a frightened field-mouse. First one goal is in danger, and the players crowd so thickly about it that you cannot see the goal-keeper. Then a long throw from his skilful stick sends the rubber away off to the side, or perhaps almost down to the other goal, and two dangers are over for the time. Next an artful dodger will catch the ball on his crosse, and turning, twisting, dodging this way and that, dropping the ball when checked, only to pick it up again deftly after the checker is eluded, will, amid the shouts and cries of spectators and players alike, carry it clear down the whole length of the field, and perhaps, if he be very lucky, send a "grounder" between the goal-posts ere the goal-keeper has time to recover from the surprise of his onset.

In the throwing, catching, checking, running, and dodging which the game calls for, every muscle and sinew is given fullest exercise, and every man in the team has a share of the work. There is no "loafing" possible in lacrosse, as there is in base-ball and cricket, when the out-field are getting nothing to do. Even the goal-keeper has plenty of hard work, for whenever the ball goes behind the goal-posts he must go after it, and struggle for it until he can send it either to one of his own side or far down the field. Indeed, the ability to play well "behind the flags" is as important a quality in a goal-keeper as an argus-eyed watchfulness over what is going on in front of him.

While individual brilliancy—"grand-stand play," as it

is sometimes called—is all very well in its way, good team-playing is far more effective in the end, and it is just because the whites excel in the latter that they have become more than a match for the redskins, from whom they have adopted the game. One of the prettiest sights imaginable is to see two expert players "tobying" to one another for perhaps half the length of the field before they can be stopped. This tobying consists in their running along ten or fifteen yards apart, and throwing the ball from one to the other so soon as there is danger of the one carrying it being checked.

Another valuable accomplishment in a lacrosse-player is knowing how and when to "uncover"—that is, to stop away from the opponent who has been deputed to cover him, and consequently be free to snatch up the ball the moment it comes his way. When one team understands this better than the other, the result is to convey the impression that it must have more players, because there always seem to be two of them at least wherever the rubber is.

The game is won by the ball being thrown between the goal-posts, not higher than an imaginary line drawn across their tops. It must, of course, be thrown through from in front. Formerly a match was decided by the winning of three games, "best three out of five;" but in one of the two lacrosse associations now existing in Canada a change has been made, and unless one team wins three games straight, play must be continued for two hours, and then the team having the most games wins the match. The reason of the change was that in some cases a team would take three games from their opponents in a few minutes, and at this the spectators grumbled.

The most interesting recent event in the history of the game in Canada is the visit of the famous Toronto twelve to Great Britain. They are a splendid lot of players, and seem to have it all their own way, as might be expected. The fact, however, that there are enough lacrosse clubs in the Old Country to make it worth their while to go over, proves that the game is making progress round the world. Indeed, it has been already heard of from Australia, India, China, and other far-away quarters of the globe.

In the United States it is spreading rapidly, and the time cannot be far distant when we shall have international struggles for supremacy in lacrosse as well contested as we already have in some other sports. Some years ago a team from the United States crossed the Atlantic to contend against their British cousins, and succeeded in winning every match they played but one.

A PILLOW-SLIP FULL OF APPLES.

"A. & H. O. A. S.

"The arch-room—ten o'clock to-night. Bring a sheet and pillow-slip.   ABRACADABRA."

CHARLIE DRAPER gazed at the piece of paper containing these simple words and mysterious signature with mingled feelings of pride and trepidation—pride because it was the first time since his coming to Twin Elm Academy that he had been the recipient of one of these much-prized missives, and trepidation because he had very vague notions of what his accepting the invitation it bore might entail.

He was a new boy, just finishing his first month at the academy, and being of rather reserved disposition, had been slow in forming acquaintances. Indeed, but for an incident that suddenly brought him into prominence, he might have made still poorer progress in this direction than he did.

A few days before this communication from "Abracadabra," a party of the boys were bathing in the river near Deep Pool. A youngster who could not swim rashly ventured too near the pool, and disappeared in its dark depths. There arose an immediate chorus of cries from his companions, but no intelligent effort was being made at rescue, when Charlie Draper, who had not been of the party, came rushing up, threw off his cap and coat, plunged into the pool, and brought out the drowning boy at the first try.

Of course he was a hero at once, and the leaders of the "A. & H. O. A. S."—the secret society of the academy, of which Charlie had already heard much, and admittance to which was the desire of his heart—lost no time in deciding that he was beyond question one of the right sort, and that he must become one of them forthwith. Hence the short but significant summons whose contents have been already given.

Promptly at ten o'clock, Charlie, in his stocking feet, and provided with pillow-slip and sheet, crept cautiously up the long stairs that led to the arch-room.

All the students, except those who belonged to the society, were already sound asleep, and the two tutors who lived in the building, knowing nothing of this exception, and imagining that every cot was duly occupied, had settled down for a comfortable smoke and chat in the cozy sitting-room of Mr. Butler, whose quarters were farthest away from the arch-room.

Upon all this the members of the society had astutely reckoned, and the coast was accordingly clear for them to do as they pleased as long as they did not make too much noise about it.

Bearing his note of invitation as a passport, Charlie approached the door of the arch-room. Suddenly out of its shadow a masked and draped figure darted, and putting its hand to his throat, inquired in a very husky voice,—

" What doest thou here ?"

For answer, Charlie held up his sheet and slip of paper.

" 'Tis well. Pass on," said the husky mystery.

And with palpitating heart Charlie tiptoed through the door.

The moment he passed the portal, two other masked and draped figures seized him by either arm, and hurried him before a fourth figure, who occupied a sort of throne at the far corner of the room.

" Whom do you bring before me ?" asked this potentate, in the husky tone which seemed to be characteristic of the society.

" Charles Draper, may it please your sublimity," was the reply, accompanied by a reverent obeisance, in which Charlie was directed to join.

" He hath been well recommended to us. Let him be put to the tests. If he doth survive them and will take the oaths, he may be admitted into membership."

Then followed a lot of the usual elaborate nonsense such as boys delight to invent and execute in connection with their secret societies; and at the end of fifteen minutes or so, Charlie, flushed and excited, but triumphant, was handed a gown and mask, and informed by the figure on the throne, whose official title was the same as the signature to the invitation, that he was duly admitted into the membership of the society, whose full name he now learned was The Ancient and Honourable Order of Apple Stealers.

The next piece of information he received rather staggered him. It was that, according to the rules of the society, he must at once justify the confidence its members had reposed in him by proving his prowess as an applestealer.

The August pippins in Squire Ribston's orchard were reported to be ready to drop into one's mouth. Upon the novice, Charles Draper, devolved the perilous duty of securing a generous sample of those juicy golden globes, so that the ancient and honourable order might pronounce judgment on their excellence.

So soon as he understood this, Charlie began to wish he had not been in such a hurry to join the society. He had been at Twin Elm long enough to learn that old Squire Ribston's dogs were as good in their way as his apples were in theirs, and he did not at all relish the prospect of having an argument with them in their own territory at the dead of night.

But he was too stout of heart to back out, or even to show any signs of flinching, as his sublimity proceeded to give him his instructions.

Each member had brought a sheet with him. These were quickly converted into a rope, which reached from the window of the arch-room to the ground.

Stuffing the pillow-slip into his pocket, and putting on his shoes, Charlie, amid the whispered commands of his companions—to " Be sure and fill the pillow-slip," " Don't call the dogs bad names," "Give the compliments of the order to the squire if you happen to meet him," and other inspiring injunctions—climbed carefully out of the window, and let himself down hand over hand to the ground.

Pausing only to kiss his hand circus-fashion to the faces at the window, he hastened off noiselessly over the dew-laden grass in the direction of the squire's orchard.

He knew his route well enough, and the distance was not quite half-a-mile, so that a few minutes' quick walking brought him to his destination.

The Ribston mansion stood well back from the road, and the orchard lay to its rear.

Charlie therefore thought it well to leave the road before he reached the gate, and to take a slant through the fields that brought him up to the orchard fence about fifty yards behind the house.

Here he crouched down, and listened, with strained ears and throbbing pulses, for the slightest sound that might indicate the proximity of a dog. But not a growl, or bark, or even sniff, broke the clover-scented stillness.

As it chanced, he had hit upon a particularly favourable night for his enterprise, the good squire being wont to spend his Friday evenings with admirable regularity at Doctor Aconite's, where the genial rector of St. David's and important Judge Surrebutter helped to make up a quartette that could play whist by the hour without so much as winking.

For the sake of company on the way home the squire always took his dogs with him, so that until his return, which was never later than eleven o'clock, the Ribston premises were entirely unguarded.

Encouraged by the perfect silence, Charlie gently got over the fence, and making his way to the August pippin-tree, set diligently to work to fill his pillow-slip.

The boughs were bending low beneath their weight of juicy fruit, and he had no need to shake them. There were far more apples within easy reach of his hand than he could carry home.

Five minutes sufficed to fill the pillow-slip, and then, with a vast sigh of relief, he crawled back over the fence, hastened across the field, and came to the fence beside the road.

Knowing nothing of the squire's whist club, he took it for granted that all danger was practically over, and without looking to right or left, he tossed his bag over the fence and vaulted lightly after it.

Hardly had his feet touched the ground than a sharp, suspicious bark came from only a few yards away, and the next moment a collie dog, followed closely by a fox-terrier, bounded toward him, barking fiercely, while looming dimly through the darkness the portly form of their owner could be descried, as he demanded angrily,—

" Who are you ? and what are you about ? "

Charlie could have answered both questions easily enough had he chosen to do so. But the time did not seem to him altogether favourable, and instead of a verbal reply he picked up his pillow-slip, threw it over his shoulder, and took to his heels, with the dogs after him in full cry.

"Catch him, Grip; catch him, Oscar!" shouted the squire to his dogs, as he joined in the chase with all his might.

Although hardly in condition for a sprinting match, Squire Ribston had been renowned for fleetness of foot in his younger days, and he showed a surprising turn of speed as he dashed down the road after the fleeing boy.

Now, had Charlie dropped his heavy pillow-slip, he might have distanced his human pursuer easily, and as the dogs seemed to be content with barking, and to have no idea of biting, the irate squire would never have known more about the daring raider of his orchard than his strong suspicion that it was one of those rascally Twin Elm boys.

But to let go his burden was the last thing Charlie thought of doing.

To his daring, determined nature only two alternatives presented themselves—escape with his booty or capture red-handed.

So away he sped, holding tight to the pillow-case, the collie and terrier punctuating his strenuous strides with short, sharp barks.

After his first furious spurt, the squire's speed rapidly slackened until it became little more than a laboured jog-trot; and by the time he reached the entrance to the long avenue leading from the main road to the academy, Charlie was under the window and jerking the sheet-rope by way of a signal to the boys to haul him up.

Unfortunately, they were so occupied with some of their nonsense that they did not at first observe the signal, and

precious moments were lost before
they responded, so that Charlie's
anxious ears caught the sound of
the squire's panting as he toiled
gamely along the avenue.

" Hurry up, boys!" he called, as loudly as he dared;
" the squire's after me!"

The boys responded with a sudden jerk that snatched
him off the ground, and nearly made him drop the apples.
Then up he went more steadily, foot by foot.

But he was not half-way to the window when the squire,
guided by his clever dogs, arrived upon the scene, and in
spite of the semi-darkness his keen old eyes took in the
situation at a glance.

" Aha, you young scoundrel!   I have you now.   Take
that!"

And he hurled his stout oak cane at the ascending boy.
The result greatly exceeded his expectations, for the stick,
going straight to its mark, gave Charlie such a stinging
blow that he involuntarily let go of the weighty pillow-
slip, and down it dropped full upon the squire's pate,
crushing his tall gray beaver over his eyes and sending
him headlong to the ground.

It was some moments before he could pick himself up
again, and by that time Charlie was safe inside the window.
Beside himself with wrath, the squire assailed the front
door with furious blows, bringing both the tutors out in
startled haste.

To them, as well as his breathless, disordered condition
permitted, he explained himself, and was at once invited
to enter, while Mr. Butler went for Professor Rodwell.

On the professor's arrival all the boys were summoned
to appear in the school-room, and presently in they flocked,
all but the members of the A. & H. O. A. S. (who, by the

way, had managed to get into their night-gowns with marvellous celerity), manifesting their innocence by their unmistakably startled, sleepy faces.

"Are all the boys here?" asked the squire suspiciously, on finding every one arrayed in his night-gown.

Professor Rodwell counted heads carefully.

"Yes, squire, all the boys are present," he replied.

"Humph!" snapped the squire. "A clever trick; but they can't pull the wool over my eyes in that way."

An anxious, expectant hush following, Professor Rodwell addressed the boys in grave yet not unkindly tones :—

"Young gentlemen, it is clear beyond possibility of denial that some of you have been guilty of robbing Squire Ribston's orchard. Now, I dare say, it will not be difficult to trace out the culprits, but I would much prefer that they should acknowledge their wrong-doing of their own accord. I therefore wait to give them the opportunity."

There was but a moment's pause, and then Charlie Draper, stepping forward, said in a steady voice, looking full at Professor Rodwell,—

"It was I that took Squire Ribston's apples. Let me bear all the punishment."

A look of mingled surprise and relief came into the professor's troubled face, and even the squire's anger-wrinkled countenance seemed to take on a softer expression, touched with approval of this frank avowal.

"Charles Draper, I am very sorry," said Professor Rodwell slowly. "Although you've been but a short time with us, I had thought better things of you than this."

Charlie's eyes fell and his lip began to tremble. He was already feeling deep regret for his part in the matter, and these gentle words touched him to the heart.

He was just about to express his contrition and ask for sentence upon himself, when the squire exclaimed,—

" Charlie Draper ! is that Charlie Draper ? "

" It is," replied Professor Rodwell, wondering why the squire asked.

" The same boy that saved my little grandson Hughie from drowning in Deep Pool a week ago ? "

" Yes, squire, the same boy," replied the professor, now beginning to catch the old gentleman's drift.

" Then," cried the squire, who was as quick of generous impulse as he was of temper, jumping from his seat and advancing toward Charlie, " I don't want this thing to go any further.—Here's my hand, my brave lad. You're welcome to every apple on the tree, if you'll only come after them in honest, manly fashion, and not be playing such foolish pranks, skulking through the fields when you ought to be abed.—Come, now, Professor Rodwell, let's cry quits. I'm willing to let the matter rest. Boys will be boys, and if your boys will promise never to go out robbing orchards again, I'll promise to let 'em into my orchard on Saturday afternoons and take every apple they find in the grass so long as the crop lasts."

For a moment the boys were so bewildered by these astounding words that they could hardly credit their ears.

Then a spontaneous cheer burst from their throats, and the upshot of the whole matter was that they heartily gave the promise the squire asked; and the professor, relieved beyond measure at the turn affairs had taken, dismissed them with the understanding that the night's doings should be no further inquired into, provided good behaviour was maintained in future.

The pledge thus given, taking away from the A. & H. O. A. S. its principal reason for existing under that name, did not, however, put an end to its career. It simply altered its title and amended its ways, and continued to flourish as vigorously as before, with Charlie Draper as one of its most popular and active members.

LOST ON LAKE ST. LOUIS.

THE great river St. Lawrence, as if not content with its ordinary ample breadth, a few miles above the city of Montreal spreads out into a wide sheet of water which is known as Lake St. Louis. Lake St. Louis is about twelve miles long by eight in width at its widest part, and being famous for its cool breezes, the people from the city go out there in throngs every summer, so that its shores are well populated as long as the thermometer keeps well above the seventy point.

In winter, however, it is very different. Then Jack Frost has a confirmed habit of sending the mercury away down, down, down, not only below freezing-point, but below zero even; and the blue waters of the lake turn into a floor as hard as steel, over which the snows drift and pile up and scatter again in fantastic windrows, until the warm spring sunshine melts them into soggy slush, and a little later rends the solid floor itself asunder and sends it careering down the current in great jagged ice-floes.

There is nothing undecided about a Canadian winter. The frost-king means business from the start, and for three long months keeps a tight grip upon the land. Some winters, of course, he is more tyrannical than others. The Ross boys, for instance, thought that he had never before in their experience been so unmerciful as during the season that the event happened about which I am now going to tell. Day after day for weeks at a time the thermometer would not get up to the zero mark at all, while it would at night drop as much as thirty points below it.

"'Pon my word, this sort of weather isn't fair at all," said Bob Ross, in an impatient tone, at the breakfast-table one morning. "A fellow can hardly stir out of doors without getting his nose or ears nipped. My nose was frost-bitten for the third time last night, and that's a little too much of a good thing for me."

"Right your are, Bob," chimed in Phil, his elder brother, from across the table. "My poor ears have been nipped nobody knows how often. I expect one of them will drop off some fine day."

"It's a keen winter, boys, no doubt," assented Mr. Ross. "I don't remember many as sharp. But the longest winter has an end, and you'll forget all about the cold the first warm day that comes."

"That may be, father," answered Bob, "but I'd like a little mild weather right now if the weather-clerk has no objections. You know we're going over to the church festival at Beauharnois to-morrow night; and an eight-mile tramp in this cold weather is not just what I'm hankering for—though I mean to go all the same."

"Tut! my lad, when I was your age I would have thought nothing of double the distance, if only a certain person were at the end of it," replied Mr. Ross, with a meaning smile at his wife as he added, "But perhaps you have no such attraction."

"Not I," laughed Bob. "I'm going for the sake of the supper; but I won't answer for Phil," looking quizzically at his brother, who blushed violently and made a timely diversion by springing up and saying,—

"Come along, Bob; let us get at our work, cold or no cold."

Whereupon the two lads went off together.

Mr. Ross owned one of the largest and finest among the many farms that bordered upon Lake St. Louis. Although he was what might be called a gentleman farmer, he was a thoroughly practical farmer too. He made his farm pay him handsomely, and thought so well of his occupation that he had brought up his two boys to follow it also. When they were grown men he would divide the greater part of his property between them, reserving only sufficient to keep himself and his wife in independent comfort during the remainder of their days.

The two sons, Phil and Bob, at the time of my story about sixteen and fourteen years of age respectively, were as satisfactory a pair of boys as parents could wish. One, the elder, tall and dark, the other short and fair, both were strong, healthy, hearty lads, full of spirit, and fond enough of having their own way, but thoroughly sound at heart and passionately fond of father and mother. Although trained to all kinds of farm work, their education had not been by any means neglected. They had had a good share of schooling, and Mr. Ross never went into the city without bringing back a new book or the latest magazine, so that they might keep up with the spirit of the times.

The church festival Bob spoke of was to take place the following evening at Beauharnois, a village that stood straight across the lake "as the crow flies" a distance of about eight miles. The snow was in capital condition for snow-shoeing, and the two sturdy boys thought nothing of the tramp there and back. They would start from home at four in the afternoon, make Beauharnois about six, enjoy themselves there to the best of their ability until ten, and then set off for home, where they ought to turn up soon after midnight.

Much to their gratification, the cold next morning showed signs of moderating.

"Looks as if the weather-clerk was interested in the festival," remarked Phil in the course of the morning, his beaming face revealing clearly enough that others than the weather-clerk were interested in the same event.

"I'm glad it isn't quite so keen as yesterday," answered Bob. "A fellow will enjoy the spread all the better for not going to it with his nose frozen."

"I shouldn't wonder if we had a regular change," said Mr. Ross, casting a searching glance at the sky, which was evidently losing its sharp blue tinge and becoming ashen gray in colour. "We often do have a soft spell about this time of the year. There'll most likely be snow soon. I hope it won't begin before you get home, boys."

"Oh, I think not," replied Phil confidently. "It can't come much sooner than the morning."

The hours of the day slipped quickly by, and sharp at four o'clock the two boys set forth on their long tramp. They certainly were a prepossessing pair in their white blanket-coats, that became them so well, tied with broad scarlet sashes, and blue caps with scarlet tassels on their heads. Bidding good-bye to their parents, who stood at the door watching them with fond pride, Phil and Bob strode swiftly down the slope to the lake, and soon were tramping over its broad bosom, upon which the snow lay deep in undulating waves. Barring the leaden hue of the sky, the afternoon could hardly have been finer. The stinging cold was gone, yet the air was keen enough to be bracing. There was little or no wind. The snow was well packed; and, full of joyful expectations, the brothers walked on side by side, their broad snow-shoes bearing them easily upon the very surface of the drifts. Eight miles in two hours was no remarkable performance for two such expert snow-shoers as they, and they accomplished it without difficulty, reaching their destination just as the bell in the tower of the church boomed out six solemn strokes.

Leaving their coats and snow-shoes at a friend's house, they hastened to the place where the festival was in full swing, and entered heartily into the enjoyments, each following his own bent. The expectations of both were fully satisfied. The supper presented more dainties on its generous bill of fare than even the capacious appetite of Bob could comfortably sample, and Phil was not disappointed in the light that shone from a certain pair of brown eyes that for some mysterious reason had more attraction for him than anything else the entertainment offered.

Ten o'clock came all too soon for him, especially as the festival was not entirely over, although some of those who lived at a distance had already left; but Bob was rather glad, as the last hour had been somewhat slow, from his point of view. So siding up to Phil, he whispered discreetly in his ear,—

"Time to go, Phil: it's 'most ten o'clock."

Phil pulled out his watch with an incredulous look; but, alas! it told the same story as Bob, and dearly as he would have liked to linger, he knew well enough that the sooner they started now the better. So, with a very regretful adieu to the one whose presence had "made the assembly shine," he joined his brother at the door.

When they got outside, the look of the night and the feel of the air told them that the snow was nearer at hand than they had expected. In fact, a few soft, sly flakes were already dropping noiselessly. The friend at whose house they had left their coats and snow-shoes suggested their staying all night; but although Bob was nothing loath, Phil would not be persuaded.

"Father said he'd wait up for us," he objected, "and he'll get anxious if we're not home by twelve o'clock.— Come along, Bob."

Accordingly, off they went into the darkness of the night. When they reached the shore of the lake, they could just see the glimmer of the village lights by which they were to be guided—their home lying about half-a-mile to the left. Although their pace was far from a loitering one, they did not get over the snow by any means so fast as in the afternoon.

Bob was not only tired and sleepy, but provoked with Phil for refusing to stay all night at their friend's house. Indeed, he hoped his brother would yet repent and return, and so his feet dragged not a little. Noticing this, Phil said briskly, -

"Step out, Bob; we'll have all we can do to get across before the snow comes."

"All well enough to say 'step out,'" answered Bob gruffly. "Why couldn't you stay overnight? I'm too tired to walk fast anyhow, snow or no snow."

"Oh, you're not tired, Bob. You've eaten a little too much supper, that's all," rejoined Phil pleasantly.

Bob vouchsafed no answer, and for some time the brothers tramped along in silence. As they neared the centre of the lake, the snow-flakes, which had at first been few and far between, thickened rapidly, and the wind at the same time rose into gusts that blew them sharply into the boys' faces.

A thrill of alarm shot threw Phil, and grasping Bob's arm he called out,—-

"It looks nasty, Bob; let's put on a spurt."

At this appeal Bob roused himself; and quickening their pace to a trot, they hastened onward, their snow-shoes rising and falling in steady, unbroken step. Every minute the snow and wind increased, until at length the storm in full force burst upon the boys and almost blew them off their feet.   All around them the air was filled with flakes of white whirling about in bewildering myriads, splashing like fine spray into their faces and stinging like small shot, for the wind was bitterly cold.   Presently Phil halted, and, peering hard into the blinding storm, cried anxiously,—

"What's become of the lights, Bob?   I can't see them a bit; can you?"

"N-n-no," panted Bob.   "Let's turn back."

"THE FORMS OF THE TWO BOYS WERE EXPOSED TO VIEW."

"No use in that," replied Phil, turning round.   "I can't see those behind us either.   There's nothing for it but to push ahead."

"O Phil! are we lost?" asked Bob, with quivering lips.

Phil was more than half afraid they were; but to reassure Bob he answered cheerfully,—

"It's all right.   I know how to steer.   Come along." And grasping Bob's hand he started off again.

On and on they plodded through storm and snow, Phil half dragging Bob, who, between fright and real weariness, found difficulty in making progress at all. For half-an-hour more they struggled thus, until at last Bob dropped his brother's hand and flung himself down in the snow, sobbing out despairingly,—

"It's no use, Phil, I'm dead beat; you'll have to go on without me."

"Nonsense, Bob," said Phil, taking him by the shoulder. "Jump up and go at it again."

Thus helped to his feet, Bob made another attempt, but had not gone more than a quarter of a mile in a way that was staggering rather than walking before down he slipped again; and this time all that Phil could do failed to rouse him from his stupor. The cold and exhaustion had completely overcome him. He had but one thought, and that was—to be allowed to sleep. Phil fully realized the danger, and, tired as he was himself, put forth every exertion to keep his brother awake. He even tried to drag him along by his sash in what he thought was the right direction, but of course soon found this impossible.

Desert his brother he would not, though they died together; so, in order to keep himself from falling into the same state, he made a circle around him, walking slowly. While doing this he encountered a high drift whose lee afforded some shelter from the blast. An idea flashed into his mind which he instantly proceeded to execute.

Returning to Bob he dragged him with infinite difficulty to this spot. Then slipping off one of his snow-shoes, he proceeded to cover his body with snow, leaving nothing but his head exposed; the poor boy, now fast asleep, offering no objection to such strange bedclothes. Then sitting down beside him, with the big drift protecting his back, he let the snow gather over himself, hoping he hardly knew for what, and praying for the Lord who sent the snow-storm to have mercy on them both.

In a vague way—for the stupor was fast creeping upon him too—he wondered if his father had begun to miss them yet, and whether he would come out in search of them. He even dimly pictured his father sitting in the parlour at home reading his book, and pausing every now and then to listen for his boys' voices. His mother, he knew, would have gone to bed long ago. He felt relieved that the snow no longer stung his face, and that the wind had gone down completely, and so his thoughts wandered on until he knew no more.

One hour, two hours passed, and the drifting snow had hidden the forms of the two boys from sight, when a long line of men might have been seen coming from the village and scanning carefully every mound and swell of the snow as they hastened onward. In advance of the rest strode Mr. Ross, his face full of grave anxiety, his eyes intent upon the white plain before him that seemed to have so little to tell. Now bounding on ahead and now returning to look up in his face with inquiring eyes was his wise old collie, Oscar, without whom he never went abroad.

" Find them, Oscar, find them, good dog," would Mr. Ross

say encouragingly, and the sagacious animal would dart on again. Presently he stopped beside a drift now grown to huge proportions, sniffed sharply at the snow, and then proceeded to dig into it with eager, vigorous paws. Observing his action, Mr. Ross uttered a cry of joy and sprang forward to the dog's side. Going down on his knees he tore at the snow-bank in a frenzy of haste. In another moment a red tassel appeared, then a blue cap, then a white, still face, and, others coming to his aid, the forms of the two boys were exposed to view, Phil still sitting up with his head bent over his knees, and Bob lying comfortably beside him. That they were both alive was clear enough, for they were breathing—very faintly, to be sure, but undoubtedly breathing.

Mr. Ross caught up one after another in a passionate embrace. Then litters were quickly improvised out of blanket-coats stripped from willing backs, and soon the unconscious boys were speeding homeward as fast as stalwart arms could bear them.

The rest of the story is quickly told. Thanks to the sturdy frames and perfect constitutions, the brothers were only temporarily the worse for their experience. They both were frost-bitten, of course, Bob's poor nose and Phil's feet coming in for the worst of it; but a few weeks' good nursing cured everything, and no scars remained to remind them, had they ever been likely to forget it, of the night they were lost.

ICE-SKATING IN CANADA.

IT is a glorious winter afternoon, and having left the smoke and din and dust of the city far behind, we are standing together at the foot of the first of the Dartmouth lakes. Straight before us, and spreading far out on either hand, lies a glistening expanse, whose polished surface flashes back the cheerful sunshine. Three unbroken miles in length, and more than one in width, this icy plain awaits us in its virgin purity. It were strange, then, did not our fingers tremble with impatience and our acmes snap with feverish haste. They are on at last, and now for the supremest luxury of motion. The crisp, cool air is charged with electricity; every answering nerve tingles delightfully, and the blood leaps responsively through the throbbing pulses. Once out upon the ringing ice, and we seem to have passed from the realm of solid flesh and blood to that of "tricksy, dainty Ariel." We have broken loose from the bonds of gravitation, and as with favouring wind we speed away to the farther shore, every stroke of our steel-shod feet counting good for a quartette of yards, the toiling and moiling of the work-a-day world seem to have found at the margin of the lake a magic barrier beyond which they may not follow us, and with spirits light and free we glide off into a new sphere where care and labour are unknown. Mile after mile flashes past, yet our muscles weary not, nor does the breath grow short. But what is this? Is our flight already ended; and must we turn back so soon? The fir-clad shores, which were a little while ago so far apart, have drawn together, until they seem to meet not far ahead, and put a bar to further progress. A cunning turn, a short, quick dash over the dangerous spot, where the current runs swiftly and the ice bends ominously, and, behold! we are out again upon a second lake, still larger than the first, and dotted here and there with tiny evergreen islets that look like emeralds in a silver setting. For three miles more our way lies before us smooth and clear; and then at last, as having reached the limit of our enterprise we throw ourselves upon a fallen tree, to rest our now tired limbs and catch our diminished breath, I ask which, of wheelman, horseman, yachtsman, sculler, or skater, enjoys the finest exercise?

No country in the world presents better facilities for indulgence in the luxury of skating than Canada. Holland may with propriety boast of her smooth canals, Norway of her romantic fiords, Scotland of her poetic lochs; but for variety of lake, river, canal, pond, and frozen sea, from the majestic St. Lawrence to the humblest stream that affords delight to the village red-cheeked lads and lasses, Canada is unsurpassed. It is no wonder, then, that the

Canadians are a nation of skaters, and that the skating-rinks should be as indispensable an adjunct to every city, town, and village as the church and the concert-hall. With a season extending over four and often five months, the managers of rinks can count upon receiving profitable returns upon their capital; and so those institutions multiply.

Owing to the great quantity of snow which every winter brings, the season for outdoor skating in Canada is very short, consisting usually of the middle weeks of December, when Jack Frost, by thoughtfully anticipating the snow, allows of a fortnight's skating in the open air before the mantle of winter hides his handiwork from sight and use. As a natural consequence, Canadians are not remarkable for long-distance skating; and two winters ago the swiftest fliers of our land had to lower their banner before Mr. Axel Paulsen, the renowned Norwegian skater, who made a triumphant tour through Canada and the United States.

On the other hand, the long season enjoyed by the rinks enables all who will take the trouble, and do not shrink from a novitiate of bumps and bruises, to become exceedingly expert at fancy skating: and it is hardly debatable that the rinks of Toronto, Montreal, Halifax, and St. John can send forth skaters who, for grace, precision, and intricacy of movement, would find no superiors in the world. When Mr. Paulsen attempted to teach the Canadians fancy skating, he was somewhat chagrined to find himself soon reduced to the position of learner. As an ice-acrobat he did indeed perform one or two feats that were novel, but they had only to be seen to be immediately copied; while some of the Canadians were able to open his eyes to possibilities of "didoes" which he thought it not best to hurriedly attempt. His visit was of permanent value, however, because it awakened a deeper interest in long-distance skating; and one may safely venture to prophesy that, should Mr. Paulsen come this way again, he will find the defeat of his whilom opponents at long distances not quite such a holiday task as on the occasion of his last visit.

What is known in England as "figure-skating," and there very ardently indulged in by well-to-do members of the various clubs, who can afford to acquire the art in Norway or Scotland, is but little practised in Canada. It is not suitable for rinks, as it requires so much room, and can only be done to advantage in large, open spaces, which the "figurists" may have all to themselves.

Figure-skating is undoubtedly very effective and striking when executed by a band of well-disciplined skaters who thoroughly understand one another. But it is so elaborate, and takes so much time both in preparation and performance, that it is not suited to the latitude of a colony where the majority of those who skate have no surplus leisure, and want to make the most of the time at their disposal for recreation.

There is one phase of figure-skating, however, which does flourish throughout Canada—to wit, dancing; and it would delight the heart of Terpsichore herself to watch a well-skilled quartette of couples gliding through the mazes of the lancers or quadrille, or sweeping round in airy circles to the music of the waltz. The evolutions differ somewhat, of course, from the steps taken on the floor, but the identity of the dance is far from being lost, and the pleasure of the dancer is greatly enhanced through the surpassing ease of motion. This dancing on the ice may be seen in its perfection at Halifax, the capital of Nova Scotia, which, being a garrison city, enjoys the unique privilege of military bands; and the officers as a rule becoming enthusiastic skaters, the ladies who grace the fashionable rink by their presence have a grand time of it gliding entrancingly about to the bewitching strains of delightful music, and bringing all the artillery of their thrilling eyes, tempting cheeks, and enslaving lips to bear upon the gallant sons of Mars, who oftentimes find the slippery floor more fatal than the tented field.

The finest rinks in Canada are those in Montreal, Halifax, and St. John. The rink at Halifax is really the Crystal Palace of the exhibition grounds, and for size, appearance, and convenience is surpassed by none. One of the most cheerful sights imaginable is this vast building on band-night, when the snow-white arena is almost hidden beneath a throng of happy skaters, youths and maidens, circling round hand in hand—the maiden glowing with pride at her admirer's dexterity, the youth enraptured by his charmer's roseate winsomeness. Here doth Cupid bid defiance to the chilling blasts of winter, and although the poets and painters have conspired to confine him to a garb appropriate to the dog-days, the sly wielder of the fatal bow must in winter enwrap himself in furry garments, and like a tiny Santa Claus perch his chubby form unseen among the rafters, and from that coigne of vantage let fly his shafts thick and fast into the merry company beneath.

One of the chief attractions of skating for the ambitious disciple is that there is practically no limit to its possibilities in the way of invention and combination. It would be extremely difficult to prepare for any skating tournament a hard-and-fast programme which would meet every requirement. Hence in competitions of this kind the custom is to lay down some twenty or thirty of the best-known feats which every competitor is supposed to do, and then leave each contestant to superadd thereto such marvels of skill as he may have picked up or invented. At the same time, of course, there may be almost as many degrees of skill represented in the execution of the set programme as there are competitors, and the judges must take this fully into consideration when making their award, and not allow their judgment to be dazzled by some particularly striking "extra." Skating tournaments, however, are not as frequent as they ought to be. While every other recognized sport has its regularly recurring trials of proficiency, skating has hitherto been inexplicably neglected. Surely nothing could be more interesting or attractive than a gathering of accomplished skaters of both sexes vying with one another in the ease and grace with which they can illustrate the intricacies of

the "grape-vine," the difficulty of the "giant swing," or
the rapidity of the "locomotive." Trials of speed are
common enough at all rinks, and are undoubtedly more
popular and exciting than trials of skill, but the more
refined and less demoralizing competition should not be
entirely neglected.

The speed attained by those who race in rinks, it need
hardly be explained, affords no criterion whatever whereby
to judge of what fast skaters are competent to accomplish.
The incessant turns, the sharp corners, the confined area,
all tend to materially reduce the rate of progression; and
only out on some broad lake or long-extending reach of
river can the skater do his best. I have no records at
hand as I write, but my own experience justifies me in
venturing the assertion that a champion skater in perfect
form, and properly equipped with long-bladed racing
skates, would prove no mean antagonist for Maud S——
herself over a measured mile, while at longer distances he
would have the field to himself.

Like all other amusements, skating in Canada waxes
and wanes in popular estimation, according to the mysterious laws of human impulse. One winter skating will be
voted "not the thing," and the rinks will be deserted; the
next, they will be crowded, and even the heads of families
will be fishing out their rusty "acmes" from the lumber-
closet, and renewing their youth in the icy arena. As
a means of exercise during the long, weary months of
winter, when the deep snow renders walking a toil devoid
of pleasure, and the muscles are aching for employment,

the skating-rink is an unspeakable boon, especially to him whose lot it is to endure much "dry drudgery at the desk's dead wood." An hour's brisk spinning around will clear the befogged brain, brace up the lax frame, and give a keenness to the appetite that nothing else could do. Then the rink has its social as well as its sanitary advantages. During the winter months it affords both sexes a pleasant and convenient rendezvous, where, unhampered by the conventionalities of the ball-room, and aided by the cheerful inspiration of the exercise, they can enjoy one another's society with a frequency otherwise unattainable. On band-days, indeed, the rink becomes converted into a spacious *salle d'assemblée*, where the numbered programme of musical selections enables Corydon to make engagements in advance with Phyllis, and thus insure the prosperous prosecution of his suit.

A carnival on ice—and every rink has one or more during the season—affords a rarely interesting and brilliant spectacle. For these occasions the building dons its gala dress, the gaunt rafters are hung with banners, the walls are hidden beneath variegated bunting and festooned with spruce embroidery, lights gleam brightly from every nook and corner, and the ice is prepared with special care. Then, as the motley crowd glides swiftly by, one may behold representatives of every clime and nation mingling together in perfect amity. It is true the tawny Spaniard, the dark-eyed Italian, the impassive Turk, the appalling Zulu, the soft and silent Hindu, and others whose home lies beneath the southern skies, betray a familiarity with the ice which seems to cast some doubt upon its genuineness.

But when his Satanic Majesty himself, with barbed tail and cloven hoof, confesses to an intimacy with the mazy evolutions of the " Philadelphia grape-vine," the incongruity attaching to visitors from cooler climes appears less striking, and they may go on their way unchallenged. Sometimes masks are *de rigueur* at these carnivals, and then the inevitable clown and harlequin have unlimited license, till even Quakers and friars, infected by their bad example, vie with them in mad pranks, and the fun soon waxes furious. Masked or unmasked, the carnival skaters have a joyous time, and the hours steal away with cruel haste.

Such are some of the phases of ice-skating in Canada. If this article has seemed to be devoted principally to indoor skating, it is because that can be pursued through so much greater a portion of the winter than the outdoor kind. Skating in its perfection is of course only to be had in the open air, and my most delightful recollections are associated with the Dartmouth lakes, of happy memory. Connected with the same lakes, however, there is a recollection too thrilling to be delightful, and which, in view of what might have been, brings a shudder even now while I rehearse it.

It happened in my college days. I had been skating all the afternoon, and, as the dusk grew on apace, found myself away down at the head of the second lake, full six miles from the point where I had got on the ice; so, girding up my loins, I set my face towards home, and struck out lustily. After going about one hundred yards, I thought I heard the sound of my name come faintly to me over the ice.

Wheeling sharply about I saw nothing, except a dark form some distance away, which through the gathering gloom resembled a log or tree-branch ; and I was just about to start off again, when once more my name was called, this time so clearly as to leave no chance for doubt, the sound evidently coming from the seeming log. Hastening over to it with all speed, I was startled to find the professor of classics at my college—who did not allow the loss of an arm to debar him from the pleasure of skating—lying on the ice, with his left leg broken sharp and clear a few inches above the ankle, the result of a sudden and heavy fall. Here, indeed, was a trying situation for a mere lad to cope with. We were alone in a wilderness of ice, and six miles away from the nearest house. The shadows of night were fast closing around us. Those six miles had to be gotten over in some way, and there was not a moment to be lost. Hurrying to the shore I cut down a small spruce tree. Upon this the helpless sufferer was laid as gently as possible, and bound to it with straps. Then upon this rude ambulance I slowly dragged him down the lake, while he, with splendid self-control, instead of murmuring at his terrible agony, charmed away my weariness by his unconquerable heroism. It was a toilsome task, but help came when we reached the first lake, and once the shore was gained, a long express waggon filled with mattresses made the homeward journey comparatively painless. "All is well that ends well." The broken leg soon mended, and the following winter found the professor skating as briskly as ever.

Yet I cannot help wondering sometimes with a shudder how it would have fared with the interpreter of Greece and Rome had not that first faint call reached my ears. A bitter cold night, a wide expanse of polished ice, a solitary man lying prone upon it with one arm missing at the shoulder, and one leg broken at the ankle—it were little less than a miracle if ice-skating in Canada had not been clouded by one more catastrophe that winter night.

THE WILD DOGS OF ATHABASCA.

OLD Donald M'Tavish was a wonderfully interesting
character. In the service of the Hudson Bay
Company, which for nearly two hundred years held regal
sway over the vast unknown north-west of Canada, he had
spent half a century of arduous and exciting service, living
far away from civilization, one of a mere handful of white
men in the midst of a wilderness sparsely inhabited by the
Indian and the half-breed, but abounding in deer, buffaloes,
bears, wolves, and the smaller wild animals.

He had risen rapidly in the service, for he was a fearless,
stanch, trustworthy man, and for the latter half of two
terms had filled the important post of chief factor at
different forts; for it was his somewhat undesirable if
honourable lot to be sent to those stations that gave the
most trouble and the least returns to the company. Such
was his reputation for shrewdness, courage, and fidelity,
that it was felt by the authorities that no other man
could so soon set matters straight as Donald M'Tavish.

Having filled out his fifty years with entire satisfaction
to his employers and no small credit to himself, he had

retired on his laurels to spend a hale and hearty old age, in the enjoyment of the comfortable pension awarded him by the company which he had served so well.

It was the delight of his declining days to recount for the benefit of younger ears the many thrilling incidents of his adventurous career, and one of his favourite stories was that which I shall now attempt to tell, as nearly as possible in his own words.

"It was early in the Fifties, when I had charge of old Fort Assiniboine, away out on the Athabasca River, not far from the Rockies. Sir George Simpson, the governor of the colony at Red River, like the thoughtful man he was, had sent out to me by the spring brigade a splendid Scotch stag-hound, one of half-a-dozen he had just brought with him from the dear old land.

"O man, but he was a dog! His back was on a level with my belt, and when he raised himself on his hind legs he could put his fore paws on my shoulders and rub noses with me; yet I stood a good six feet in my stockings in those days.

"His hair was as grizzled as old Ephraim's, and coarse, and curled like what they stuff beds with. His body was long and lean, and so was his head, but he had a noble eye; and then the way he could run, and leap over everything that came in his path, it was a sight to see, I warrant you.

"We soon got very much attached to each other, and wherever I went Bruce went too. He did not seem to take to any one else, and I was just as well pleased that he did not, for I never wanted him out of my sight.

"That same summer a new hand was sent to the fort. He was an Englishman, who gave his name as Heathcote, and he brought with him a pure white female bull-dog that was one of the most dangerous-looking brutes I ever laid eyes on. She minded nobody but her master, of whom, to do her credit, she seemed fond enough.

"I never much cared for that breed of dog, but I must say Vixen was about perfect in her way. As to good-breeding, there certainly wasn't much to choose between her and Bruce.

"I was a little uneasy as to how the two dogs would get on, and at first it did look as if there might be trouble, for Bruce, who utterly despised the rabble of curs hanging about the fort, evidently felt disposed to resent the coming of this possible rival; but almost before I knew it, the two were the best of friends, and would eat their dinner side by side like two well-behaved children.

"After a while they took to going out a-hunting together, and grand times they had. They would work along in company until a herd of deer was started, and then Bruce would make for the fattest doe, his tremendous speed soon bringing him to her throat; while Vixen, following at her best rate, would come up just in time to help him to finish her, and then they would have a fine feast.

"Once the dogs got into these ways neither Heathcote nor I had much more satisfaction out of them. They were never on hand when wanted. They kept growing wilder and wilder, and finally, toward autumn, they disappeared one day, and were never seen at the fort again.

"We hunted for them high and low, sending out the half-breeds as far as Lake La Crosse on the east, and to the foot-hills of the Rockies on the west, but not a sign or trace could we find of them. When winter came and they did not return, we gave them up as lost, thinking that something must have happened to them on one of their hunting forays, or that perchance they had been killed by the Indians.

"Two years went by, and Bruce and Vixen were almost forgotten, when stories began to reach the fort of a strange and fierce kind of wild dog that was being seen now and then by hunters and trappers in the out-of-the-way valleys and ravines of the foot-hills.

"It was not an easy job to get at the bottom of these stories, for they passed from mouth to mouth before reaching us; but at last a trapper turned up who had seen a pack of the dogs himself, and after hearing his description I had no longer any doubt but that these wild dogs which were making such a stir were the offspring of our two former pets which had gone away in company.

"By all accounts they were evidently dangerous brutes to meet. From Bruce they had got wonderful speed and endurance; from Vixen, ferocity and fearlessness. Swift, savage, stubborn, and always going in large packs, there was not an animal on the plains or up among the mountains for which they were not more than a match.

"I felt eager to get a sight of the creatures, even though it should mean some risk; for while, like all wild dogs, willing enough to give men a wide berth, there was no telling what they might do if pressed by hunger. It was therefore good news when, a year later, orders came from Red River for me to make a trip to Fort George on the other side of the Rockies, where there were some matters that needed straightening up, as either going or coming back I would run a good chance of seeing something of the famous dogs.

"I left Fort Assiniboine in the autumn, and although a sharp look-out was kept by all the party as we went over to Fort George, not a sight nor sign of the dogs did we stumble upon.

"But on my way back in the spring I had better luck, and I certainly shall never forget my first and last sight of those terrible brutes.

"We had crossed the Rockies, and were descending the eastern slopes, getting down among the foot-hills. One day Heathcote and I pushed on together in advance of the rest, both of us having the dogs on our mind.

"Early in the afternoon we came to a bluff that overlooked a lovely little valley, which we at once decided would be our camping-place for that night. A bright stream ran along the centre of the valley. Having a thought that perhaps a herd of deer might put in an appearance if we kept out of sight, we stretched ourselves out comfortably on the bluff and awaited developments. They proved to be interesting beyond all our expectations.

"We had been there about an hour, perhaps, when Heathcote, who had been looking over at the opposite bluff, suddenly grasped my arm, saying under his breath,—

"'Look there, M'Tavish!   What do you think of that?'
"A break in the bluff had made a sort of easy descent

"AGAIN AND AGAIN WOULD THE BEAR, RISING ON HIS HIND QUARTERS,
HURL THE DOGS FROM HIM."

into the valley, and down this were coming, in single file,
one, two, three, four—no less than a dozen bears of the

large and dreaded silver-tip kind; splendid fellows most of them, bent on having a good time on the sunny slopes beside the stream.

"We hardly dared to stir or breathe. To have attacked them would have been utter madness. Thankful might we be if we could crawl away without their attacking us.

"While lying there motionless, and wishing to the bottom of our hearts that the rest of the party were on hand to make matters even, a fierce bark came from the bluff a little above where the bears first showed themselves. It was followed by a whole chorus of deep-mouthed baying, and an instant later there rushed into view, fairly tumbling over one another in their impetuous haste, a great pack of dogs that we at once recognized as those we wished to see.

"They were certainly a fearsome lot of creatures. Some were long, lean, and shaggy, like Bruce; others were thick-bodied and smooth of hair, like Vixen,—and all were powerful, ravenous-looking brutes, a dozen of whom might eat a good-sized buffalo for dinner without feeling uncomfortably overloaded after their meal.

"They sighted the bears the moment they reached the edge of the bluff, and at once rushed down to the attack, barking as though they would split their throats. The bears made ready to receive them by massing together at the top of a little knoll near the water, and before we could fully realize what was taking place the fight had begun.

"So far as we could make out the dogs numbered fifty at least, so that, considering their size and strength, the

odds were a good deal in their favour; but the bears
fought like heroes.

"At first they crowded together in a sort of circle, with
heads facing out; while the dogs ran round them, snarling
and barking, and watching their chance to spring. A few
moments later the circle was broken up into a dozen roaring, writhing, yelping groups, composed of a bear with
four or five of the dogs clinging tenaciously to different
parts of its body.

"It was the Vixen strain that told now. Again and
again would the bear, rising on his hind quarters, hurl the
dogs from him with mighty sweeps of his huge fore paws,
only to be penned at once, and brought to the ground by a
fresh attack.

"At frequent intervals an agonizing death-howl would
pierce its way through the horrible clamour, as some unfortunate dog, caught in the grasp of its maddened enemy,
would be crushed to death in his resistless embrace.

"The minutes slipped by, and the fight still raged, but
there could be no doubt how it would result. The dogs
had the best of it as to numbers, and they were the equals
of the bears in courage, ferocity, and endurance, if not in
sheer strength.

"One by one the big brown bodies rolled over in the
stillness of death. At the end of about half-an-hour the
fight was over. Not a bear breathed, and around their
torn carcasses lay between twenty and thirty of the dogs,
as dead as themselves—the best possible proof of how
fiercely and obstinately they had fought.

"Not a word had passed between Heathcote and myself while all this went on. We were too much taken up with the extraordinary conflict going on before our eyes even to look at each other; but when it was all over, and the surviving dogs, having satisfied themselves that the bears were really all dead, lay down to lick their many wounds before they began upon the feast their brave victims had provided for them, I touched Heathcote on the shoulder, and whispered,—

"'We've seen the dogs; let's take good care they don't see us.'

"After such a proof of their powers as we had had, we were in no mind to claim a nearer acquaintance with them on the score of having once owned their ancestors. Accordingly we crawled noiselessly away, and making a long circuit, rejoined our party in time to prevent their turning down into the valley, which we no longer considered a good place to camp in for the night.

"That was my first and last sight of the wild dogs of Athabasca. The following autumn I went east, and never returned to Fort Assiniboine. Whether the dogs have since been all killed off or are still running wild among the far recesses of the Rockies, I don't know; but that wonderful battle in the valley was one of the greatest sights of my life, the like of which no one perhaps will ever again see on this continent."

BIRDS AND BEASTS ON SABLE ISLAND.

IF you will take your atlas and turn to the map of Canada, you may, by looking very carefully, discover a small spot in the Atlantic Ocean almost due east from Nova Scotia, and close beside the sixtieth parallel of longitude. This little lonely spot is Sable Island. There it lies in the midst of the waves, a long, low bank of gray sand without a single tree upon it from end to end; nay, not so much as a bush behind which a baby might play hide-and-seek. It seems, therefore, at first sight to be one of the most unfavourable places in the world for the study of either birds or beasts. Yet, strange as it may seem, this island, which is now but twenty miles long, and at its greatest breadth but a mile and a half wide—once it was quite double that size—has a wonderfully interesting history of its own, of which not the least entertaining chapter is that relating to its furry and feathered inhabitants.

Although when first viewed from the sea Sable Island appears to be nothing better than a barren sand-bank, on closer acquaintance it reveals inside its sloping beaches vales and meadows that in summer-time seem like bits out of a Western prairie.   There are green, grassy knolls, and enchanting dells with placid ponds in their midst; and if you only come at the right time and stay long enough, you may gather pink roses, blue lilies, China asters, wild pea, gay golden-rod, and, what is still better, strawberries, blueberries, and cranberries in bountiful profusion.

Our concern at present, however, is not with the fruits and flowers, but with the fur and feathers of this curious place.

Seeing that Sable Island has no trees on the branches of which nests may be built, it follows naturally that its winged inhabitants are altogether of the water-fowl and sea-bird variety.   All over the sides and tops of the sandhills, which rise to the height of thirty, forty, or fifty feet, the gulls, gannets, terns, and other aquatic birds scrape together their miserable apologies for nests, and hatch out their ugly little squab chicks, making such a to-do about the business that the whole air is filled with their chattering, clanging, and screaming.

They are indeed very disagreeable neighbours; for besides the horrid din they are ceaselessly making, they are the most untidy, not to say filthy, of housekeepers. After they have occupied their bird-barracks, as their nesting-places might appropriately be called, for a few weeks, the odour the wind bears from that direction could never be mistaken for one of those spicy breezes which are reputed to "blow soft o'er Ceylon's isle."

Then they have not the redeeming quality of being fit to eat; for unless one were on the very edge of starvation, one taste of their flesh, rank with suggestions of fish and train-oil, would be sufficient to banish all appetite.

They have one or two good qualities. They are brave; for at the peril of their lives they will dauntlessly attack any rash intruder upon their domains, swooping down upon him with sharp cries and still sharper beaks.

Their movements illustrate the poetry of motion, as they come sailing grandly in from the ocean spaces, and circle about their own particular hillock in glorious dips and curves and mountings upward, that fill the human observer with longing and envy.

Much more satisfactory, however, are the black duck, sheldrake, plover, curlew, and snipe, which nest by uncounted thousands in the dense grass that girts the fresh-water ponds, and afford dainty dishes for the table. It is easy work to make a fine bag on a favourable day, and grand sport may be had by any one who knows how to handle a double-barrel.

Many are the interesting stories connected with bird life on Sable Island, but a single one, and that the oddest of them all, must suffice. I give it upon the unimpeachable authority of Dr. J. Bernard Gilpin.

About forty years or more ago a lot of rabbits were sent there as an experiment. The idea was, if they prospered, to furnish the human inhabitants of the island with a pleasant variety from the salt junk which generally adorned their tables.

The experiment succeeded admirably. Bunny found the firm, dry sands just the thing for his burrows, while the abundant wild pea and other herbage furnished unstinted food for his prolific brood. But one fateful day in spring—a dark day in the annals of rabbitdom—a big snowy owl, that had somehow lost his bearings and been driven out to sea by a westerly gale, dropped wearily upon the island to rest his tired pinions.

While sitting on a sand-heap, thankful at his escape from a watery grave, he looked about him, and to his amazed delight beheld—of all sights the most welcome in the world to a hungry owl—*rabbits!* Rabbits young and rabbits old, rabbits plump and rabbits lean, rabbits in sixes and rabbits in sevens, were frisking about in the long grass and over the sand, merrily innocent of their peril.

At first Sir Owl could scarcely believe his eyes, for it was a bright, sunny day, and owls cannot see very well when the sun is shining; but presently, as he still squatted on the sand, perfectly motionless except his eyelids blinking solemnly, a thoughtless little rabbit, which had grown too much excited over a game of chase with his brother to look where he was going, ran up against the bewildered bird.

This awoke the owl thoroughly. With a quick spring that sent all the other little cotton-tails scampering off to their burrows in wild affright, he fastened his long claws in the back of his unfortunate disturber, and, without even stopping to say grace, made a dinner off him on the spot.

That was a red-letter day in the owl's calendar. Thenceforth he revelled in rabbit for breakfast, dinner, and supper, and, had he been a very greedy owl, might have kept his discovery of a rabbit bonanza all to himself; but he didn't. With a splendid unselfishness which some bipeds without feathers might advantageously imitate, he had no sooner recruited his strength than off he posted to the mainland to spread the good news.

Four days later he came back, but not alone this time. Bearing him company were his brothers, his sisters, his cousins, his uncles, and his aunts, in such numbers that ere the summer ended there was not a solitary bunny left upon the island!

Since then the place has been restocked, and there having been no return of the owls, the rabbits, despite the fact that great numbers of them are killed for food, have so multiplied as to become a positive nuisance, and the experience of Australia being in view, the advisability of their extermination is seriously considered.

Besides the rabbits, there have been, at different times, the following animals upon Sable Island—namely, the black fox, white bear, walrus, and seals; wild horses, cattle, and swine; rats, cats, and dogs. That makes quite a long list. Of course so small and bare an island could never have held them all at once.

Now they are all gone except the rabbits, the horses, of which several hundreds still scamper wild over the sand dunes, and the seals, which come every year to introduce their shiny little whelps into the world, and to grow fat on the fish hurled continually upon the beach by the tireless breakers.

It is a great many years since the black fox, white bear,

and walrus were last seen upon the island. Too much money could be made out of them when dead for the fishermen, who knew of their presence, to let them live long; and so with powder and shot and steel they were ruthlessly exterminated. The beautiful skins of the black fox, worth one hundred golden crowns each, went principally to France, where they were made up into splendid robes for royalty.

Just how the wild horses and cattle found their way to Sable Island is not positively known.

They were first heard of in those early days when ships loaded with cattle, grain, and farming utensils were coming over in little fleets from Europe to help to settle America. In all likelihood some of these vessels got cast away on the island—for it has ever been a dreadful place for wrecks—and in some way the animals managed to scramble safe ashore, and thus the place became populated.

The wild cattle disappeared early in the century; but the horses, or rather ponies, are still there, and very interesting creatures they are.

Winter and summer they are out on the sand in all weathers. Indeed, they scorn to go under cover even in the wildest storms; and although shelters have been built for them, they will not deign to enter them. Another curious thing about them is that they are never seen to lie down, and apparently go to sleep standing.

There are now about four hundred of these ponies, divided into troops, each under the charge and control of an old stallion, whose shaggy, unkempt mane and tail sweep the ground as he stands sentinel over his numerous family.

They belong to the Dominion Government, and it has been usual to cull out some forty or fifty of the best of them each year and send them up to Halifax, where they command good prices.

They are stanch, sturdy little animals, and very serviceable when properly broken. In my boyhood days I rejoiced in the possession of a fine bay that, barring a provoking habit of pitching an unwary rider over his head, was a great source of enjoyment.

The manner of catching the ponies is for a number of mounted men to surround a band and drive it into a corral in which a tame pony has been placed as a decoy. This is often a very exciting experience: the cracking of whips, shouting of men, neighing of ponies, combine with the plunging of the frightened captives and the gallant charges of the enraged stallions to make up a scene not readily forgotten.

Once safely corralled, the best males are picked out and lassoed, and the rest turned loose to breathe the salt air of freedom once more.

As the breed has been observed to be degenerating greatly of late years, means have been taken to improve it, and it is probable that ere long Sable Island ponies will be more desirable than ever.

A very amusing thing in connection with animal life on Sable Island is the story of the rats, cats, and dogs.

First of all were the rats, who are reputed to be very

clever about deserting sinking ships, and who here found plenty of opportunity to show their cleverness, for wrecks are always happening. They thus became so plentiful that they threatened to eat the human inhabitants out of house and home. Indeed, they did make them do without bread for three whole months upon one occasion.

This state of things, of course, could not be tolerated. A large number of cats were accordingly imported, and they soon cleared the premises of the rapacious rodents. But it was not long ere the pussies in their turn grew so numerous, wild, and fierce as to become a source of serious trouble. A small army of dogs was therefore brought upon the scene, and they made short work of the cats, thus rounding out a very curious cycle.

Did space permit I could tell something about the seals, and their very quaint and attractive ways and manners. But perhaps enough has been already written to convince readers that however lonely, barren, and insignificant Sable Island may seem, it has an interesting story of its own which is well worth the telling.

THE BORE OF MINAS BASIN.

UPON the side of one of the rounded hills that rise up gently from the wonderful sea of verdure which Longfellow, without ever looking upon it for himself, immortalized in his "Evangeline," Acacia Villa nestled cozily in the midst of many trees. Long lines of poplars stood sentinel-like up and down the house front, and marked out the garden boundaries, furnishing abundant supplies of "peppers" for the boys in spring-time; and, better still, a whole regiment of apple and pear trees marshalled itself at the back, filling the hearts (and mouths) of both young and old with delight in the autumn, when the boughs bent so temptingly beneath their burden of fruitage. There could hardly be a more attractive location for a boarding-school; and seeing what comfortable quarters Mr. Thomson provided, and how thoroughly he understood the business of teaching, it was no wonder that boys came not only from all parts of Nova Scotia and New Brunswick, but even from the United States, to be grounded in classics, mathematics, and literature under his direction.

The last boarder left Acacia Villa long ago, but twenty

years back its dormitories were filled to their utmost capacity with lads of all ages and sizes, and the whole neighbourhood felt the stirring influence of twoscore lively, hearty, noisy boys in its midst. For nearly ten months out of the year the school was like a hive of bees in honey-time — the term beginning in September and finishing in June. It was coming on toward midsummer now, and excitement ran high throughout the school; for while the drones were looking forward longingly to the holidays which would release them from all horrid lesson-learning for a couple of months, the workers were even more eagerly expecting the final examinations, when books, bats, balls, knives, and other things dear to the schoolboy's heart, were offered by wise Mr. Thomson to the boys who came out ahead in the different branches of study. The two boys strolling down toward the river this fine summer afternoon were good representatives of the two classes— Frank Hamilton being one of the brightest and most ambitious, as Tom Peters, or " Buntie " in the saucy slang of his schoolmates, was one of the dullest and least aspiring in the school. Yet, somehow or other, they had been great chums ever since they came by the same coach to the Villa two years before. One could easily understand that lazy, good-natured " Buntie " should find much to admire and love in handsome, manly, clever Frank, who was indeed a born leader; but just what Frank found in Tom to make him so fond of him puzzled everybody, from Mr. Thomson down. In whatever lay the secret, the fact was clear that the boys loved each other like brothers;

and the master, who delighted in classical allusions, used to greet them as Damon and Pythias when he encountered them together. They were discussing the approaching examinations, and speculating as to the prizes Mr. Thomson would offer this year.

"No apples for me on that tree," said Tom; adding with rather a rueful smile, "If Mr. Thomson would only offer a prize for the most lickings and impositions, I guess I'd run the best chance for it."

"Never mind, old boy," said Frank, consolingly. "You weren't cut out for a scholar, that's clear; but you'll come out all right at something else, and perhaps make a bigger name than even 'Yankee' himself, although it wouldn't do to let him hear you say so."

"I'm 'fraid I'd have a poor sight to beat Yankee at anything," answered Tom. "But say, Frank, how do you feel about giving him the go-by for the Starr prize? It 'ud break my heart if you didn't come out first."

"Well, to tell the truth, Buntie, I don't feel any too cocky about it. Yankee's a tough customer to beat," replied Frank. "But, hush! he's coming right behind us. Must be going down to the river too, though it's more like him to stick in his room and grind."

And as a tall, slight, dark-faced lad of about sixteen went past them without exchange of greetings, the two friends stopped talking and went on in silence.

"Yankee" was the nickname given to one of the American boys at the school. He had been thus distinguished because both in face and figure he bore some resemblance to the typical Uncle Sam, being longer, leaner, and sallower than any of his companions. He was of a quiet, reserved disposition, and had few friends. Indeed, he did not seem to desire many, but kept very much to himself, so that a lot of the boys disliked him. Yet, on the other hand, others respected although they might not love him; for not only did he divide with Frank Hamilton, whom they all worshipped, the highest honours in scholarship, but once, when scarlet fever broke out and seized upon six of the smallest boys before they could escape to their homes, " Yankee," or, to give him his proper name, Emory Haynes, although he had never had the fever himself, stayed with Mr. Thomson through many anxious weeks, and watched night after night by the sufferers' bedsides, showing such tact and devotion as a nurse that the doctor said at least two of the boys would never have been saved from death had it not been for his help.

Walking with a rapid, almost impatient step that was characteristic of him, Emory Haynes passed the two friends, all three directing their course toward the Gaspereaux River, which cuts a wide red gash through the Grand Pré before adding its turbid torrent to the tossing waters of Minas Basin.

" If Yankee beats me for the Starr prize, it will be the biggest disappointment of my life," continued Frank. " It's not every day that a fellow can get hold of five pounds in bright big gold pieces: and father has promised if I win it to chip in as much more and buy me a splendid boat."

"O Frank, you're sure to get it. Yankee works like a slave, to be sure, but he hasn't half as good a head on him," answered Tom confidently.

"I'm not by any means certain of that, Tom. Just see how easily he gets through his mathematics. He's sure to beat me on that, and I'll have to make up for it by beating him in classics. Anyhow, it is no use worrying about it now. Let's hurry up and have a dip."

So dropping the subject, the two boys ran off at a rate that soon brought them to the river bank.

Here a lovely picture awaited them. From their feet the red banks of clay and sand stretched hundreds of yards away (for the tide was out), until they were lapped by the river, now shrunk into a narrow, sluggish stream. To right and left and beyond the river the wide, level marsh lands, redeemed from the water by the patient toil of the Acadians, were waist-deep in verdure that swayed in long lines of light and shadow before the summer breeze. Not far off began the great dikes that sweep clear round the outer edge of the Grand Pré, the only elevation on all that vast plain, and now waving to their summits with "dusty-blossomed grass." Behind them the hills rose gently in fold upon fold, their broad shoulders flecked with frequent patches of golden grain or the dark foliage of the orchards; while over all rose a glorious summer sun that seemed to thrill the whole landscape with life and warmth and glory.

But the boys had no eyes for all this beauty. They were far more concerned about the tide, and felt inclined to resent very warmly the fact that it should be out just when they wanted to have a swim.

" What a fraud!" exclaimed Frank.   " 'Pon my word, I believe the old tide is twice as much out as it is in; now isn't it, Buntie ?"

" It is, sure's you're born," assented Tom.   " There's nothing for it, I suppose, but to wait ;" and so saying, he threw himself down in the long grass, his friend immediately following his example.

Twenty yards away Emory Haynes was already seated with his face turned riverward; apparently lost in deep thought.

" Wonder what Yankee's thinking about ?" remarked Tom.   " Puzzling out some of those confounded problems he does so easily, perhaps," he added feelingly, for he had had some humiliating experiences of his own inability to get over the *Pons Asinorum* safely, or to explain why a was equal to x under certain perplexing circumstances.

" More probably planning what he'll do with that five pounds," said Frank, half petulantly.   " I guess it's more likely to go into books than into a boat if he gets hold of it."

" But he isn't going to get hold of it," objected Tom ; and then, without giving Frank a chance to reply, he burst out, " Oh, I say, Frank, suppose instead of waiting here we go down to meet the bore and have a race back with it."

Frank hesitated a moment before answering, for what Tom proposed was a very rash thing to do.   What is

known as the " bore " is the big wave produced by the on-
rush of water in a place where the tides rise forty, fifty,

"THEY SAW THEIR COMPANION EMBEDDED NEARLY TO THE WAIST IN A QUICKSAND."

or even sixty feet, according to the time of year. The
Bay of Fundy, of which Minas Basin is a branch, is fa-

mous for these wonderful tides, and the movements of the
water make a sight well worth watching. The two boys
had often looked on with lively interest as the returning
flood rushed eagerly up the channel and over the flats,
until in an incredibly short time what had been a waste
of red mud was transformed into a broad expanse of turbid
water.

"Rather a risky business, Tom, but I don't mind trying
it. I'm in the humour for almost anything to-day; so
come along."

And without more ado the boys doffed their boots and
stockings, rolled up their trousers, and set out for the
water's edge. Emory Haynes watched them in silence
until they had gone about fifty yards. Then, as if divining their foolish design, he called after them,—

"Frank—Tom—where are you going to?"

"Going to meet the bore. Don't you want to come?"
Frank shouted back. "Come along, Yankee, if you're not
afraid," he added, in a half scornful tone.

Not the words, but the tone in which they were uttered,
brought an angry flush out on Emory's sallow cheeks, and
without stopping to think of the folly of the thing, he too
flung off his boots and started after the others.

"Blessed if Yankee isn't coming, after all," said Tom,
under his breath, to Frank. "The chap's got plenty of
grit in him."

Side by side, but in silence— for somehow or other they
felt ill at ease—the three boys picked their way carefully
over the slippery mud and soft sand, keeping a sharp

look-out for the sink-holes or quicksands, in which they might easily sink to their waists, or even deeper, at one plunge. Hardly had they reached the edge of the channel when Frank, who had been gazing down intently toward the Basin, called out,—

"There it comes, fellows. Doesn't it look grand?"

A good way off still, but drawing nearer with astonishing speed, a wall of dark foam-topped water came rushing up the channel and over the thirsty flats. It was several feet in height, and behind it followed the whole vast volume of the tide.

The three lads had never been so close to the bore before, and they stood still and silent watching the grand sight until a shout from Emory broke the spell.

"Now then, boys, let's run for it."

As fast as their feet could carry them they sped over the treacherous greasy flats, leaping the gaping gullies, turning aside from the suspicious spots, and steering straight for the place where they had left their shoes. Frank and Tom were both famous runners, and soon outstripped Emory; in fact, they were more than half-way to the bank, when a sharp cry of alarm made them stop and turn to see what was the matter. One glance was enough to tell them. Twenty yards behind they saw their companion embedded nearly to the waist in a quicksand, from which he was madly struggling to extricate himself, while his efforts seemed only to sink him the deeper. His situation was one of extreme peril. The bore had somewhat spent its force, but still advanced steadily. Unless Emory was rescued without delay, he would be buried beneath its pitiless flood.

For one brief instant Frank hesitated, and Tom, as usual, waited for him to lead. Thoughts of the personal risk, the small chance of succeeding, and even—though ever after the mere recollection of it made his cheek burn with shame—of the advantage it would be to have his rival out of the way, throbbed through his brain. But it was only for an instant; and then with a shout of "Keep cool, Yankee; we're coming!" he grasped Tom's arm, and together they sprang to the rescue. Running with all their might, they reached their imperilled schoolmate just a second before the bore did, and standing on either side the treacherous spot were able to each seize a hand, and with one tremendous effort draw him out of its deadly embrace ere the great wave came sweeping down upon them, tumbling them over like nine-pins into the midst of its muddy surges. Fortunately, however, all three were good swimmers, and they had only to allow the water to work its will with them, for after a little tossing about it landed them safely on a sand-bank, whence they could easily wade ashore.

Emory did not say much to his rescuers. It was not his way. But no one could mistake the depth of feeling expressed in the few words,—

"Frank, you've saved my life, and I'll never forget it."

Two weeks later the examinations came off, and amid the applause of the school Frank Hamilton was declared winner of the Starr prize, Emory Haynes being only just a few points behind him.   Mr. Thomson was very well pleased at the result ; but there was one thing that puzzled him a good deal—Emory, who was by far the best mathematical scholar in the school, had somehow or other done by no means so well in that branch as usual.   In fact, he had actually left several not over-difficult questions altogether unanswered, and this more than anything else had lost him the prize.   Mr. Thomson mentioned the matter to Frank Hamilton, at the same time expressing his surprise.

"I'm not surprised," said Frank, as something that looked very like tears welled up in his eyes.   "When I saved Yankee's life he said he'd never forget it.   That's how he kept his word."

Mr. Thomson needed no further explanation

THE GAME OF RINK HOCKEY.

THE part performed by Canada in making contributions to the list of the world's amusements has been by no means slight. Lacrosse and canoeing for the warm bright days of summer, snow-shoeing and tobogganing for the crisp cold nights of winter, these make up a quartette of healthy, hearty sports, the superiors of which, in their appropriate season, any other country might safely be challenged to show. But apparently this ambitious colony is not content with the laurels already won, and in the bringing of the game of rink hockey to perfection would add another to her garland; for this fine game, as played in the Canadian cities to-day, is, without question, a distinctly home product.

Not that hockey is native to the soil in the same sense as lacrosse. In a simpler form, and under different names, it has long existed in England; but the difference between the game as played there on the green and played in Canada on the ice, is as great as that between an old-fashioned game of rounders and a professional game of base-ball.

The most ancient account of hockey is to be found in that dear, delightful old book, Strutt's "Sports and Pastimes of the People of England," where it figures under the name of "bandy ball,"—what is now called the hockey stick being then known as the "bandy;" and there is attached to the description a comical little woodcut representing two boys in short frocks, each wielding bandies almost as big as themselves, playing with a ball half the size of their heads.

As first played in Canada, hockey went by various names, some of which were apparently merely local—hurley, shinny, rickets, and so forth. It was played only upon the ice in winter-time, and there was not much pretence to rules, each player taking part as best he knew how. No effort toward systematizing the game appears to have been made until the year 1875, when the members of the Montreal Football Club, in search of some lively athletic amusement for the long winter months, recognized in hockey the very thing they wanted.

At first the rules adopted for the regulation of the game were modelled upon those of the English Hockey Association. But as the game developed, many changes were found necessary in adapting it to the requirements of a rink, and the rules now used by the Amateur Hockey Association of Canada are in the main original with it.

Starting from Montreal, the game has made its way to Halifax and St. John on the east, and to Ottawa and Toronto on the west, and from the enthusiasm with which it has been taken up at these cities, it actually threatens to displace tobogganing and snow-shoeing in the affections of the young men.

Let me now try to give my readers some idea of the game and the way in which it is played. Please picture to yourselves a skating-rink with an ice surface one hundred and fifty feet in length by seventy-five feet in width. At either end, close to the platform, are the goals, consisting of two slender poles placed six feet apart, and standing four feet high, with small red flags at their peaks. Such is the field of battle, and upon it the players take their places. They are dressed much as they would be for football, except that their feet are shod with skates of a peculiar make, the heel projecting more than in an ordinary skate, in order to guard against getting a nasty fall when heeling up suddenly. Each player is armed with a hockey stick, as to the size of which the only rule is that it shall not be more than three inches wide at any part. A good stick should be made of a single piece of ash, bent, not sawed, into the proper curve, of the length and weight the player finds to suit him best. The bone of contention between the contending sides is called the puck, and is a circular piece of vulcanized rubber one inch thick all through, and three inches in diameter. It is slightly elastic, and will rebound from the board sides of the rink if sent violently against them; a fact which enables an expert player to evade an opponent charging down to wrest it from him, as by striking the puck against the boards, and picking it up again on the rebound, he can keep on his way unchecked.

The teams are arranged in the following manner :—Goal-keeper takes his place between the posts, and a little forward of them; point stands about four yards out, and a little to one side, so as not to interfere with the goalkeeper's view down the centre; cover-point's position is from ten to fifteen yards out from goal, and on the opposite side to point; centre's post is indicated by his

name; and the same may be said of the right and left forwards, and the half-back, who supports centre.

For the control of the game there are a referee, who follows it about as does the referee at football, and two umpires, one at either goal, the sole business of the latter being to decide whether or not the puck has passed between the posts, and not above the flags.

Play begins with a bully—that is, the puck is placed

between the two centres in the centre of the rink, and they, after solemnly striking their sticks together three times, scramble for its possession, trying either to drive it ahead into their opponents' territory, or behind to the half-back, who immediately passes it to one of the forwards. Then the game goes on in lively earnest; and when the teams are expert and well matched, there is nothing on ice to compare with it for brilliancy and excitement. The exceeding swiftness of the players' movements; the sudden variations in the position of the puck as, under the impulse of sinewy arms, it darts from end to end, from side to side, of the rink; the incessant grind and clatter and ring of the skates; the crack of the hockeys, and the shouts of the eager players—all combine to work up the deepest interest among the spectators; and the announcement of a match between two good teams always insures a large and enthusiastic attendance.

The rules by which the game is governed are easily understood. So long as the puck is on the ice it is in play, even though it be behind the goal line. Of course a goal can be won only from the front; but an opponent who is not off-side may follow the puck behind the goal line, and fight for the privilege of bringing it out again. The rules as to on-side and off-side are precisely the same as in Rugby football; that is to say, a player must always be between his own goal and the puck when he plays on it. A violation of this rule calls for a bully at the spot where the wrong stroke was made. The referee is the sole judge in all matters of this kind, and from his decision there is no appeal. The puck may be stopped, but not carried or knocked on by any part of the body. In striking it the stick must not be raised above the shoulder. The object of this rule is to check violence, and the effect of it is to make the stroke more of a push than a blow, insuring greater accuracy in shooting for goal or a fellow-player, and adding greatly to the grace of the game. A practised player will, with wonderfully little manifest effort, send the puck from end to end of the rink if the ice is at all in good condition.

Another mode of propelling the puck which is at present permissible, but is in danger of being ruled out, is "lifting." I cannot very well explain in words how it is done; but by a deft turn of the wrist, gained only by diligent practice, the rubber is made to spring into the air and fly in the desired direction. It is a very effective but dangerous way of gaining ground, the danger consisting in the liability of players to be struck by the weighty missile, and ugly blows have often been received in this way. A "lift" at the goals is very hard to stop, if sent in low and swift, as I know by personal experience; for once, when tending goal, the point of my opponents charged down the length of the rink, and, without slackening speed, "lifted" the puck, and sent it past me like a bullet, while I was making ready to receive it on the ice, not imagining that he could lift successfully while at full speed.

No charging from behind, tripping, collaring, kicking, or shinning is allowed; and if any player offends after two warnings, it is the duty of the referee to order him off the ice for the remainder of the match. If the puck goes off the ice behind the goals, it must be taken five yards out, at right angles from the goal line, and there "faced" as at the beginning of the game. When it goes off the ice at the sides, it must be faced five yards at right angles from the side boundary.

The goal-keeper must not during play lie, kneel, or sit upon the ice, but must maintain a standing position. He may stop the puck with his hands or feet, but may not throw or kick it away from the goal. He must play it properly with his stick.

Two half-hours, with an intermission of ten minutes to regain breath and wipe off the perspiration, is the time allowed for a match, the team winning the most goals being the victors. There are no other points than goals to be scored.

Such are the principal rules; and now for a few words in conclusion of a general character. Only those who are in good condition and at home on their skates should undertake to play hockey. It is a violent game, and tests both wind and muscle to the utmost. The player must make up his mind to many falls, and no lack of hard knocks on shins and knuckles; for such things will happen, however faithfully the contestants try to keep to the rules. At the same time, these very characteristics make hockey one of the manliest of sports. Strength, speed, endurance, self-control, shrewdness, are the necessary qualities of one who would excel in it. Combination play is just as effective in it as in football, and there is no practical limit to the skill that may be attained.

A very important feature of hockey is that it may be played at night. Since the introduction of the electric light our rinks are made as bright as day, and then the many hard-working young men who are too busy all day to take part in any sport have the opportunity of an hour's splendid exercise after their work is over.

Take it all in all, there is perhaps no winter sport exclusively for men that is destined to become more popular, or have more enduring favour. In Canada new associations are rapidly springing up, and local leagues that arrange a schedule of matches for the season. The boys are taking hold of the game with great zest, closely imitating the tricks and artifices of their big brothers, and it is safe to say that hockey has definitely taken its place among the national sports of Canada.

"HURRAH, Lon! we've got the sort of day we've been looking for at last," cried Alec Pearson, as he met his chum one lovely still summer morning. "No trouble about getting over to Deschenes to-day."

"Right you are, Alec! This is just the correct thing. We'll start straight after breakfast—hey?"

"As soon as you like, provided mother's got the grub ready. Can't think of going without that, you know."

"No, sir. A basket of grub's half the fun. And mother's promised me a big one."

"Ditto mine," responded Alec. "So there's no fear of our starving for a while, even if we get cast away on one of the islands."

"Cast away on one of the islands!" echoed Lon. "That's a great idea! Wouldn't it make a great sensation?"

"Perhaps it would," replied Alec, who was of a more cautious and unimaginative cast of character. "But I'm not hankering to try it all the same. To get over to Deschenes will be enough fun for me."

The speakers were two boys of about sixteen years of age, sitting upon the front steps of a summer cottage, and looking out across the splendid stretch of water that flashed like a flawless mirror beneath the fiery morning sunshine.

They had come out to Britannia for the summer, and were enjoying its fine facilities for boating, bathing, and canoeing as only city boys, pent up in close quarters for three-fourths of the year, can enjoy such exhilarating sports.

The great Lake Deschenes filled them with profound admiration. They exulted in its magnificent breadth, its mighty length, its cool, limpid depths, and most of all the glorious rapids which marked the place where it gathered itself together to become the River Ottawa again, and resume its steady course seaward.

Nearly all their time they spent upon the water or in it, and in the course of a month had become tolerably expert canoeists, so that they did not hesitate to take long trips up the lake or across to the farther side.

The visit to Deschenes village, whose cottages were scattered along the lake shore almost opposite to Britannia, had been put off until they felt themselves to be thoroughly masters of their cranky craft; for in order to get there it was necessary to cross the head of the rapids, and to do this successfully would require both strength and skill.

For a week past Alec and Lon had felt themselves to be equal to the task, but had been delayed by unfavourable weather. Great, then, was their delight when this particular Saturday morning dawned clear and calm, promising to be the very kind of a day they desired.

They started at nine o'clock, taking with them for company, besides their well-filled baskets, Wad, Alec's handsome hunting spaniel, who had learned to behave perfectly on board the canoe.

Their craft was of the most approved make, of which they were joint-owners, completely equipped with paddles, cushions, sails, and steering-gear.

There being not a breath of wind, they had no use for the sail, so the mast was not put up nor the rudder shipped. In his enthusiastic eagerness to realize their long-cherished plan, Lon set to paddling with all his might; but Alec, who had the stern, laughingly checked his ardour, saying,—

"Take it easy, Lon; take it easy, my boy! There's lots of work ahead of you. Better not waste your muscle now!"

Alec had taken care to make inquiries of some of the Britannia folk as to the course he should steer, and they had all impressed upon him to go a good way straight up the lake, and away from the rapids, before turning toward Deschenes, as the current was tremendously strong, and made itself felt far higher up than one would imagine, looking at it from the Britannia side.

Accordingly he pointed the canoe almost due north, as though he had Aylmer in mind rather than Deschenes, and kept her on that course until Lon began to grow impatient.

"What's the use of going up so far?" he protested; "you can't feel the current here."

"Because old Lark told me to make that point before striking across, and he knows all about it," replied Alec.

"Ugh! Lark's an old fuss. He goes away up there only because he's too lazy to pull straight across where the current's strong." grumbled Lon, who had a passion for short cuts, and who kept urging his companion to head the canoe more directly toward their destination, until at last Alec, for very peace's sake, and against his better judgment, altered their course in compliance with his wishes.

For a hundred yards or so the paddling was no harder than before, and they made no leeway, so that Lon could exclaim triumphantly,—

"There now, didn't I tell you? It's only a waste of time going so far up."

But when another hundred yards' advance had brought the canoe fairly into the middle of the mighty stream, moving with majestic flow toward the angry rapids, the paddlers soon awoke to the fact that while they were still making good headway, they were making considerable leeway also, and that the task of getting across was going to be made much harder thereby.

Although both noticed this, neither made any remark about it at first: Alec, because he did not wish to alarm Lon; and Lon, because he shrank from admitting that it would have been wiser to follow shrewd old Lark's advice.

So they paddled away in silence, putting plenty of muscle into their strokes, and anxiously measuring their progress by landmarks on the farther shore.

Presently their exertions began to tell upon their young frames. The perspiration beaded their faces, their breath came short, their backs began aching, and their arms grew weary.

Lon's heart was already sinking within him, and Alec deeply regretted having yielded to his companion's ill-advised solicitations to disregard old Lark.

But there was no time for reconsideration or exchanging of regrets. They were beyond a doubt in the grasp of the current, and must strain every nerve to extricate themselves.

Then, to add to their anxiety, the weather showed signs of betraying the fair promise of the morning. Clouds began to obscure the deep blue of the sky, and a breeze to ruffle the calm surface of the lake. Unable to control his feelings any longer, Lon broke out with more than a hint of a sob in his voice,—

"O Alec, I wish we hadn't started! I'm getting awfully tired, and we don't seem to be making any headway at all."

"Oh, yes we are, Lon," responded Alec, doing his best to be cheerful. "Paddle away; we'll get across all right."

Thus encouraged, Lon put a little more life into his strokes for the next few minutes, and the canoe did seem to be gaining ground. But the gain was only temporary. The further they advanced the more they felt the force of the current.

Yet it was too late to turn back. Their only course was to keep on until they had shaken themselves free from the power that was dragging them downward to destruction.

Whether they would have been equal to this feat can only be guessed; for in trying to change his position to relieve his cramped legs, Lon lost his balance for a moment, and on attempting to recover himself did what was even worse—let slip his paddle, which was instantly whirled out of his reach.

"O Alec! what shall we do now?" he cried in dismay.

Alec's face was white and set.

"Nothing—we are powerless," he said quietly.

It was, of course, futile for him to try to contend alone with the pitiless current. The little canoe, as if glad at having no longer to fight its way foot by foot, glided gaily down towards the rapids, and all that Alec could do was to keep it straight in its course, and not allow it to swing around broadside.

Poor Lon, utterly overcome with terror, crouched down in the bow, sobbing so that he shook the frail canoe. But Alec was not one to yield to despair so long as anything could be done.

His brain was busy seeking some scheme for escape from their exceeding peril, and as he glanced anxiously ahead, a thought flashed into his mind that caused his eye to brighten and his pale face to light up with hope and determination.

Right on the edge of the rapids, just before the smooth swift stream broke up into tumultuous billows, stood a little island—a mere patch of rocks, crowned with half-a-dozen straggling trees.

If he could only beach the canoe on this island they

might yet be saved. It was all that remained between them and certain death.

The island was not more than two hundred yards distant, and to reach it he must make the canoe cut obliquely through the current. Summoning all his energies for a supreme effort, he bent to his task, in the meantime saying to Lon,—

"Be ready to jump the moment the canoe strikes."

For a boy of his age, Alec put a wonderful degree of strength into his strokes, and he had the joy of seeing his frail craft obey, in spite of the opposing waters, until it was pointing fair for the island. Then with a glad hurrah he ceased fighting the current, and joined forces with it, so successfully as to drive the canoe straight towards the rocks.

He did not miss his aim. With a leap, as though it were alive, the canoe rushed at the island and ran half its length out of the water, a sound of splintering wood telling that its bottom had suffered in so doing.

With feelings of indescribable relief the boys sprang out upon the solid ground, and instantly embracing one another, danced about in sheer exuberance of joy.

The rapids were cheated of their prey, and the worst of the peril was passed.

Having thus given vent to their feelings, they proceeded to examine the canoe, and were glad to find that its bottom was not very badly injured, and could be easily repaired.

Their next thought was, how could they get off the

island ? They were safe enough there for the present, of course, and they had sufficient provisions, if carefully husbanded, to keep them from starving for three or four days.

But they had no idea of playing the part of Robinson Crusoe and his man Friday, even for that short space of time, if it could possibly be helped. So they got on the edge of the island nearest Britannia, and Alec held up his paddle with his coat on it as a signal of distress, while both shouted at the top of their voices.

Their shouts were drowned in the ceaseless roar of the rapids ; but after a while their signal of distress was observed, and soon a crowd had gathered on the shore opposite them, and there was great excitement.

Everybody was eager to help, but nobody knew just what to do. All sorts of schemes were suggested for the rescue of the boys, the most feasible of which was to have a large boat go out above the rapids and anchor there, and then send down a smaller one secured by a rope, with which it could be hauled back again, for no boat could by any possibility be rowed back against that mighty current.

But there were two difficulties in the way of this plan. There was no boat at the village big enough and no rope long enough for the purpose, so some other way must needs be devised.

The morning wore away and the afternoon shadows lengthened without anything being done, and it looked as though the boys would have to stay on the island all night, when the cry was raised that there was a raft coming down; and sure enough the great towing steamer, followed by a huge raft of square timber, hove into sight far up the lake.

The problem of the boys' deliverance need no longer be worried over. The raftsmen would solve it in short measure.

The big raft reached Britannia just long enough before dark to allow of the rescue being accomplished. The moment the foreman heard of the boys' situation he detailed six of his best men, three being Indians and three French Canadians, to bring them off.

Landing their largest bonne, a kind of boat peculiar to lumbering, being flat on the bottom and very high at both bow and stern, they rowed off briskly towards the rapids, laughing and chaffing one another, and evidently deeming it quite a bit of fun, while the crowd gathered on the shore watched their every movement with breathless attention.

Managing their clumsy-looking but most seaworthy craft with perfect skill, they made an easy landing on the island, took the boys on board, and then waving their hats to the admiring onlookers, continued gaily on into the very midst of the boiling rapids, the big bonne bobbing about like a cork, seemingly at the entire mercy of the waters, yet all the time being cleverly steered by her crew, and after an exciting passage, during which the boys hardly breathed, shooting out into the smooth stretch below the rapids without having taken so much as a single drop of water on board.

A hearty cheer broke from the delighted spectators at this happy conclusion to the affair, and a few moments later the boys were in their midst, receiving the embraces of their overjoyed parents and the vigorous congratulations of the others.

The rescuing raftsmen were well rewarded for their timely service, and Master Lon learned a lesson in caution that he is not likely soon to forget.

THEO'S TRIUMPH.

Page 363.

THEO'S TOBOGGANING TRIUMPH.

THE boys of Bridgetown were all agreed that there had not been such a winter for tobogganing since they could remember; and if they ever thought of the weather-clerk at all, it was with feelings of the deepest gratitude.

In the first place, it began with a frost that made the ground as hard as iron, and the waters were, in Bible language, "hid as with a stone." Then upon this came one fall of snow after the other, until there was nothing left to wish for in that direction, and the boys were thoroughly content.

Not only was the weather-clerk thus considerate, but nature had already been kind enough to provide them with the finest site for a toboggan slide imaginable. The placid stream which bore the name of Bass River spread out into a broad reach just before it came to their town, and on one side the bank rose up into a steep bluff whose grass-grown face, slanting right down to the water's edge without a break or gully, seemed intended for no other purpose than to afford the boys a splendid coasting-ground when well sheeted with snow. And the boys knew right well how to appreciate their privileges, I can assure you. To go out to Bass River Bluff on a Saturday afternoon was to witness a scene well worth seeing. The hill would fairly swarm with boys and girls enjoying themselves to the top of their bent. From Patsey Kehoe, the washer-woman's ragged urchin, with his curious apology for a sled constructed out of old barrel staves, on which he dared to take only short slides from a little way up the hill, and which he sorely regretted was not big enough to carry him and Katey at the same time, to Ralph Masterton, the eldest son of the rich and haughty judge, with his big toboggan, so finely varnished and comfortably cushioned, that could take four persons down every trip, the young people of the town would turn out and make the valley ring with their laughter and shouting.

One of the most regular attendants at Bass River Bluff was Theo Ross, who, with his widowed mother, lived in a cozy cottage on the opposite side of the river from the town, and consequently was looked upon as one of the country boys, although he came in every day to the high school. There was a good deal of rivalry between the boys of Bridgetown and those who lived in the scattered settlement across the river, which was known as Riverside—a rivalry that led to all sorts of matches, and now and then to fights. No one took more hearty interest in this rivalry than Theo. He was a strong, stout, hardy lad of sixteen, up to anything, as the saying is, and was generally looked upon by the Riverside boys as their leader. One Saturday evening he came home in high spirits.

"Hoop-de-dooden-do!" he shouted, as he burst into the house.

"Why, Theo, what are you so excited about?" inquired his mother, looking up with a glad smile of welcome for the boy that was the joy and pride of her life.

"Excited? Perhaps I am; and no wonder, for aren't we going to have the biggest tobogganing match next Saturday afternoon that you ever heard of!" replied Theo, at the same time giving his mother a hug and a kiss that were a credit to both, for it showed how thoroughly they understood one another.

Mrs. Ross was a wise not less than a loving mother, and one of the proofs of her wisdom was the hearty interest she took in her son's sports as well as in his studies. He had lost his father when but a baby, and she had determined to fill the vacant place to the best of her ability. So from the very first she entered heartily into his amusements, and made herself his companion as far as she could. Theo never played cricket or lacrosse so well as when his mother was looking on, and no applause was sweeter to him than the clapping of her hands. He therefore felt sure of an attentive listener as he proceeded to unfold the cause of his excitement.

"Well, you know, mother, the Bridgetown boys have been boasting all winter about their toboggans, and saying that they can run away from anything in Riverside, and our fellows have been talking back at them, until both sides have begun to feel pretty hot over it. We've had a lot of races, but they didn't settle anything, because sometimes the Bridgetown boys would win and sometimes the Riverside; so this afternoon I proposed to Ralph Masterton that next Saturday afternoon he should bring a team of four tobogganers from the town, and I would bring four from the country, and we'd settle the question without any more talk."

" Well, but, Theo dear, won't it be dangerous for so many as eight to coast down together?   You might run into each other," asked Mrs. Ross, rather anxiously.

" O you dear innocent !" laughed Theo, " that's not the way we'll do at all.   Only two will go down at a time. You see there will be, first of all, four heats, and we'll draw lots for our places in the heats; then the four winners will run against each other, making two more heats ; and then there will be a final heat in which the two winners will run together, and that will decide."

" That seems a very good arrangement," said Mrs. Ross approvingly.   " Whose idea was it ? "

" Mostly mine, mother.   It's the best way to get fair play all round," answered Theo.

" Will you have any difficulty in choosing your team ? "

" Oh, not much.   Walt Powell and Rob Sands will be on for sure.   They have good toboggans, and they can steer splendidly.   The fourth chap I'll pick out through the week."

" Well, Theo, you must do your best to win, for I'll be there to watch you."

" You may depend upon it I will, for your sake as much as for the honour of Riverside," replied Theo, giving his mother a loving kiss before he went off to his room for a wash.

It seemed an awfully long week to the excited boys, impatient for the coming contest. Theo had many applicants for a position on his team, and having, after careful deliberation, decided in favour of Fred Fellows, the four boys had many an earnest consultation as to the best way of securing success. On Friday evening the others brought their toboggans over to Mrs. Ross's, and they spent an hour or two in seeing that the bottoms were perfectly smooth, the gut lashings all taut, and the cushions secured beyond the possibility of slipping. They were not a little disturbed at some rumours that had reached them of Ralph Masterton having sent off to the capital and got a new toboggan of a kind just lately patented, which was made differently from the others and reported to be much faster. If this was true, Ralph had done rather a mean thing; for although not expressly stipulated, it was generally understood that the toboggans to be used in the contest were such as they already had, and not new ones imported for the purpose. But, as Theo sensibly said, it was no use worrying until they knew for certain; so, hoping for the best, they parted for the night.

Saturday proved as fine as could be wished, and early in the afternoon a crowd began to gather on Bass River Bluff.

Besides the honour of the championship, Judge Masterton had offered a handsome prize to the winner in the shape of a silver cup, and there was no end to the excitement. The judge himself and all his family were present. So, too, were

Theo's mother and the parents of the other contestants. So, too, was Patsey Kehoe, holding Katey with one hand and dragging his forlorn little barrel-stave sled with the other. Everybody in Bridgetown and Riverside that could come had come, and the flat top of the bluff was fairly black with spectators.

By three o'clock all the competitors had arrived. When Ralph Masterton appeared, Theo gave one sharp glance at his toboggan, then turned to his companions with his face the picture of indignation.

"It's true, boys, after all; Ralph's got one of those new-fangled affairs I read of in the papers. They say they can go like smoke. He hasn't done the square thing. But we're not beaten yet, for all that!" and Theo looked proudly down at his toboggan, which had won as high a reputation for speed as the owner had for skill.

It took half-an-hour to draw lots for the heats, and then at last all was ready, and Judge Masterton, acting as starter, called out the first pair. Besides the steerer each toboggan was to carry another person for ballast. Fred Fellows was the first of Theo's team to try his fortune. Amid breathless silence and suspense he put his toboggan in position beside his opponent's.

"Are you ready?" asked the judge. They both nodded. "Then—go!" and with half-a-dozen quick steps they pushed their toboggans over the brow of the hill, and flinging themselves on sideways with one leg extended for a rudder, shot down the steep slope like arrows from a bow. For some time they kept side by side. Then Fred was seen to swerve and slew, and the Bridgetown boy to slip ahead. The advantage was not much, but he kept it to the end, and the first heat went against Riverside. The Bridgetown boys cheered lustily, and the Riversiders looked rather glum, until the next heat was run and resulted in a win for the latter, thus making things even. The Riverside entry took the third heat also, and their hopes ran high, but cooled down again when the fourth heat went to Bridgetown.

The result of the first round, accordingly, was that two of each side had won their heats, Theo and Ralph being, of course, among the winners. The excitement grew more and more intense as, after a little breathing-space, the second round was called.

Curiously enough, Theo and Ralph did not come together in this round either, having each another opponent, whom they vanquished easily. As they stood on the hill together at the conclusion of the round, Ralph turned to Theo with a smile which betokened perfect confidence in himself, and pointing to his new toboggan, said,—

"She's a hummer: there's nothing on the bluff to touch her."

"Do you think it was just the square thing, Ralph, to get that toboggan when it was understood we were to race with what we had already?" asked Theo quietly.

"Pooh!" replied Ralph, tossing his head defiantly; "everything's fair in love and war."

As he turned away and swung his toboggan round, it came in contact with Patsey Kehoe's barrel-stave sled.

With a muttered oath Ralph sprang toward the obstruction, and kicking it high into the air, the clumsy little thing fell to the ground shattered into useless fragments. Poor Patsey gave a cry as he saw his plaything demolished, but Ralph's angry face silenced him again, and with tears running down their cheeks he and Katey proceeded to gather up the pieces.

"Get ready for the final heat," called out Judge Masterton.

Mrs. Ross pressed forward to Theo's side and whispered in his ear, " Good luck to you, my boy."

With every eye upon them, Ralph and Theo drew their toboggans into position. The difference between the two toboggans was very marked. Theo's was a particularly fine one of the ordinary kind, but Ralph's was made of narrow hard-wood strips secured by screws instead of thongs, and had a sharp racing look that could not be mistaken. Just as the contestants were ready to receive their ballast, Theo's glance fell upon Patsey Kehoe pressing forward eagerly on the edge of the crowd, watching him with his whole soul in his eyes. He knew well how intensely the little fellow hoped for his success, and suddenly an idea flashed into his mind which caused him to call out to Judge Masterton,—

" A minute's time, please, sir."

" All right, my lad," replied the judge.

Then, to the surprise of everybody, Theo, after whispering to Walter Powell, whom he had first intended to be his companion on the toboggan, and who now drew aside, beckoned to Patsey Kehoe. Patsey approached bashfully.

"Jump on in front, Patsey," said Theo briskly. "You're to be my ballast this time."

There was a murmur of astonishment from the crowd as the ragged little chap awkwardly got into his place, and Theo did not miss the contemptuous curl of his opponent's lip, but neither did he fail to catch the pleased, approving look his mother sent him. A moment more and everything was in readiness. The spectators held their breath as the judge, lifting his right hand, asked,—

"Are you ready?" and then bringing it down with a crack into the other, shouted, "Then—go!"

As if shot from a bow the two toboggans leaped over the bluff and went rattling down the smooth slope side by side and head to head. Down—down—they went; Theo and Ralph with iron grip and hard-pressed toe keeping them straight in their course, and Patsey and the other ballast clinging fast to the hand-rail. It was the proudest moment of Patsey's life, and one that he would never forget. Just as the toboggans, still perfectly even, approached the bottom of the declivity where the track ran out on to the bosom of the river, Ralph's struck a slight obstacle, which caused it to swerve and then to slew. With a vicious dig of his toe he tried to bring it round straight again. In his hot haste he overdid it, and the head swung round until the toboggan went broadside to the track, scratching, bumping, cracking, until like a flash it came bang against the side of the slide, pitching its passengers out upon their heads and splitting one of the thin strips clean in two. In the meanwhile Theo and Patsey, amid the cheers of the crowd on the hill, were speeding smoothly over the level ice, winners by nearly a hundred yards.

Great was the delight of the Riverside folk at their champion's victory, and many of the Bridgetownians joined in congratulations too, for Ralph Masterton was far from popular among them. When Theo reached the top of the bluff his mother hastened to him, her face beaming with pleasure as she said,—

"I am very proud of your victory, Theo, but I am prouder still of the heart that prompted you to take Patsey Kehoe."

THE END.